Readers Love Amanda Meuwissen

A Model Escort

"The aspect of "Beauty and the Geek" is subtle but effective here…. This would be an attractive story for readers looking for more STEAM/STEM in their romances."

—*Library Journal*

Their Dark Reflections

"I thoroughly devoured this book. Amanda Meuwissen has a gift for creating multi-dimensional characters, full of moral ambiguity, and making you fall in love with them. This book is no exception."

—Paranormal Romance Guild

"The concept of the story was simple, the execution – delightful – one that kept me turning the page."

—Love Bytes

After Vertigo

"With its endearing main characters and a story that held my attention, *After Vertigo* was a fun read and perfect to unwind with at the end of long day."

—Joyfully Jay

Coming Up for Air

"*Coming Up For Air* by Amanda Meuwissen is the first book that I've read by this author, but it won't be the last…"

—OptimuMM

By AMANDA MEUWISSEN

Coming Up for Air
Their Dark Reflections

DREAMSPUN DESIRES
A Model Escort
Interpretive Hearts

MOONLIGHT PROPHECIES
By the Red Moonlight
Blue Moon Rising

TALES FROM THE GEMSTONE KINGDOM
The Prince and the Ice King
Stitches

Published by DSP Publications
After Vertigo

Published by DREAMSPINNER PRESS

BLUE MOON
Rising

AMANDA MEUWISSEN

DREAMSPINNER
PRESS

Published by
DREAMSPINNER PRESS

5032 Capital Circle SW, Suite 2, PMB# 279, Tallahassee, FL 32305-7886 USA
www.dreamspinnerpress.com

Blue Moon Rising
© 2022 Amanda Meuwissen

Cover Art
© 2022 Kris Norris
https://krisnorris.com
coverrequest@krisnorris.com

Cover content is for illustrative purposes only and any person depicted on the cover is a model.

Trade Paperback ISBN: 978-1-64108-385-0
Digital ISBN: 978-1-64108-384-3
Trade Paperback published May 2022
v. 1.0

Printed in the United States of America
∞
This paper meets the requirements of
ANSI/NISO Z39.48-1992 (Permanence of Paper).

Chapter 1

SOMETIMES JAY forgot how beautiful Brookdale was.

The city came to life as the train rounded a corner out of the countryside, bathed in sunlight since it was early afternoon. It was mid-November, so that sunshine presented a false backdrop, given the air would be brisk outside, but it hadn't snowed yet. In many ways, Jeffrey "Jay" Russell's home was very much like Centrus City, where he was coming from, with skyscrapers and sprawling residential areas, even a river lining one side—a river that connected the two cities, despite them being almost six hundred miles apart.

Originally, Jay had anticipated leaving Centrus with an even stronger connection having been forged, linking that city's shifter pack with his own, but his marriage to Centrus City's Alpha, Bashir "Bash" Bain, had fallen through. Jay's mind still reeled from all that had happened the past couple of weeks. Discovering Bashir was a Seer, for one, but more than that, the son of a Seer and a Focus, just like the newly turned vampire, Ethan Lambert.

Seers could see the future, Focuses could amplify the abilities of those around them, and Bash and Ethan could do both. Jay had discovered that Centrus City even had a Null, someone who could nullify abilities so people like shifters, vampires, and natural-born witches seemed little more than human.

"Finally," Maximus grumbled across from Jay, gazing out at the city as well. Maximus Thornton was Jay's Second, a large man with dark skin, long braided hair, and a general surliness to him that had been pushed to its limits during their trials in Centrus. They'd faced mind-controlled shifters under the vampire thrall of Ethan's father, Gordon, and even under Ethan's thrall once, before he beat his father's influence. "It'll be good to be home. No offense to Bain—well, maybe a little offense—but I'm glad to be away from that city's insanity. Never thought I'd make nice with a vampire," he added with a huff.

Jay never thought he'd lose what he'd hoped would be the love of his life to one either.

But he didn't love Bashir. He hadn't gotten the chance. Bashir and Ethan were drawn to each other and much better suited for one another. Losing Bashir to Ethan was just something that happened, a prophecy being fulfilled that Jay couldn't possibly have beaten. It was insanity, but the kind he hoped would be for the best.

A laugh erupted from the seats behind them in a voice like but also not like Bashir's. Bari Bain was entirely different from his twin brother, no matter how much they looked alike. He had the same bronze skin, wavy dark hair, and golden-brown gaze, but his smile was wider and crinkled his eyes. He was also an incredibly stylish dresser.

Not to downplay Bashir's classic style in dark colors, but with a subtle glance over the top of Jay's seat, he admired the clean lines of the outfit Bari had donned before they left Centrus City that morning. He wore a long charcoal jacket similar to his brother's style, but beneath was expertly tailored slacks that couldn't possibly be off the rack and an emerald-and-black patterned button-down, tucked in, with a chic belt and handsome watch as accessories, and something Jay hadn't noticed before was that Bari's right ear was pierced with a diamond. Jay was fairly certain Bashir didn't have any piercings.

He didn't want to keep comparing the brothers, but it was difficult not to, especially after Bari had invited himself to return with them to Brookdale as a sort of ambassador from Centrus City's pack, despite not living there anymore. He'd also offhandedly mentioned that if they still wanted to join the cities, a marriage between Jay and a member of Bashir's inner circle wasn't unheard of—or between Jay and a member of Bashir's family.

He only had the one brother.

Bari noticed Jay staring and promptly winked.

Jay turned back around like a flustered teenager. He was thirty-five, but that face had made his insides jelly ever since he first saw it on Bashir and hoped to find love in a marriage of convenience. Maybe he still could. After all, as he and Ethan had bonded over, both brothers were super-hot, and Bari was much more Jay's type.

"Then again, we are bringing some of that insanity with us," Maximus griped. "You aren't seriously considering marrying that one now, are you? He's a bit… much."

Jay gave a nervous laugh. They hadn't even talked to Bari during the trip, since they'd separated themselves from where Bari was sitting with Maximus's wife, Theresa, and son, William, to catch up on pack business ahead of their arrival. "It's a little early to jump from one arranged marriage to another, Max." Much as the idea made Jay's face feel flushed. "And he's not much, he's... energetic, friendly—"

"Annoying."

Jay snorted. "Your family seems to like him." He could hear Theresa and William laughing too, thoroughly enjoying Bari's company.

"At least we're not bringing the vampire home," Maximus said, glancing at his phone. "Urs is going to have enough of a field day with everything that happened as it is. She's been texting me all day."

Ursula was Jay's Warden, a sort of sheriff among their people who kept the peace and had agents all over the city.

"I thought we already went over the circle's daily reports," Jay said, deciding to not remind Maximus that Bashir and Ethan were scheduled to visit in a week.

"We did. I told you everything they sent. They want a report back."

As Alpha, every shifter in Brookdale was Jay's responsibility, but he didn't run things alone. Besides Maximus as his Second and Ursula as Warden, there was also a Magister who watched over magic and those who could wield it, a Councilor to ensure the people were cared for and loyal, and a Shaman for healing and protection against being discovered by normal humans. And, unlike Bashir's inner circle, all of Jay's advisors were wolves.

He'd been an Alpha for less than five years, half the length of Bashir's time in leadership, yet Bashir was the one who made other cities nervous. Bashir's father, Centrus City's previous Alpha, hadn't exactly been a stable leader, but the real reason other packs doubted Bashir's reign was because, after killing his father to usurp him, Bashir had slowly replaced the old inner circle with all non-wolves. The marriage had been a way for Bashir to gain favor with other cities by uniting with a more traditional pack, but what Jay wanted out of the deal was to show his people that intermingling the tribes could work. It didn't have to only be wolves on top, with all the races segregated.

Five years of trying to prove that to his people had gone nowhere. In fact, tribal wars were worse than ever in Brookdale, and Jay had to find a way to fix it, even without Bashir's influence.

"We'll be home soon enough," Jay said. "I'm not texting or calling with what went on in Centrus City. Those events need to be explained in person. What's Ursula asking?" he added as an aside, curious if she'd heard anything from the rumor mill.

"She knows you well." Maximus scrolled through some of the messages. "Wondering if you're bringing home any strays with your new husband."

Jay cringed. He wasn't even technically bringing home a fiancé anymore. It was better things hadn't worked out between him and Bashir, but that didn't mean what happened didn't hurt. Instead of breaking things off between them from the start, Bashir had slept with Ethan— twice—before Jay backed out of the marriage himself. Jay just wanted to be someone's first choice, but being a hopeless romantic didn't mean he had luck in love.

"You're not still poring over pack reports, I hope." Bari appeared as if summoned, depositing himself gracefully in the seat next to Jay with a dramatic crossing of one leg over the other and leaning toward him. Bashir smelled like sandalwood, but Bari smelled like jasmine, another sign Bari was more Jay's type, because that smell made his insides quiver, and scent was a common factor in choosing a mate. "Even an Alpha needs to take breaks, darling. And we're nearly home! Well, home for you. Speaking of...." He batted impossibly long lashes, and his exaggerated nature reminded Jay like a slap to the face how different he was from Bashir in every way. "Foolish little ol' me forgot to look into any hotels. I hope everything won't be booked."

Maximus scoffed at the obvious lead-in, but Jay had already intended this offer.

"No hotel necessary," Jay said, enjoying Bari's scent but trying to stay focused and hopefully not look as red in the face as he felt. "Only Max and our Magister are mated, so we have plenty of spare rooms at our den. We'll head there once the train arrives so you can get settled and I can address my circle about what's gone on the past few weeks."

"You haven't told them anything?"

"Not yet, but I'm sure they've heard whispers. While I intend to tell my circle everything, I'll make sure it's understood that talk of Seers, Focuses, and Nulls needs to be kept as only gossip for everyone else."

"My pack thanks you for that," Bari said with a gentle touch to Jay's arm. He was very casually physical, another contrast to his brother.

"I know you were gone much longer than planned. I hope everything ran smoothly without you."

"Smooth enough," Maximus growled, reminding Jay that they weren't alone. "Are you an ambassador or a spy?"

"Max," Jay chided him.

"It's okay," Bari dismissed. "I was prying. I won't pretend like Bash didn't ask me to keep him informed of the state of your city. But allies should be honest with each other." He looked squarely at Maximus and grinned. "When I spy, I'll warn you first."

Maximus turned away with another scoff.

"But before any espionage, I'm looking forward to a better meal than the train food we had for lunch." Bari returned his attention to Jay. "Would you like to get dinner later?"

In an instant, Jay was a flustered teenager again because he couldn't think of a response. He wasn't used to anyone being so forward with him, especially someone who'd almost sort of already proposed.

"He's been gone for weeks," Maximus broke in, "and you think he's going to immediately start playing tour guide just because—"

"Max," Jay chided again, which at least helped him find his voice. He knew his Second was only looking out for him, but being a good Alpha meant taking time for himself too, something he often forgot. "Pack business comes first, always," he reassured Maximus, and then looked to Bari. "But I do have to eat. I'd love to take you to dinner tonight."

There was that unique crinkle at the corners of Bari's eyes that Jay had never seen on Bashir. "Marvelous. It's a date. That is a very fetching shirt on you, by the way." He lightly tugged Jay's collar and stroked once more down his arm before getting up and heading back toward Theresa and William with a sly smirk.

It wasn't that special of a shirt, Jay thought, just black with a few horizontal stripes in gray, but since he'd taken his jacket off during the ride, he supposed the short sleeves flattered his biceps well, which was where Bari had touched.

Jay realized he'd followed Bari's retreat almost to the point of turning in his chair and quickly sat forward again.

Maximus stared at him deadpan.

"What? It's just dinner."

As soon as Maximus huffed and looked back out at the city, Jay couldn't contain his smile. Just dinner—for now.

BARI WAVED at Theresa and William as he passed them on his way to the bathroom. He liked those two. Theresa was a beautiful blond bombshell with a marvelously fierce attitude and had been regaling Bari with all the places he would have to see while in Brookdale, and William was a famously sharp and well-spoken ten-year-old who, except for the shorter hair, was the spitting image of his father. Both were far more welcoming than brusque Maximus, though Bari didn't mind being scowled at. He understood it coming from an Alpha's Second toward a virtual stranger.

And besides, Max wasn't the one Bari was trying to get to like him.

Jay was an absolute treat—for the eyes and for company. He was like an NFL quarterback. Tall, broad-shouldered, as impressively muscled as big brute Maximus, and effortlessly handsome, with blue eyes, tan skin, and a distinguished amount of early gray coming in at the temples of his short sandy blond hair. The best part was the adorable way one of his ears stuck out just the tiniest bit more than the other, like it was crooked.

Bari had seen Jay changed into his various shifter forms—Stage One being the glow of a shifter's eyes, Stage Two being partially transformed with fur sprouting and claws and fangs coming out, Stage Three morphing them completely into bipedal fur-covered beasts like what people thought a werewolf should look like, and finally, Stage Four like a normal wolf in the wild.

Bari hadn't been paying much attention to Jay's ears at any of those stages and wondered what they looked like. Maximus had always been with Jay while they were in Centrus City. Finally, Bari was going to get the chance to get to know Jay with just the two of them.

He looked at himself in the bathroom mirror. Not too shabby, he thought, much as he'd come in here to freshen up. He'd change before dinner, though. He could definitely up his game, and four hours on a train left him grimy.

Feeling his phone buzz in his pocket, Bari assumed it was Bash checking to make sure they'd arrived safely. He adored his brother's overprotectiveness. Even though they'd lived apart most of their lives, they texted or called each other practically every day. Bari never envied his brother, but he almost would have envied Bash's recent love story with a beautiful young redheaded vampire, if not for how it meant Jay was now available.

Bari had never minded Bash rising as Alpha either. Bash had even asked Bari if he wanted to be part of Centrus City's circle, but Bari hadn't wanted anything to do with that much responsibility. He liked being able to tuck himself away into his work as a museum curator, lost in the cataloging, arranging, and procuring of artifacts. He also hadn't been ready to leave his museum or his city back then.

He was ready now.

Talk to me. Please. We can work this out.

Bari's smile dropped along with his stomach as he read the text. Not from Bash but Joseph, Bari's very recent ex.

Bari had complained to Bash about having a fiancé without telling him, but Bari had been seeing Joseph for weeks without saying anything about the relationship to Bash or Deanna, who was practically their sister. He knew they wouldn't approve, because Joseph was Bari's boss, the museum director. He was a lizard shifter, but they wouldn't have cared about that. They just would have worried Bari was setting himself up to get hurt, so he'd decided to wait to tell them until he knew if the relationship was going anywhere.

Ultimately, Bari hadn't seen a future together, so he'd tried to end it—and the bastard threatened to fire him, so Bari quit. That was the real reason he'd shown up in Centrus City when he had.

Don't message me again. I already told you I'm not coming back. Bari sent the response and then blocked Joseph's number. He'd tell Bash and Deanna the truth someday when the pain was less fresh. He'd left his whole life behind because of a stupid mistake, but for now, he was glad to be headed somewhere new, even if it meant, once again, he'd run when things got tough.

Taking in a cleansing breath, Bari exhaled all possible thoughts of Joseph and kept his sights on Jay. It was just a maybe for now, a possibility, but it was something. Staring at his reflection, Bari could honestly believe this new start was the best thing for him, however it turned out.

At least he thought that until his smile dropped at the sight of his brown eyes flashing blue and the whites going black, with a third eye blinking into existence on his forehead.

The vision struck Bari all at once.

A figure, indistinct but female from her silhouette, was growing larger and larger above the cityscape of Brookdale until she was like some apocalyptic beast, with Centrus City and even nearby Glenwood seen beneath her as well, as if her influence was spreading. As Bari saw it all, he heard his own voice and knew he was speaking, though he had no control over what was said.

Plans set in motion spanning years in the making
Her desire for the past still ripe for the taking
One city saved won't prevent a revising
Keep watch on the lonely for the blue moon rising

Then it was over, and Bari was left looking at his normal reflection, gasping for breath. He'd just had his first-ever prophecy at thirty-three, proving to have Seer abilities like his brother after a lifetime assuming he didn't, and it wasn't a nice prophecy either.

"Shit."

Chapter 2

IF BARI could pretend with ease like nothing was wrong concerning his exodus from his old life, old city, old job, and secret old ex, then he could pretend he hadn't just had a dooming prophecy about Brookdale. At least until he had the chance to speak with Jay alone.

He smiled and chatted and played the role of tourist all throughout their arrival and subsequent car ride from the train station to the circle's den, but internally he felt queasy. He'd witnessed Bash have prophecies before and heard his brother describe the experience, but this was the first time he'd had one himself, and all because he'd spent too much time the past week in the company of other Seers and Focuses.

Bari and Bash were twins, so they were both the son of a Seer and a Focus, which was exceedingly rare, but Bari had always privately hoped to stay the "ordinary" twin. Besides Ethan also being the son of a Seer and a Focus and just how powerful Bari had felt being around Bash and Ethan at the same time, Ethan's father, Gordon, and friend Rio were Focuses too and had been within close proximity to Bari on multiple occasions.

It's a wonder he wasn't projecting prophecies in technicolor.

"And you're the only child in the entire household?" Bari asked William, valiantly trying to distract himself. A shifter driver had picked them up in a large SUV, with Theresa up front, Bari and William in the immediate back, and Jay and Maximus behind them. "Excuse me, I mean… young man."

William smiled. Whatever that prophecy was warning about, Bari sincerely hoped no harm would ever come to this sweet child. "I don't mind. I have tons of friends at school, though they do wonder sometimes why they can't come over to play. A lot of them are human."

"That sort of curiosity wanes, don't you worry," Bari assured him. "They probably just think you're part of a mob family."

"They do!" William giggled. "Everyone says Dad looks like a hit man."

Jay snorted, but when Bari glanced at the back seat, Maximus didn't look as amused. He could be as grumpy as he wanted. Bari caught Jay's gaze and held it before turning back.

"I'm sure you have shifter friends as well," Bari said. "Do you spend free time at the Shelter like you did in Centrus?"

During the time the visitors from Brookdale had been in Centrus City, Theresa and William had spent a fair share at the city's Shelter, which was exactly that—a place for shifters to take shelter when they had nowhere else to go. That could include people who'd recently moved to the city, people who'd lost their homes for whatever reason, and orphans. Residence at the Shelter was intended to be temporary, but finding homes for displaced families and children wasn't always easy.

William had wanted to go to Centrus City's Shelter to gauge the people's opinion of Bash, but after a suggestion from Ethan, he'd also begun a science experiment there for an upcoming school project. To show the scientific method in action, William had done an eyewitness study, showing how easy it is for facts to get misaligned days, hours, and even mere minutes after people witness an event. Bari had only heard about it second-hand, but he was certain the final report for William's science fair would be brilliant.

"I've been to our Shelter," William said slowly, "but…."

"Unfortunately, tribal unrest is a problem," Jay spoke up, "and it's worst at the Shelter, so I only allow the circle to go there for now, for safety's sake. I wish I could say your brother provided some good tips on how to combat that—he did—but I can't exactly commission a vampire to come in and show everyone that how we often think of each other isn't always correct."

Bari caught Jay's gaze again. "Well, you can and you are. Ethan and Bash are visiting in a week, remember, to see William's final project presented in person. Maybe just point that sweet-fanged smile toward the Shelter and see what happens!"

"Absolutely not," Maximus rebuffed, though Bari had seen a smile twitch to life on Jay's face, despite the worried glance he threw at Maximus. "And ugh, I forgot that. But your brother didn't have as big an issue to begin with. Showing off a neutered vampire isn't going to change anyone's opinion here about lizards mixing with cats mixing with rats and humans."

Bari sorely wanted to comment about how Ethan was hardly "neutered" but knew that would be in terribly poor taste in front of Jay, given Ethan stole Jay's fiancé. "Just an idea."

"Here you are, ma'am, sirs," the driver said as he pulled to a stop.

William leaped for the door, clearly excited to be home, and Bari was excited too, eager to see what Jay's den looked like. The inner circle of a pack always lived together in a group home, which could be anything from a dingy apartment setup to the beautiful manor Bash had inherited. But while that den was modern in structure and décor, Bari could tell this place would be different.

The outside looked like a dollhouse or bed-and-breakfast in deep plum, with black trim and teal accents, as well as a fountain in the front, a high stone perimeter wall, and perfectly manicured topiaries and other colorful landscaping.

"Wow," Bari said as he stepped onto the sidewalk. The neighborhood was nicer than he was used to as well, just that extra bit of upscale that made his inner princess swoon.

While Bari was busy gawking, the others exited behind him, and Maximus helped the driver unload their bags. Afterward, the SUV took off down the road, and Maximus and Theresa hurried ahead to catch up with William, who was already bounding toward a woman waiting for them outside the front doors.

She was tall, with long blond hair, blue eyes, and sharp but perfectly symmetrical features. If Theresa was a bombshell, then this woman was a star pinup—just in an all-black pantsuit like a member of the Secret Service.

"That would be Ursula," Jay said, coming up beside Bari.

Bari watched her hug William tight and greet Maximus with the same informal enthusiasm, but when it came time to welcome Theresa, Ursula didn't even acknowledge her but turned away to usher William inside. Theresa looked slighted but didn't say anything, and Maximus didn't seem to notice.

"You see the problem," Jay continued softly. "Even my own circle has issues with mixing races in pack leadership, or mixed couples, especially when one is human." He gestured for Bari to walk with him, and they grabbed their bags to follow the others at a leisurely pace.

"I'll admit," Bari said, "I'm surprised Maximus is the type who'd fall for a human."

"He had help." Jay grinned. "I saw how he'd look at her when they first met. It was right after I became Alpha. They've only been married for about two years. After losing his first mate when William was a baby, I knew Max would never make a move, so I gave him an ultimatum. I told him if he didn't ask her out, I was going to introduce her to Reggie."

"Reggie?"

"You'll meet him," Jay said cryptically.

"Blackmail!" Bari chuckled. "What a lovely meet-cute."

"I'm a sucker for a good romance."

"Me too." Bari made a point of biting his lower lip as he looked at Jay and saw the way Jay's eyes strayed right where Bari wanted them to.

Then Bari remembered his prophecy and felt his insides twist. Now wasn't the time to bring it up. Through the open double doors of the den was a cluster of chaotic movement among what was obviously the entire circle awaiting their arrival. Revelations of potential doom would have to come later.

Bari's brother would have made a point of memorizing the people first and gauging their risk factors or some nonsense, but Bari's attention was drawn to the house. Even only seeing the foyer, a winding staircase, and a living room beyond, Bari noticed countless antiques, old chandeliers, and brilliantly vintage wallpaper. He wanted shirts in every pattern and color he saw. The grandeur was an immediate testament to the pack's traditionalism, and while in principle Bari hated that, he'd put up with it for style like this.

"I'm in love," he said as he and Jay finished crossing the threshold. Jay gaped at him.

"With the house, darling, but we have time." He winked and watched Jay's cheeks redden. It was seriously endearing. They had mere seconds before they would be accosted by the crowd fussing over Maximus, William, and Theresa, so Bari leaned in close to Jay and whispered, "I'm aware I can be a bit... what was it Max said quite loudly for any shifter to hear? Much?"

Jay opened his mouth to say something, but Bari shook his head.

"It's fine. It's true. So feel free to ignore me or tell me to stop anytime. I won't, but you can still tell me." Bari grinned.

Jay laughed, and that too was wonderfully endearing.

"We'll see you two later." Theresa came over with William. Bari could tell her expression was tight, maybe only from Ursula's behavior, though Bari wondered how many of the others were staunch traditionalists unhappy with her presence. "Someone needs to make sure this guy's extra homework is finished before he returns to school tomorrow."

"Bye, Bari!" William waved as the pair headed for the stairs. "Bye, Jay!"

"Did we hear that right? This isn't Bashir?"

Two women approached who couldn't have looked more opposing in appearance. The one who'd spoken was exceptionally tall and thin with a deep-dark complexion, brown eyes, glasses, and tightly coiled short hair dyed to have a hint of auburn. She wore a lovely peach-colored jumpsuit like a high-powered fashionista.

The woman with her was Asian, with medium-length straight black hair, black eyes, and was nearly half the other woman's size, as well as flatteringly soft and voluptuous. She looked like a '50s housewife, in a collared sleeveless A-line dress covered in polka dots.

"This would be Bari Bain," Jay introduced him, "Bashir's brother. Bari, this is Clara, our Magister, and her mate, Daisy."

Bari shook Clara's hand first, the taller of the two, and then Daisy's. "A pleasure. I must confess, I'm used to being the best dressed wherever I go, but I clearly have competition here. You ladies look fabulous." He spread his fingers to encompass them both, almost like an appreciative jazz-hands.

They scoffed in mirrored dismissive but flattered manners and gave a natural lean in toward one another, as if reminded of why they'd first found each other attractive. Neither seemed standoffish like Maximus, which was something, at least.

"You don't have any magical affinity, do you?" Clara asked Bari.

Again, he thought of his prophecy, which made his mind go blank. "Um...."

"Ignore her," Daisy said fondly, latching on to Clara's arm. "She treats magic in this city like her own personal R & D department. It is super cute, but she forgets magic is the exception among our kind, not the rule."

"She says that," Clara countered, hugging her mate close, "but Daisy is a wizard in the kitchen."

"I made cookies!" Daisy declared.

Bari thought he might just love it here, if these two were an example of the rest.

"While I try to encourage group participation with making meals," Jay put in, "Daisy took over most kitchen duties after these two mated. It's hard to argue when everything she makes is so delicious."

The petite woman beamed, which made Bari feel a bit guilty.

"I hope you won't be offended I convinced Jay to take me out for dinner tonight."

"Oh, you're… really?" Clara asked with a curious look between them.

"I'll explain," Jay began. "Let's—"

"You're not marrying Bain?" another female voice boomed with the approach of a far less hospitable figure. "Then why is that one even here?"

She was beautiful. Maybe an inch taller than Theresa's more average height, but with a subtlety of muscle to her movements beneath a simple T-shirt, leather jacket, and jeans that reminded Bari of Deanna—a powerhouse in a deceptive package. She had long wavy black hair, light brown skin, and vibrant green eyes.

"Bari, this is Anjali," Jay said with the edge of a sigh, "our Councilor."

This was their Councilor? Clara and Daisy might look like opposites, but they had a similarly sweet, bubbly nature. Other than the casual clothing, this woman was the true antithesis of Luke, Centrus City's Councilor, who was affable and patient and acted like one of the people, because that's what he was. Not wanting to admit his surprise, however, Bari held out a hand with a broad smile.

Anjali didn't take it.

"What is going on?" she barked at Jay. "People are talking vampires and an army of mages at Bain's disposal. Is all that true?"

"Bit of an exaggeration," Bari began.

"Was I talking to you?" Her green eyes were like glimmering pools of acid when they snapped to Bari.

"Anji, please," Jay tried to temper her, "Bari is our guest, and you know better than anyone not to listen to rumor."

"Ah, but rumor keeps the blood pumping!" The final unknown figure in the foyer joined them, looping an arm around Anjali's shoulders, who tensed but didn't brush him off, like she was used to his behavior. "And they sometimes have more truth to them than we'd admit. Hello there, lovely. I'm Reggie."

Last but not least meant this was the Shaman. Despite an English accent, Bari couldn't help being reminded of a slightly younger version of Jeff Bridges as the Dude, because the man was average height and build, with maybe a bit of jolly pudge, wearing comfortable pants that might be sweats, a white linen tunic covered by a burgundy kimono cardigan, and he had the Dude's signature long brown hair, beard, and sunglasses indoors.

"Reginald Edith Lancaster, if you can believe it." He bowed somewhat grandly with his free arm. "But call me anything but 'Reggie' and we'll have words. Bari, was it? Mm. Aren't you the fine specimen? And there are two of you? Well, if a little polygamy is JJ's idea of balking at conservatism, consider my vote in the affirmative."

"Reggie," Jay hissed. It seemed he was forever correcting his circle from saying things he didn't like, but Bari didn't mind. He laughed. He liked a bit of scandalous charm. If he wasn't interested in Jay, he might have been a little scandalous himself if Reggie's pleased perusal of him was genuine. "That is not what's going on here."

"Then if I may ask, Alpha, what is?" Ursula asked now that the din in the foyer had hushed. She had a raspy deeper voice and remained beside Maximus, stoic in a way very unlike the others. Most of them were friendly, a couple downright rude, but Ursula was like the calm center of a storm, which said a lot about what she could weather. "I think we're due for explanations."

"That you are," Jay agreed. "Come. Let's take a seat."

They gathered in the living room, and Bari held his tongue so as not to gush even more that he was ready to move in forever, thank you. This place was gorgeous. Dark wood, fleur-de-lis wallpaper with actual gold leaf, and the upholstery on the antique furniture made him afraid to sit on it. But since everyone else did without hesitation, Bari claimed a burnt orange wingback chair that felt like butter beneath his hands.

Throughout Jay's explanation of events in Centrus City, the circle members cast glances at Bari, some in suspicion, others in amazement. It was quite the tale, with Bari's brother, Bash, revealed to be a Seer with Seer and Focus blood, and Ethan the same, a vampire turned by his own father, Gordon, who'd been thought dead. Leo, the man who raised Ethan, had been a vampire first, and turned Gordon after accidentally going feral and nearly killing him when Ethan was a boy. Ethan and his mother arrived home at the worst time, and Gordon attacked and killed his wife in his own feral state.

All these years later, Gordon wanted to make it up to Ethan somehow, having gone mad from grief, with a plan to use his superior vampire thrall to enslave all of Centrus, giving Ethan an entire city to rule over with a worthy partner beside him in Bash.

Together with Bari, Bash's inner circle, Jay and Maximus, and the human mayor of Centrus City, who was a Null, they'd defeated Gordon, but decided to keep him alive in the hopes that Ethan could reach his father someday.

"And you went along with all that," Anjali spat at the end of Jay's tale, "instead of killing those vampires the moment you had the chance?"

Anjali sat with Maximus and Ursula on a sofa across from Bari. Clara and Daisy shared a love seat at Bari's right, with Reggie lounging on a chaise at Bari's left, nursing what might have been whiskey, and Jay stood in the middle, not shying from the varied reactions centered on him, most of which were barely veiled shock.

Bari understood. He too had been raised to believe vampires were parasitic monsters, unworthy of mercy, and he might have gone on believing that for the rest of his life if he hadn't met Ethan and taken such an easy liking to him.

"I trusted Bashir," Jay answered.

"You mean the man who humiliated you by sleeping with someone else?" Ursula asked, still coolly collected but not hiding the sneer that curled her lip.

Anjali's disgust was more prominent. "A fanger too? It's bad enough Bain created a circle from the lesser races, and now—"

"Excuse me?" Bari interrupted. He'd told himself to stay quiet, to let Jay handle this, since it was his pack, but he couldn't let prejudice like that slide. "First, I'll ask you not to call a friend of mine 'fanger.' And who exactly is lesser just because of their tribe? You think us so superior because we howl at the moon?"

If Jay disliked Bari stepping in, he didn't show it, since he peeked at Bari with the shadow of a smile creeping into his expression.

Anjali rose to her feet. "If I don't have respect for an Alpha who'd rather fuck a fanger than mate with an honorable man of his own tribe, I'm certainly not going to listen to the reject brother."

"Anji!" Jay whirled on her.

"Now, now, can't we all just get along?" Reggie called from his reclined position, clinking the ice in his glass and seemingly nonplussed by it all, though it was difficult to tell with the sunglasses.

"Your stance is well-noted, Reggie," Ursula droned. "You'd sleep with anything with a pulse, whether human, whiskered, or scaly."

Reggie shrugged.

Jay still had his gaze on Anjali, and though his back was to Bari in that position, Bari knew the moment when Jay stared her down with an Alpha challenge, because it was more than the flash of eyes Stage One would have provided, but a flex of claws at his sides proving he'd gone straight to Stage Two.

Anjali lowered her head and sat.

The small display of machismo made Bari shift in his seat. That was hot, though now wasn't the time to enjoy it.

"Personally, I can't imagine not being with another wolf," Clara spoke softly, holding her wife's hand between them, "but we're not talking about a lizard or some other tribe here. Bashir chose a vampire over you. It's...."

"Creepy," Daisy said with a shiver.

"Concerning," Clara corrected, squeezing Daisy's hand. "I mean, can someone like that ever be trusted? Can Bashir? How do you know they're not biding their time to try taking everyone over again now that you and Max are gone?"

"My brother would never do that," Bari affirmed.

"Maybe not normally," Clara placated, "but none of this is normal, is it? Statistically, all this happening at the same time, in the same city, is... well, not just improbable. If I hadn't heard it happened, I'd say it was literally impossible. The vampire was able to control Bashir, you said. How do you know he isn't still controlling him? Even if he's not, letting the father live too, who's clearly unhinged and dangerous, just seems...."

"Suicidally stupid," Anjali groused.

"Incompetent," Ursula said when Jay returned his attention to the sofa. "You do always want our honest opinion, don't you, Alpha?"

If Jay had been about to tout his position and power again, he reconsidered at that question, and any sign of his inner wolf had retreated by the time he answered. "Always, but don't think I made any of my decisions or concessions lightly. Max," he beseeched his so far silent Second, "a little help?"

Maximus scooted to the edge of his seat, but his expression didn't look like he was about to say what Jay was hoping for. "I can vouch that I don't think Bain or the vampire intend on anything nefarious on purpose, but I'm not going to say I agree with letting the older vampire live. Clara's worries are valid. The power in that city, the threat it could pose… I don't agree with just leaving things be and hoping for the best."

"That vampire," Jay said with stress on how Maximus had yet to use Ethan's name—none of them had, "saved Theresa and William's lives."

"He did, after being the reason they were at risk in the first place. I'm sorry, Jay." Maximus hung his head, having spoken softer than he was known for, but he was being honest, not simply telling his Alpha what he wanted to hear, which was a Second's duty.

"What would you have me do?" Jay asked the room. "Pull our support? Challenge Bashir directly?"

It was clear the circle was hesitant to voice their answers with Bari in the room.

When no one else said anything, Ursula cleared her throat. "All we would ask is for you to keep your eyes open and be receptive to the possibility that you're wrong. That's enough. For now." Diplomatic but direct—just like a good Warden should be.

"Obviously, we will monitor the situation carefully," Jay conceded. "There is a lot of power in Centrus City, but that doesn't mean their pack is a threat. Until I have reason to believe otherwise, they are still our allies."

No one spoke against that, but Bari had a feeling if Jay asked for a vote on whether to unite the packs through a different marriage, no matter who the new candidate might be, he'd be hard-pressed to get even an equal split.

Bari had his work cut out for him, and that was without anyone knowing he was a Seer, though considering he and Bash were twins, they might already suspect.

Like before, what broke the silence was Ursula clearing her throat. "Apologies, Alpha. We want what's best for our people. Always. Anything beyond that is something we can be patient about."

"Thank you," Jay said again, calming himself with a deeper breath. "Now, I want to get back to my city and her troubles. You all had rather unfortunate accounts in your reports. It's time we started coming up with solutions. In the meantime, Bari is our guest, and I expect everyone to treat him as such. I'm sure he'll be happy to answer any questions you have about what happened, his brother, and Centrus City."

"Yes, I'm sure his opinion won't be skewed at all," Anjali added a final barb.

It hit Bari then that his prophecy was about a woman, and just like Bash's inner circle, Jay's was made up of three men and three women equally, with the addition of Clara's wife, Daisy. Could any of them be the one Bari had to worry about?

Her desire for the past, the words of the prophecy said. Clara, Daisy, Anjali, and Ursula all seemed to be traditionalists to some degree, even if some were nicer about it than others. A few cities had other tribes in control—lizards, cats, rats—but even that would have been unheard of a few decades ago. Once, every city was run by wolves, every inner circle made of wolves only, and the other races were like a caste system beneath them. Things had been getting better, but not everywhere was like Centrus City, where Bash had fought to keep the races equal.

Bari's straying thoughts meant he almost missed the others dispersing. Anjali stormed off, Maximus and Ursula went somewhere together, and even Clara and Daisy offered Bari no more than weak smiles. Only Reggie was the exception, who sidled up to Bari as he stood from the chaise.

"If JJ's too busy later to give you a proper tour, love, the lower level is all mine. Stop by anytime." Reggie may have winked, though again, the sunglasses made it difficult to tell.

"If I forget to knock, will you be decent?" Bari volleyed back.

"Never," Reggie purred and unabashedly eyed Bari up and down.

Bari laughed.

At Jay's approach, Reggie nodded in farewell and made a swift retreat. Reggie would be a good time, no doubt, but Jay was something else—something more that Bari hoped he didn't have to give up on yet.

"Don't forget I warned you about him," Jay said, nodding after Reggie.

"Oh, he's harmless. Sweet, though. I'm not so sure I'll get as warm a welcome from any of the others anymore."

"I hope all that didn't give you too poor of an opinion of my city." Jay motioned into the foyer where they'd left their bags and led Bari from the living room.

"Not at all," Bari said. "You have a passionate circle, firm in their beliefs. If I hadn't been in Centrus City myself, I might not be as open-minded about what happened either. That is quite the crew you have, though."

"And Bashir's isn't?" Jay said with a chuckle.

"Fair." They collected their bags, and Bari followed Jay up the spiral staircase. Everyone else seemed to have vanished. "Were they all your choices for circle members?"

"For the most part. Maximus was my first choice as Second. He recommended Ursula, and she recommended Anji. I chose Clara myself, and Reggie is leftover from the previous circle."

"Brookdale votes on your Alphas, don't you?"

"We do. We might be traditional about wolves running the city, but we've voted on our Alphas for generations instead of following familial lines. I was voted in after the previous Alpha chose to retire. I was Councilor then, started young, just like your Luke back in Centrus."

"Really?" Bari grinned. "I can see that. Which is also why, forgive me for saying this, but Anjali seems an odd choice as your replacement."

"I know she's intense, but that's what was needed," Jay defended, keeping a close pace in the upper hall so he only had to look over his shoulder to meet Bari's eyes. "I was voted in because I had the Alpha's backing and was considered the most levelheaded choice, but the people who didn't want me thought I was too sympathetic toward the plights of other tribes. Choosing to surround myself with known traditionalists helped appease those voices, and whatever else Anjali might be, she does keep the peace."

"I thought you said tribal unrest was a problem?"

"It is, but in my day, things had gotten so bad, there were fights in the streets, and the Shelter was practically a war zone. Our Alpha said the only reason it wasn't outright civil war was because of me and my efforts, and enough of the people agreed to choose me to succeed him. Things had been getting better, but it's not enough. Every time I think we're making headway, something counteracts our progress—a fight, a house being burned down, a family run out of the city. I'm hoping we can find a way to finally settle things down. Here we are."

Bari startled. He'd gotten so caught up in their conversation, he hadn't realized how far they'd walked—all along an open hallway that seemed to span the entire den and looked down on the rooms below. They had just entered a closed section of the hall with doors on either side and what looked like a second staircase at the other end.

"This will be your room." Jay gestured to their left.

"And yours would be…?" Bari asked with a not-so-subtle bat of his eyes.

Jay huffed a laugh, so sweetly bashful that Bari couldn't help ruffling him every chance he got. "My room is at the end of the hall." Jay pointed to the final door on the left, a few rooms down. "There's work I need to do, but… dinner at seven? You have free rein anywhere in the house until then. I'll find you. I have a place in mind I think you'll really love."

"Sounds perfect," Bari said, and it would have been, even with the sour circle members, but that wasn't the only thing plaguing Bari. "Um…."

"Something else?" Jay prompted when Bari didn't finish his thought.

They were alone, and if they were going to trust each other, Bari should tell Jay what he saw. He really, really should.

But he didn't.

"Don't let the naysayers get to you," Bari said instead. "They're right to be skeptical. Even I am a little, and I adore Ethan. All you can do is continue to make decisions with your people's best interest in mind. That's being a good Alpha, which you clearly already are."

If possible, the flush Bari kept bringing to Jay's face reddened darker than ever, and his smile went wider too. "Thank you. I needed to hear that. I'll see you soon." He continued down the hall, and Bari watched after him a pace or two, before he pulled out his phone.

Bari wanted to tell Jay the truth, but things were tense already, and Jay would want to tell his circle, who might turn this into a witch hunt—or prove to be the witch needing hunting. For now, Bari had to keep this in the family.

He texted Bash the words from his prophecy, adding afterward, I'm not attempting bad poetry, brother. I had a vision. Help.

Then he tucked the phone away and slipped inside his room.

Bari's jaw dropped. There was the same vintage décor, with a four-poster bed, vaulted ceiling with exposed beams, his own bathroom, including a clawfoot tub he could see through the open door, and a balcony he at first thought looked out over a nearby park, until he realized it was a courtyard within the den, complete with rose bushes and an herb garden that only a house with the magically inclined could keep so vibrant this late in the year.

All that alone would have been worthy of the jaw-drop, but that wasn't why Bari stood stunned.

The balcony doors were busted open, and a body lay in front of them, facedown on the carpet in a pool of drying dark-red blood.

"Fuck."

Chapter 3

JAY WAS ready to yank Anjali back by the hair to keep her from digging her claws into Bari, but thankfully, Reggie looped a hold on her elbows first. Reggie might look disarming, but he was deceptively strong.

"Why aren't we tearing this spy apart right now?" Anjali snapped her jaws, at full-on Stage Two, nearly Stage Three with how the seams of her jacket were straining to reveal tufts of dark brown fur peeking through.

"I found the body!" Bari defended, while Maximus and Ursula of all people were standing guard in front of him, with Clara and Daisy beside Jay, holding each other after the revelation of a murder having occurred inside the manor.

So much for anything settling down.

"Finding the body only makes you more the likely suspect!" Anjali countered.

Jay had barely had time to open his suitcase to unpack when a frantic knock sounded at his door, revealing Bari, wild-looking and out of breath. Once Jay saw the grisly scene, he knew there hadn't been time for Bari to be the culprit, and they'd started gathering the others to explain.

It had been almost an hour now since the body was found in the guest room prepared for Bari. Anjali had been last to join them in the living room, having stormed out after their previous meeting.

"Reggie and I inspected the corpse," Ursula said sternly, flashing her eyes at Anjali in warning, one hand outward and the other back toward Bari. "That rat had been dead for over an hour when we found him. The killer wasn't Bain."

"Thank you," Bari said with a huff, crossing his arms indignantly.

"He's still the cause!" Anjali shrugged Reggie off, but only because he let her, since the sprouting of fur had started to dissipate and she no longer looked ready to launch herself forward. "People knew he was coming. People have been spreading rumors about vampires and magic in Centrus City for days. Someone is trying to send a message, and it's clearly to Bain. Or to us for having him here."

"Enough," Ursula said before Jay could bark the same. She calmly approached Anjali, and Jay let her take the lead. "Remember who your Warden is. It isn't your job to be a detective, only to know the people. So, Councilor, who was that man?"

They had already brought the body down to the lower level for Reggie to do an autopsy. Since this was shifter business, they would not be contacting the police, though damage control would likely be necessary. No one else recognized the man, but they could smell that he was rat tribe, and when Anjali finally arrived and saw his face, the rage that had erupted from her proved she knew him.

"Stoltz," she said, smoothing out her clothing. "Angus Stoltz. Rat tribe, yes. He and Alice Leer were just mated."

"That can't be true," Daisy sputtered in disbelief. "Alice has wanted to be a mother since I've known her."

"What does that matter?" Bari asked.

"Alice is a wolf," Clara answered.

Mixed races couldn't procreate. Different types of wolves could, as could different cats, even occasionally, very rarely, a larger cat with someone of the smaller housecat subrace, but a rat and wolf weren't compatible.

"Last I heard," Anjali said, softer, maybe even sympathetic, which was rare from her in the worst of situations, "she was willing to adopt if it meant being with Angus."

They had a moment of silence for the deceased and who he'd left behind, and then Jay stepped forward to retake the room. "Anji, did you have any reason to suspect Angus was in danger?"

"Not to the point of being murdered on our doorstep."

"I've already contacted my network of agents throughout the city," Ursula said. "If there's anything to discover, they'll find it. I'll join them now and check in later." She nodded at Jay, back at Maximus, and took her leave.

"I need to make a sweep of the den," Maximus offered, "figure out where and how our security was breached. If I have any doubts about our safety afterward, no one is staying here tonight. I'll check on Theresa and William again first, and then I'll get to work." He nodded at Jay as well before exiting.

Jay's advisors were nothing if not adept in their autonomy; it was why he'd chosen them.

"I think I'm going to be sick." Daisy grimaced.

"I've got you, honey." Clara drew in the air in front of Daisy's stomach a rune Jay knew to be used on nausea, usually for travelers or mothers with morning sickness. It glowed a pleasant green and faded into Daisy, where it dissolved, spreading the verdant light outward through her body and causing her to instantly look soothed.

Clara would have made a wonderful Shaman if she wasn't better at offensive spells.

"Thanks." Daisy leaned up to kiss her wife's cheek. "I'll make some tea. Anyone else?"

Bari and Reggie both shook their heads, and Anjali said nothing.

"No, thank you, Daisy," Jay said, and she and Clara left.

"I'll see what more I can learn from the body," said Reggie, more serious than usual, but then they rarely dealt with deaths, let alone murder. "Once I'm through, I'll clean it up and contact the kin."

"I'm coming with you," Anjali said with little room for argument—not that Reggie would have made any; it was customary for the Councilor to lead in such matters.

"When you're ready," Jay said, "I'd like to come too."

Anjali nodded once, stiffly, while Reggie pulled on a smile.

"Of course, JJ."

Déjà vu, Jay thought, only this time, left by his advisors to be alone with Bari Bain, the mood was far more somber.

"Do you really think that man died because I'm here?" Bari asked.

"No." Jay went to him, drawn to offer comfort, though not quite certain how.

Bari had his arms crossed around his middle, but Jay didn't think they knew each other well enough for an embrace to not feel awkward. Given Bari's penchant for being physical, however, he gave a firm squeeze to Bari's shoulder and felt him relax.

"No one knew you'd be here. If anything, they thought your brother was the one I'd be bringing home. I realize that might not be much comfort, but this is not your fault. I am so sorry you had to find that."

"I'm sorry," Bari said, lifting one of his hands from his tightly crossed shield to rest atop Jay's. "And honestly, at least Anjali's outburst made me like her more."

"Really?" Jay asked in surprise.

"She clearly cares about the people here. Even if only for a fellow wolf left widowed." Bari grinned, patted Jay's hand, and let his arms drop to his sides. "I guess this means dinner is cancelled."

"No," Jay said without hesitation. "This isn't how I wanted my homecoming, but like I said, I need to eat. I have different tasks now to complete before tonight, but I'd still like to keep our date. If you're up for it?"

Bari's grin widened into something more genuine. "Is wine on the menu? Because by then, I might need a glass or two."

"I think we might need a few bottles," Jay joked, and as terrible as everything else had turned out, hearing Bari laugh eased Jay's turmoil. "I'll find you," he promised.

This wasn't the homecoming Jay had hoped for one bit. Despite the reports from his circle members of the usual unrest while he'd been away, some of which had been rather brutal brawls, he'd never expected a homicide. That didn't happen in his city, let alone a few feet from where he slept.

First, he followed up with each of his advisors. Clara reported no magical residue on the body or in the room, and so far, Reggie could only confirm the killing blow was dealt by claws. It would take some time to narrow down suspects.

Ursula had checked with the neighbors, all wolves, but no one had witnessed anything. All she learned from her agents was that plenty of people, Alice's family and other wolves in particular, weren't happy with the mixed marriage, but that was to be expected.

Angus was a recent member of the Brookdale pack, after moving there for work. He was an accountant at a firm nowhere near the den and had been at his office less than an hour before the attack would have occurred.

Their one reprieve in the case was that Maximus declared the den safe, having found where Angus snuck inside the grounds. The circle kept everything warded with runes and other magic, but there was a crack in the stone gate hidden by shrubbery, which had allowed Angus to climb over. Blood smeared the stone, proving he'd been attacked before reaching the den. Maybe he'd simply been looking for sanctuary. Regardless, Clara and Reggie sealed the crack and restored the wards, leaving the rest to be solved later when they had more to work with.

Anjali didn't apologize for yet another outburst at Bari, but then she was never one for regrets. "Alice may have questionable taste in men," she said with the usual sneer, "but she loved Angus. She's going to be devastated."

She was when it was time to deliver the news. Since Angus's family lived in Glenwood, Alice was the only kin they could tell in person, and she broke down in Anjali's arms.

By the time Jay had the chance to return to the den, shower, and change for dinner, he was more than ready for that wine.

He probably fussed too much over his outfit, but Bari was always so fashionable. Jay was a sucker for a well-dressed man, but he rarely got the opportunity to enhance his own wardrobe. The best he could manage after rummaging through his closet was nicer gray slacks and a black button-down with light blue accents along the collar, inside where it buttoned up, and inside the cuffs, which he rolled up just enough to show off the contrast. It was basic but better than a T-shirt.

When Jay knocked on Bari's door, there was no answer, so he peeked inside. Reggie and Clara had worked together to magically clean everything after the evidence was gathered. Jay had offered to let Bari stay in any other room—they had plenty—but Bari said he refused to be scared off.

And he really didn't want to give up the balcony, which was standard in only a handful of rooms.

It was off that balcony, down in the courtyard, where Jay heard Bari's voice. He hurried down to meet him. When Bari hadn't answered the knock, Jay almost worried he'd find him in the basement with Reggie, knowing how… friendly both men could be, but while Reggie was with Bari, Jay was pleased to discover them merely chatting at one of the small terrace tables.

Naturally, Bari looked incredible. He too had changed for dinner, his wavy hair flawlessly styled, face shaved while leaving a purposeful amount of scruff that suited him handsomely, and now wearing white fitted slacks, a long white tunic with a Middle Eastern flare, and a high-collared navy blazer, left open and reminiscent of Japanese school uniforms, though the blazer fell much lower past his hips. As Bari gestured while he talked, Jay noticed cuff links glittering at him in the shape of double Bs.

"Jay! Is it dinnertime already?" Bari declared as he caught Jay staring at him from the courtyard doorway. He stared right back, eyeing Jay with a ravenousness far removed from thoughts of dinner. "My, you clean up nice...."

Jay felt his cheeks flush like a teenager again. He really needed to learn to control that.

"Personally, I prefer the bulging bicep look," Reggie said with a wink.

"Reggie," Jay chastised. At least he was used to Reggie's innocuous flirting. He'd known Reggie for far too long and had too little interest in him that way to be as bashful as when the same comments and gestures came from Bari.

"And... me?" Bari had his legs crossed but uncrossed them to stand and brought his hands up with a little tap and flourish at his shoulders, spinning once in a perfect pivot.

He had an unmatched grace and raw magnetism to him that was similar and yet entirely unique from his brother's. How it could be both, Jay hadn't yet figured out.

"Nice," Jay echoed, unable to think of anything better, only to realize how inadequate that was when Bari pouted. "I mean good! Great!"

"Ahem." Reggie loudly cleared his throat and then said in a mock whisper, "I believe the word you're looking for is stunning."

"Yes!" Jay blurted in an attempt at recovery. "Obviously. So stunning, I clearly can't think straight."

Bari's pout spread into a smile.

"Don't mind him, Bari my boy," Reggie said, still kicked back in his chair with another glass of whiskey or some type of alcohol in hand, which most days seemed to be bottomless, and yet he never acted drunk or even slightly buzzed. "It's just that poor JJ hasn't been laid in ages."

"Reggie!" Jay nearly yelped, while Bari threw back his head and laughed.

"Just trying to lower expectations." Reggie shrugged. "Best hurry on off to dinner now, JJ, or I might keep your dancing partner as my own." He leered so openly at Bari that it was obviously meant as a ruse—Jay hoped.

"Now, dancing is something I haven't done in far too long," Bari said, kindly leaving the "laid" comment alone.

"Sorry to disappoint you, love, but our JJ's got two left feet."

"I do not! I mean… it's not that bad," he admitted to Bari, who once again laughed. "Shall we?" Jay held out an arm, and Bari retrieved the overcoat Jay hadn't noticed draped over the chair—black-and-white houndstooth of all things, which made Jay feel even more out of his league. After putting it on, Bari crossed to Jay with a bounce in his step.

At least Jay could embarrass himself all he wanted and Bari didn't seem fazed.

"You have a lovely evening now, Reggie," Bari said as they turned to leave.

"Don't do anything I wouldn't do!" Reggie called after them.

Jay whispered, "Wait for it…."

"Oh right—I do everything!"

Bari laughed, something that was quickly becoming one of Jay's favorite sounds. "Will Maximus be driving us? Or maybe Daisy? Wouldn't that be fun? Miss Daisy driving us."

"Actually," Jay said with a chuckle, "this is one of my favorite places because it's close enough to walk."

Jay enjoyed the way Bari had taken his offered arm and, after Jay claimed a far less spectacular overcoat from the front closet, remained close and connected to him all the way out of the house and down the sidewalk.

"I'm surprised your circle didn't insist on providing a bodyguard," Bari said.

"They tried. I insisted otherwise. I'm not a target. This is about everyone else, particularly non-wolves."

"Of which you're a sympathizer. That could make you a target."

"True, and don't think Max didn't say the same thing, but a murdered Alpha would erupt the city into complete chaos. Everyone knows that. My city's problem is traditionalists, not anarchists. But I really don't want to talk about that tonight."

"Deal." Bari smiled sweetly and hugged Jay's arm a little tighter. "So… why don't you confirm whether any of Reggie's stories about you are true?"

Jay blanched. "He started with the manure one, didn't he?"

"Right in your Alpha's face!" Bari threw his head back in delight.

"I thought it was mud! It stormed all night! I didn't know Reggie fertilized the plants!"

One small comfort to this further mortification was that Jay would likely be accompanied by Bari's laugh all the way to dinner.

BARI COULDN'T remember the last time he'd enjoyed himself so much on a date, let alone a first date. Dinner was French and flawless, as was the wine, and they were halfway through their second bottle before dessert arrived. Then again, they were wolves, so it took about twice as much alcohol to affect them.

Bari felt a lovely, mild buzz.

"I have to ask—how on earth are you still single?"

Then Bari felt suddenly, startlingly sober.

"Forget I asked," Jay said with a cringe, obviously picking up on how Bari's face must have fallen.

"No, it's… just complicated. My last breakup was recent and far from cordial. What about you? Oh shit." Bari's hand flew up to cover his mouth. "Forget I asked." He knew Jay's last breakup was also recent and far from cordial because it had been with his brother after Bash cheated on Jay with Ethan.

"It's all right," Jay dismissed, far more understanding than Bari felt he deserved. "It's not like we were really a couple. Before all that… I guess I got too invested in my role, and whenever someone did turn my head, it was purely physical, and like I've said maybe too many times now, I want romance."

"Then, if I'm being honest," Bari couldn't resist saying, "Bash was a terrible choice for you."

Jay laughed. "So I learned. I also learned that you're the brother who likes romance. Tell me then, more Danielle Steele or Jane Austen?"

Bari winced. "I hate Jane Austen, actually."

"Oh thank God," Jay said in honest relief. "Regency, right? So overdone."

"I know!" Bari leaped forward, nearly upsetting the table in his excitement. "I cannot understand everyone's fascination with it. Of course, I also read gay romance, but I'll admit, I couldn't tell you a single author's name. I'm a total cover whore. Half the time I don't even read the book jackets. It's a terrible habit."

Chuckling, Jay leaned over the table to rest his hand atop Bari's that had slapped down beside his empty plate. "I read the last page of a novel first."

"You monster," Bari gasped.

They laughed together this time, and Bari felt a tingle rush through him from where Jay had his hand.

"Crème brûlée?" The waiter appeared, and they had to disconnect to give him room to set it down. They'd only ordered the one dessert to share, so he provided two spoons, smiled pleasantly, and whisked their empty plates away. "Let me know if you need anything else."

Their second bottle of wine was a Sauternes, sweeter for after a meal, and it would pair perfectly with their dessert. They cracked the top of the crème brûlée together and took their first bites. Heaven—and even more heavenly when Bari sipped his wine.

"Mm. Between that den of yours and being wined and dined like this," Bari said playfully, "you might never get rid of me."

Maybe it was the wine or just that Jay was finally growing more comfortable around Bari, but for once, he didn't blush or stumble over his words. "Then I must be doing something right."

Even finding a dead body in his room, having his first-ever prophecy of doom and gloom, and getting a text from his awful ex couldn't spoil how this day had turned out.

"Don't think me frivolous, though," Jay amended. "Before tonight, I hadn't allowed myself to come here in… over a year? Usually a bowl of Neapolitan is good enough for me. Kind of hard to justify too many candlelit dinners when my people lack housing."

Classy all around, Bari thought with a flutter in his chest.

"So," Bari asked when the wine and dessert were gone, "what else does the Alpha of Brookdale do for fun?"

BARI DIDN'T know what he expected—maybe a board game back at the den—but it certainly wasn't taking a cab to what looked like an abandoned warehouse.

"Um… you're not taking me in there to kill me after that lovely dinner, are you?"

Jay laughed, beckoning Bari to join him. "Guess you'll have to risk it. Come on." The wine had definitely loosened him up.

They went through a nondescript door into an equally nondescript entryway, and Bari honestly might have believed something nefarious was afoot until Jay opened the next set of doors and he heard children's laughter beyond, as well as the unmistakable playful growls and yips of fellow wolves.

For at least the third time that day, Bari's jaw dropped.

The building housed an enormous indoor park, so expansive and filled with hills, trees, and other greenery, that if it hadn't been for the clear glass roof displaying the night sky above, Bari could have believed this was the real thing.

There was a good dozen other people there, adults and children, all nude and in various states of transformation. It was clear some wolves were simply there to frolic and enjoy themselves, while others were training their children to shift through each of the stages. Real parks and wooded areas could be dangerous and required lookouts to ensure normal humans didn't discover the existence of shifters, but this took care of that, since the building was clearly controlled by the pack. It was also a nice alternative to the dropping temperatures outside as winter approached.

"There are lockers through here where we can put our clothes," Jay said, gesturing Bari through yet another door, the only area remaining inside the building that wasn't a living part of the park.

"Getting me naked already?" Bari teased as he followed Jay.

Finally, Bari was afforded another bright blush across Jay's cheeks. "Unless you want to ruin that outfit!"

"Now that would be a travesty."

They undressed, hung up or folded their clothing in separate lockers, and Bari was quickly amused by just how obviously Jay was trying to not admire the merchandise. By nature, shifters weren't as caring as humans about being nude in each other's presence. There was a primal part to them that needed freedom and thrived off time spent in their animal forms, whatever stage. Being clothed for that wasn't practical. But family or even strangers was different from seeing someone naked for the first time who you planned to court.

Bari didn't want to seem like a deviant—the unspoken rule was like bathhouses in Japan: no obvious leering—but he couldn't resist a peek.

This date was turning out splendidly.

Bari caught Jay's eye and winked. "Race you to the top of that hill," he said and took off running for the door, already starting to shift.

By the time Bari's feet hit the grass outside the locker room, they were more like paws, and he was a Stage Four wolf before he was even halfway up the hill in the center of the park. Bari's wolf coat was silver like his brother's, and he'd seen enough of Jay partially changed in Centrus to know he was a brown wolf.

A handsome brown wolf that zoomed past Bari just as he was about to crest the top of the hill, trotted about in a circle of triumph, and howled.

Bari joined him, circling Jay before stopping to echo that howl, and then lowering himself with a wag of his tail and rolling over in the grass. Jay sniffed him, hunkered playfully, and Bari almost thought the Alpha was going to lick his nose, but at the last moment, he nudged it instead, tender and sweet and still more intimate than having seen each other naked.

Rolling back up onto his paws, Bari nipped at Jay impishly and took off running again down the other side of the hill. They chased each other, running and circling and rolling again through the grass and around trees, until Bari's legs burned, and he returned to the top of that same high hill, unfurling himself in human form to look up at the sky through the glass ceiling. He kept a little of Stage Two about him, his eyes cutting through the dark, since there were few lights in the park, a bit of silver fur edging his body and his fangs prominent as he swiped his tongue across them when Jay joined him in a similar state.

Jay's ears were just the tiniest bit wolflike still, trimmed in his brown fur. As they looked at each other, lying side by side, panting for breath, Bari saw that Jay's one slightly crooked ear was a tad more bent than the other even in this form, and Bari thought the way it looked was especially charming.

A shadow of discomfort crossed Jay's face, and he reached for that ear like he wished he could hide it.

"Sorry!" Bari said, assuming Jay must be self-conscious about the ear. "I didn't mean to stare. It's just so... cute." He reached over, hesitant, giving Jay plenty of time to pull away if he didn't want Bari to touch him, but when all Jay did was lower the hand that had covered his ear, it was easy for Bari to replace it. He gently stroked the edges of the furred and slightly pointed tip.

A rumble sounded in Jay's throat, almost like a cat's purr. It would have been the ideal moment to lean in for a kiss—if Bari hadn't suddenly felt several sets of eyes on him.

He sat up and looked around. The remaining people and families in the park were pretending they hadn't been watching, but Bari could tell they had all only just looked away.

Jay sighed as he sat up next to Bari, letting Stage Two fade to nothing, and Bari did the same, leaving them as just two thirtysomething naked men on a hill.

"I think we're drawing some attention." Bari leaned into Jay's shoulder with a teasing bump.

"Sadly, yes. I don't come here very often, but more than us drawing attention, I think they might be wondering how many of those rumors about Centrus City are true. It's good for them to see us acting like everyone else, normal and at ease with each other."

Bari smiled. He'd been a little worried the scrutiny would ruin the mood, but at least it had only put it on pause. He should be continuing to charm the Alpha and see where things might go, but he couldn't help thinking of his prophecy, the murder, and the unrest he knew to be rampant throughout the city.

"Seems there are only other wolves here," Bari said.

"Yes, there's a different park like this for each race throughout the city, leftover from the previous Alpha's reign. I've been trying to convert the largest one, this one, into the sole building for all races and turn the others into housing, but I'm not getting much support."

"That would be a wonderful idea," Bari agreed, "but difficult if everyone's against it. Is it really no other races allowed?"

"Not officially, but they've segregated themselves, and no one goes against it."

"Maybe you're underestimating people."

"How do you mean?"

Bari shifted onto his hip to better face Jay. "Organize mixers."

Jay laughed.

"I'm serious! If you lead by example, they'll slowly grow more comfortable too. Have mixers at all the parks, little by little, until people stop even realizing they're not only around their own kind. Then try your proposal again. Sometimes you have to be patient with people, but that doesn't mean you give up. Segregation isn't exactly the best method for finding common ground."

Jay seemed to consider that, scanning his people closely, who were still all pretending to be focused on their own matters. When he returned his attention to Bari, his smile was coy. "And you didn't want to be in your brother's circle?"

"I realize I'd be fantastic at it," Bari said grandly, "but I prefer my romance novels and a job I love."

"Speaking of, is it really okay for you to be away this long?"

The question almost caused Bari to flinch, but he still wasn't ready to talk about that. "I had vacation days coming."

Jay didn't pry. It would have been nice to frolic a bit more, especially since most of the families were leaving and they'd likely be alone soon, but it was late, and they'd both had an equally long and trying day.

All too soon, the date was ending, but it was a companionable conclusion, sitting closely in the cab back to the den, walking arm and arm again all the way inside, up the stairs, and down the hall to their rooms. Jumping into bed on the first date would not be Bari's idea of romance.

Tempting, though....

He didn't protest when Jay brought them to a stop in front of Bari's room to say good night. Then, just as Bari hoped, Jay turned to him.

"I had a wonderful time tonight, Bashir," he said and started to lean in.

"Bari," Bari said as he snapped backward. He tried to smile it off, but all he could do was grimace. "Wrong brother."

"I'm so sorry!" It helped that Jay looked properly mortified. "I—"

"Honest mistake. We are twins. Ethan was so sure I was Bash once, he kissed me."

That made Bari grimace again, since Jay had been about to do the same thing. It shouldn't bother him so much about the wrong name. They'd talked about Bash plenty today, and it was an honest mistake.

Jay looked about ready to offer another apology, but then blurted, "Ethan kissed you?"

Of course that's what Jay would focus on. "Don't be too hard on him. He only did it wishing I was Bash." Like you, Bari hated himself for thinking.

"I'm sorry," Jay said again. "This isn't how I wanted the night to end. It's only because Bashir and I had a similar date once, and I was probably reminded—"

"Wait, what?" Bari's eyes bugged out as this continued to spiral. "You did all those same things with Bash?"

"Not exactly!" Jay held out his hands, though his urgency was not helping. "Not at an indoor park, obviously, but… we did go to a wooded area outside Centrus City."

"So you were recreating a date you already had with my brother?"

"No! That wasn't my intention. I didn't think of it like that."

"Just enough to call me by his name?"

"Bari, please, I swear—"

Bari's phone buzzed, saving him from having to look at Jay's contorted face. When he took it out to look at the message, the fact that it was Bash texting him made everything worse. "Speak of the devil," he tried to say with a smile. "I was waiting for a message from him. I should answer this. Thank you again, Jay, for dinner. It was lovely."

Jay clearly wanted to say more, do more, anything, but a kiss good night was no longer on the table, and in the end, he couldn't come up with anything to say or do, so Bari offered a final bitter smile and went into his room.

At least there wasn't a body this time, but Bash's text didn't make Bari feel much better.

Bash apologized for not getting back to Bari sooner, but he had been without his phone for most of the day. He didn't have any ideas about what Bari's prophecy might mean but reminded him that Bash and Ethan were already planning to visit next week for William's science fair and asked him to keep them informed until then.

After all, some prophecies are short-lived, others take years to fulfill.

Years? Bari doubted he'd be staying in Brookdale that long.

At least not anymore. He was destined to run from one disaster to the next.

He set his phone on the dresser and started to get ready for bed. For once, he was honestly envious of his brother.

Chapter 4

"IT'S SUPPOSED to have foamed like that, right?" Jay asked, staring at the strangely bubbling and frankly unappetizing batter.

"Yes," Daisy said with an exasperated eye roll, though she had yet to lose her sunny smile. She wore a vintage-style turquoise apron with large black-and-white polka dot trim, covering an equally vintage yellow dress.

Jay wore a similar apron over his jeans and T-shirt—black with red ruffles covered in cherries. Daisy had insisted.

"I already said that, remember?" she continued. "It's how you know the yeast is working and ready for a recipe like this. If it didn't foam, it would mean the yeast was bad or we did something wrong. The batter is perfect now. All you need to do is pour it into the crumpet rings and…?" she trailed off, blinking at Jay leadingly for him to fill in the answer.

"Um… start them off on a high heat to get those weird little bubbles activated, then turn the stove down so the crumpets cook through without burning the base."

Daisy's smiled widened, telling him he'd remembered correctly. "Then just flip them over for thirty seconds or so to get a blush of color on the tops and you're done! You got this." She patted his arm supportively.

She may not be a true member of the circle, since she didn't hold an official title, other than being Clara's wife, but that was enough for her to live in the den like any member's mate and to retain a level of respect within the pack.

Daisy was also a phenomenal cook, and thank God, because Jay had only recently mastered pancakes. He didn't know what had possessed him to try crumpets.

"All your accompaniments are waiting on the table, and everything already smells delicious," Daisy encouraged after he'd poured the batter into the rings, stepping away and starting to hang up her apron.

Jay felt a surge of panic that she was leaving him to finish this alone, but then he couldn't have her hold his hand the whole time. The accompaniments were ready and waiting, along with fresh coffee. It would all be complete in mere minutes. "Thank you for this, Daisy."

"My pleasure!" she exclaimed, squeezing Jay's arm this time with a broad red-lipped smile. She really was the epitome of a '50s housewife, if said housewife was secretly a werewolf with a powerful witch as her sugar momma. "I don't know Bari that well, but he seems sweet. Still, Clara and I are sorry things didn't work out the way you'd hoped with his brother."

"Thank you," Jay said again, much more somberly.

"I say good riddance. If Bain would rather have a fanger as his mate, uniting with a pack like that would have been a disaster!"

Jay held back a cough and cringe at the comment. "I did still vow to support Bashir and his city, should any of the other packs attempt an attack."

"Without a marriage?" Daisy balked. "After he gave sanctuary to two vampires?"

"Glenwood gave a vampire sanctuary too, you'll recall."

Jay had explained that Leo, the vampire who raised Ethan and turned his father, Gordon, had been given asylum by the previous Alpha of Glenwood years ago. The current Alpha, the former's daughter, Kate, honored that pact when she took over, but Leo had strict rules to follow to be allowed to stay in her city, including using runes to keep himself undetectable by shifters.

If Kate's people knew they had a vampire living among them, it wouldn't be taken lightly.

"At least a leashed vampire is better than a free one," Daisy said.

Jay knew what she was thinking but didn't say aloud.

Better would be a dead one.

Jay had a collaborative circle, but not one that would roll over when being asked to ignore decades of indoctrination.

Still, he couldn't help saying, "If our three cities were united, no other packs would ever stand against us. Isn't that what we should be fostering? Community? Cooperation? A sharing of knowledge and power? Or would it be better to get plunged into war on all sides?"

"Don't pull me into the debate!" Daisy held up her hands as if asking for mercy. "I'm just the cook. I can't speak for Clara or any of the others on what would be best for this city. I just know that, well… turning your back on tradition is one thing, but vampires? I know you didn't expect things to turn out the way they did in Centrus, but who's to say you know what's going on now? Bari seems sweet. He seems pretty cool, actually. Just be careful, okay? He's a little too soft-hearted, like you."

"Soft-hearted? Weren't you the one who got queasy from our murder yesterday?"

"That's different! At least it was just a rat."

Speaking of queasy, Jay's stomach twisted, and he almost missed that it was time to flip the crumpets. As good as they smelled, he couldn't say his appetite was as strong anymore. "I doubt his mate would say the same."

"I didn't mean it like that!" Daisy defended, though Jay didn't think he could have misinterpreted her. "I'm sure Alice is beside herself. I should take her some cookies. Hopefully some good can come of this. Alice really would make a wonderful mother."

Again, Jay's stomach ached. "I'm sure she would have made a wonderful mother to an adopted child as well."

"Of course she would have." Daisy patted his arm once more, and it seemed so condescending, Jay was left speechless.

Daisy excused herself, and Jay tried to focus on not burning the crumpets after all his hard work. How many shifters thought like Daisy? And it was so casual, so offhanded, and something he heard or witnessed every day, whether subtle or blatant bigotry.

The former Alpha had been like Jay, accepting of everyone but not willing to force others out of their comfort zones where tradition was concerned. The marriage to Bashir was supposed to be Jay's first step toward pushing boundaries and striving to be better than that. Now he was right back where he'd started.

"Something smells incredible."

Jay jumped as he was flipping the last crumpet out of its ring and onto a plate. At least they'd all turned out perfectly golden, and just in time, because when Jay whirled around, there stood Bari.

He looked as effortlessly gorgeous and fashionably styled as ever in a dark teal button-down with a peach floral pattern over it, tucked into cream slacks, with a brown belt and a necklace bearing a long silver pendant with Arabic writing.

No one was supposed to look that good before coffee.

"Jay…?"

Jay jumped again, realizing he'd been staring without giving an answer. "Sorry! Uh… crumpets? Every possible topping you could want is on the table, as well as freshly brewed coffee, cream, sugar…." He trailed off because that was the end of the list, yet he felt like he should say more. There was so much to apologize for, but the most he'd figured out this morning was… crumpets.

"Love the apron." Bari smirked as he took a seat and claimed one of the coffee mugs. "Wouldn't have been my first guess for what you wear while cooking."

"It's Daisy's." Jay smirked back. "I am aware I look ridiculous."

"I didn't say ridiculous." Bari had his usual charm about him, spewing easy flirtations, but Jay saw it as armor now instead of sincerity. Something in Bari's eyes wasn't the same.

"You look very nice this morning," Jay tried to say with as much sincerity of his own. "But then you always look nice."

Bari's smirk twitched—sad, Jay thought. Wounded.

Jay brought the crumpets over, untied his apron, and sat across from Bari with the apron draped over the next chair. "May I ask what your pendant says?"

"Oh. Cheesy maybe. It's my name. Bari can have a few different meanings in Arabic, but this one is 'originator,' since I'm the older twin. Bash hates it." He chuckled, only for his smile to crumble at mention of his brother. He cleared his throat and quickly claimed two crumpets, starting with buttering them both. "Where is everyone else?"

"Hard at work, checking on more leads concerning the murder." Jay claimed two crumpets of his own, though he only planned to butter one. "I'll have to join them soon, but I wanted to do something for you."

"This is for me?" Bari asked with a frown.

"Fresh crumpets with butter and honey, an assortment of jams, and Daisy insisted on the clotted cream. There's also Nutella, which is my favorite. I recommend regular cream cheese and jalapenos too if you're more the savory type." Jay pointed to each item as he listed them and then picked up the Nutella to add to the crumpet he'd buttered.

Bari set down his knife. "You didn't need to do all this."

Jay set his knife down too. "I think I did. Last night—"

"Let me start. I think this might be too… hard. Too weird. You were engaged to my brother! It was ridiculous of me to invite myself here thinking—"

"You were thinking," Jay jumped in, "that you wanted to help, that we get along well, better than me and Bashir, and that maybe something could still be salvaged from this mess. Bashir and Ethan… well, they have the comfort of knowing they were destined to be together. They prophesized it themselves. Most people don't get that luxury. Most people mess up and have to work at it."

A deep furrow had overtaken Bari's brow as soon as Jay said Bashir and Ethan's names. He cringed harder now. "I'm not my brother. And I couldn't be happier about that."

"Me too," Jay asserted. "Honestly. I wasn't trying to recreate my date with Bashir. If anything, I was trying to replace it with something better, because believe me, that date ended worse than ours."

"Really?" Bari perked up.

"We kissed for the first and only time, and it was glaringly obvious we had zero chemistry. I'm sure that's why his name slipped out, because… even if I didn't think that would happen with us, I was terrified of being disappointed again. Hugely disappointed, because your brother pales in comparison to you, and this is a bigger risk for how much more I like you."

The remaining tightness smoothed from Bari's face, and he huffed a short, bashful laugh. Well, as bashful as Bari Bain ever got. He stood, leaving Jay unsure what was about to happen as Bari moved around the table to lean over him.

"In that case, rather than draw this out and torture you any further…." Bari grinned, but it was softer than usual because there was hope and bare affection in the expression as he leaned closer.

If asked when and who Jay had last kissed, other than Bashir, he wouldn't have been able to recall. One thing he knew for certain was that no kiss with anyone else, Bashir especially, had felt like this.

Bari knew just the right angle, the right amount of pressure, and how open to leave his mouth for a puff of breath to pass between them without expectation of anything deeper unless Jay wanted to deepen it. He felt Bari's hand curl around the back of his neck and nails scrape up into his hair, eliciting a low rumble from Jay like when Bari stroked his crooked ear that he'd almost grown his hair out over to cover.

Jay tilted his head the other way to push his advantage, humming when Bari opened wider at the request, and their tongues brushed with a tentative flick, and then a long, bold swipe from Bari made Jay hum and growl again. Jay deepened the kiss further with a stroke of his own, then another, and another, before they gasped apart.

"Mm… I hope the crumpets are half that good," Bari purred. "Didn't feel like a disappointment to me."

"Hm?" Jay blinked at him dumbly.

Bari laughed—outright and free and just the way Jay loved it.

"S-sorry!" Jay stammered, destined to forever act like an untouched virgin around Bari, apparently. "Yes, I'd say that was the opposite of disappointing. Shall we enjoy breakfast before I ruin another perfect moment?"

Bari chuckled more lightly as he pulled away, reminding Jay that his hand was curled around Jay's neck. Bari withdrew it slowly, leaving the lingering sensation of his fingers having been there, along with a soft brush against Jay's ear—the crooked one again that Jay wasn't minding so much anymore.

Bari returned to his chair. Jay put cream cheese and jalapenos on his other crumpet. Bari copied him, and then covered his second one in jam and clotted cream.

They were delicious if Bari's moan was any indication. Jay almost moaned himself, so it had to be more than just the after-buzz from their kiss.

"You are forgiven if this can be a weekly tradition," Bari gushed.

"Do you mean that?"

The question was more serious than making a date with crumpets. Bari looked a little unsure, but his gaze was steady when he said, "I think so."

It was a start.

"I have duties most of the day after this," Jay said, "but I do have one more surprise for you."

"Oh? You're spoiling me." Bari leaned his chin on one hand with his elbow propped on the table. "Keep it up."

Jay felt the most wonderful warmth flutter through him with the flutter of Bari's lashes.

"There you are! Ready to go, Bari?" Theresa bounded into the kitchen, smartly dressed in a simple white blouse and black pencil skirt. Before Jay could explain things to Bari, she noticed the spread on the table and squealed. "Ooo, crumpets!"

BARI WAS still taken aback by how impressive the Brookdale Institute of Art was proving to be. He wasn't usually won over by conventional artwork, paintings, and photography like his brother. He worked— had worked—in a natural history museum, more taken with artifacts, historical clothing, and written records.

But Bari could admit, after seeing the recently acquired collection of San Francisco rock posters from the sixties and the American documentary photography with some stellar black-and-whites, he was sold.

"I cannot believe we spent that entire train ride without me ever learning you work at a museum!" Bari exclaimed, mouth agape, as he continued his personal tour with Theresa—the museum's director. "And you run the place? That's it, you are my new best friend and are never getting rid of me." He looped an arm around Theresa's waist and hugged her to his side.

She was clearly eating up the praise and attention like a proud beaming momma. "I was on vacation! I didn't want to talk about work. Of course, now that vacation is over, you'll never hear me shut up about this place."

Bari doubted he'd shut up about it either, considering the next section Theresa brought him to was a high-ceilinged room covered in magazines, comic books, and what had once been underground publications for a punk, queer, and counterculture collection.

He whimpered like he had when tasting his first bite of crumpet. "Without sounding cliché, I feel like Belle being given her library."

"Too bad your beast couldn't join us."

Bari's smile widened a bit and then fell with an unfair scowl.

"What's that look for?" Theresa asked. The museum wasn't empty but quiet enough for them to have this exhibit all to themselves. "I thought things were going well between you two."

"They are. We had a hiccup last night, but this morning was… wonderful. He really is trying so very hard. I just worry sometimes he's still hung up on my brother."

"He probably is."

Bari frowned at her.

"Who cares? He likes you more. After a meeting with Bash, he always seemed troubled and unsure of himself. His expression around you could not be more different."

"Really?" That eased Bari somewhat, and after their admittedly fairy-tale first kiss, which he had initiated, he should be better at pushing aside insecurities.

"Want to see why Jay really wanted me to show you around?"

Attention piqued, Bari followed Theresa where no patrons were allowed to go. It was all very spy versus spy, clandestine trickery, for there was a book on the back shelf in Theresa's office that when pulled out opened the shelf inward to reveal a hidden passageway. She bobbed an eyebrow at him before pulling him inside and allowing the shelf to close behind them.

Back there, in what felt like catacombs, a narrow corridor led into a larger hidden room filled with what Bari at first assumed must be extremely rare, valuable, or maybe even stolen artifacts that couldn't be displayed to the public.

Then he realized the real reason they couldn't be displayed, because stolen or not, they were rare and extremely valuable—and all about shifters.

"Creation tablets!" Bari gasped in wonder.

There were books, tools, garments, and multiple delicate parchments under glass, but in a place of honor on a central table was an assortment of stone tablets, each laid flat and most having been meticulously cleaned.

"You're familiar?"

"More like obsessed," Bari admitted. "Jay couldn't possibly have known that. I doubt it would have come up in conversation with Bash."

"Serendipity, then. They're recent donations, or otherwise each of these would be under glass too. The cleaning is almost complete, and naturally, please wear gloves if you're inclined to touch them." Theresa indicated a box of gloves nearby. "They still need to be cataloged, and I'm afraid I don't have the expertise to know everything they're depicting."

"They're different pieces to a larger story," Bari explained, reaching out to hover his hand above the priceless relics, "and this looks like a complete collection, which was supposed to be lost. Countless cultures have tales of anthropomorphic animals. Many depict some of their gods that way, like the Egyptians. For shifters, legend says that's us, we existed first, born right out of the earth as the natural inhabitants. Creation tablets like these are the only stories about us by us. Pure animals without human forms were created to serve and feed us. And to be pets, of course."

"And humans?"

Bari circled the table, searching for the right account. "There. See the crude copulation etching between what's clearly a werewolf and a lizard shifter?" He smirked, though the image was barely more than stick figures. The humanoids were wolf and lizard-like, however, one bending over the other on all fours. The next image showed them holding a very human-looking baby with a sort of single-ringed halo. "A mutation. A curse, if you will, for intermingling the tribes."

"That's what I thought," Theresa said, scrunching her nose, "but it was hard to stomach being considered a mutant."

Bari chuckled. "You understand why the traditionalists aren't very happy about having humans in the pack."

"But the different tribes can't have children together anymore?"

"About 99.9% impossible. Another part of the curse, they say. For muddying the blood, our ability to muddy it again was removed, or at least lessened. After all, what sad, pitiable creatures don't have an animal form to change into?" Bari smiled wryly at her, and Theresa chuckled in turn.

"Don't think I'm not genuinely jealous of that."

Bari continued around the table. There was a tablet for each tribe, and he pointed them out to Theresa. "The story goes that every race had their own kingdom once, with the wolf kingdom being the largest and strongest, set above the others, but when shifters began intermarrying and humans were the result, only for the races to become practically sterile when mating with one another, many shifters turned on each other, the kingdoms were destroyed, and most considered humans to be a blight."

"There are more of us," Theresa said.

"Now, but if these stories are to be believed, not originally. It doesn't add up, and no genetic research I've ever heard of into shifter or human physiology supports it, yet belief persists. The alternate theory, of course, contradicts tradition, saying that humans came first and shifters were the mutation." As those words left him, Bari froze in his progression around the table. Theresa had stopped as well, across from him over the long expanse of irreplaceable history, even if the beliefs presented were faulty.

That humans came first was a far more likely story given today's population, and all Bari could think of then was his prophecy, much as he'd been trying to forget.

A woman hovered as a dark presence over the three closest main cities, ready to strike despite how Centrus had been saved from disaster, someone who wanted a return to the past, whatever that meant. Bari had assumed the villain to be a shifter, but a human was also possible.

"Do you have any magical affinity?" Bari asked as he resumed his circling.

"No…," Theresa said in drawn-out confusion. "Why do you ask?"

"No reason," Bari lied, but if the dark presence behind his prophecy was human, she'd have to be a natural witch to command enough power to affect so many people and cities. "Shifters are very careful in making sure none of our history falls into the wrong hands. You know more than most. I suppose that's the company you keep. Still, it's remarkable you've been granted guardianship over these pieces."

"More like a babysitter," Theresa dismissed. "All this belongs to the pack, so really Jay is guardian. He's the only other person who knows how to get in here besides me. Plus, I'm still learning. I didn't even know this area of the museum existed until I was brought into the fold. The old director was a wolf. He passed away, I took over, and Max brought William here as a cover to suss me out, maybe find ways to get inside these secret rooms and steal everything before I found it."

So that was how the meet-cute started. "And instead…?" Bari prompted, stopping his trek just in front of her.

Theresa smiled and held up her left hand, where a lovely diamond wedding ring glittered in the dim light of the back room. "Win-win for me."

Bari knew touch was a powerful conduit for focusing a Seer's abilities. He'd seen his brother trigger a prophecy through touch many times. The shift in conversation allowed Bari to hide his true intentions as he took Theresa's hand with the guise of inspecting her ring.

It was a risk, because if he honestly had a vision right then, he'd be found out, but it wasn't a prophecy or even images that assaulted him as their skin touched, just a feeling, like Bash's many "feelings" over the years that were never wrong.

Theresa was no enemy in disguise.

Bari relaxed. The last thing he needed was to make this a witch hunt all on his own. "What a gorgeous amount of gaudy and tasteful," he said, finishing his inspection with a kiss to her knuckles, which made Theresa giggle. "The perfect combination. You really love that handsome grouch, don't you? Him and William?"

"I know this may be hard to believe since you don't know Max well," Theresa said with a fond shrug, "but they are both easy to love."

"I'll take your word for it," Bari said. They clearly both loved her, but that brought Bari back to his previous list of suspects. "Pity Ursula acts like you don't exist."

Theresa cringed. "We agree to leave each other alone."

"Didn't seem like an agreement so much as her ignoring you."

"She's Max's oldest friend," Theresa said, like reflex, like this wasn't the first time she'd had to defend the behavior. "She never warmed to the idea of him marrying a human. The others are more cordial with me."

"If the best I got was cordial, I think I'd feel shunned. Oh, wait…." Bari smirked.

"You'll win them over eventually. At least you're a wolf."

That melted Bari's smirk into a firm frown. "When Bash took over being Alpha from our hardheaded father, I never thought I'd have to see a city run this way again. Wishful thinking, I know. Jay trusts his circle, but I think he needs to be a bit more disruptive."

"That's why I was so in favor of the marriage!" Theresa erupted and then had to cringe again. "Sorry. I just mean your brother could have brought change, and I think you can do better. Don't stop pushing. Jay will listen to you."

Trying to resummon his smile, Bari glanced again at the table covered in tablets. The one nearest him made him turn to better inspect it.

"This one's different."

"What do you mean?"

"It seems to be part of the creation story, but look there." Bari pointed without actually touching the stone. "Some of the runes have been worn away, and the ones remaining…."

"I'm not familiar, I'm afraid."

"Neither am I, but I should be. Are there any others like this one?"

"Several." Theresa scanned the whole of the table and pointed to those most central. "The ones in the middle. They also have some runes worn away, and others that are legible but unfamiliar to me, their meaning lost. Unless you know?"

Bari lifted onto his toes to scrutinize them. "I don't recognize those either. Strange…."

A beep sounded from Theresa's belt, where she had a somewhat antiquated pager clipped. Bari supposed that was easier than attaching a cellphone to a pocketless skirt. "Duty calls," she said after glancing at it. "You're welcome to stay in here as long as you'd like. I'll be around. In fact, I don't suppose you'd like to catalog all this for me?" She grinned as she swept an arm out to encompass the entirety of the table. "Fair warning, it could take weeks."

"Seriously?" Bari understood what she was really asking.

Did he want to stay?

"We're short-staffed, and I can't let just anyone see these artifacts. Not even the circle is allowed back here unaccompanied. Consider it a temp job, with room for a permanent position should the need arise." She offered a playful wave before escaping down the corridor, leaving Bari in what would have been his dream scenario if he was ever buried alive.

He examined the nearest tablet again and those in the middle. There were some shifter representations on those tablets that didn't look right. They could be shifters at Stage Two, but other tablets usually showed Stage Three or Four, and these figures looked more human, but with fangs—

Bari's phone erupting caused him to jump a whole foot away from the table. Back rooms in a museum were his literal favorite place, but the quiet and solitude meant sudden noise could still make his heart race. He checked his phone and didn't recognize the number the text had come from.

I'm not giving up on you. We were good together, Bari.

Joseph! That bastard must have gotten a burner phone!

With fury boiling inside him, Bari fired off an angry response, ready to block this number too the second he sent the message. Leave me alone!

But before he could do anything more, the phone started ringing—from the same number.

Bari should hang up and block it. He knew he should. But he was so infuriated, he had to answer, figuring it was the only way for Joseph to get the damn point.

"I do not want to talk to you!" Bari growled across the line. "Ever again. I'm not even in the city anymore!"

"I know that," Joseph said, maddeningly calm. "Your apartment was all but cleaned out."

"You broke into my apartment?"

"I have a key, remember? Bari, please. We were good together. You know we were. Everything we have in common. All the incredible nights we shared. Going into work late because we didn't want to get out of bed."

Bari clenched his eyes shut at the reminder. "It was good. For a while. But it wasn't love. Not for me. And I would have been sorry about that, because I thought we could still be friends, until you proved you were a possessive, manipulative psycho."

"I'm the psycho?" Joseph snapped. "You're the one who wants some fantasy that doesn't exist."

"Not when your boyfriend threatens to fire you for leaving him!" Bari yelled and then quickly looked around in case Theresa or anyone else was in earshot. Thankfully, he was still alone. "All I ever wanted was a big gesture, a little romance. That isn't fantasy. Not if you love someone. Not wanting to get out of bed some mornings might seem like enough for you, but the biggest gesture you could ever manage was being a dick. Do not call me again."

Not willing to risk Joseph saying something to keep him longer, Bari tore the phone from his ear, ended the call, and blocked the number.

Bari's phone started ringing again, and if Joseph had another burner phone, Bari was going to storm back home right now just to throttle him.

It wasn't an unknown number this time, however—but Jay.

Chapter 5

JAY WAITED outside the Shelter for Bari. Reggie had determined the claw marks that killed the rat shifter Angus were from a wolf, not that Jay was surprised. It did, however, mean this was almost certainly a racially driven homicide, and Jay could not let that slide.

Ursula had reported little word on the street. If anyone knew anything, they weren't talking. The Shelter might be their best bet, but after Anjali started asking questions, she'd informed Jay that Des wanted to talk to him alone, much as she wasn't thrilled with the idea.

Desmond "Des" Keyes was a lizard. He'd been at the Shelter since he was an orphaned preteen and never left, even at almost forty now. He had any number of excuses for why, but Jay had come to realize it was because Des felt a need to be there for everyone else. He was the most trusted shifter in the Shelter by almost everyone of every race. In some ways, he was unofficial Councilor, even if Anjali held the title, though no one would ever say that to her face.

If Des wanted to talk, he knew something, and if Jay was going to the Shelter after a yet unsolved murder, he wanted to do so with a semblance of control and from a position of power. Bari could help with that, since his presence proved Jay had allies the non-wolf population could trust.

At least he hoped they'd see it that way.

"I am plenty romantic!"

Jay blinked out of his thoughts and looked up toward the side of the building. He couldn't see anyone yet, but that was definitely Max's voice. He had gone to pick Bari up, and they must have parked around back, which was protocol. Too many vehicles outside the Shelter could draw attention.

"You better be, or I might steal that beautiful wife away from you," Bari's voice came next, teasing in his usual bold manner that didn't fear reprisal.

They crested the corner, and Maximus looked like he was barely holding back from clobbering Bari, who couldn't have been more at ease. Or at least he wanted to look at ease. There was tension in Bari's shoulders he was trying very hard to hide.

"Jay! You keep showing me such lovely sights." Bari indicated the building.

Like the indoor parks, the exterior of the Shelter made it look like a series of warehouses, not exactly condos with flower boxes. "I'm afraid this time the inside won't prove to be a diamond in the rough, but we're working on it." Jay moved to intercept them. "Thank you for coming."

"Of course, but I'm not sure what you need me for," Bari said.

The expression on Maximus's face said he was wondering the same thing.

"Just be your incomparable self." Jay smiled and then leaned toward Bari. "Is everything all right?"

"Couldn't be better!"

He was trying so hard to sell the lie, Jay didn't want to press.

With a gentle touch to the small of Bari's back, Jay led him inside, and a scowling Maximus followed.

Inside, the Shelter was clean, but Jay noticed the moment when Bari realized this was not like the Shelter in Centrus City. The size was similar, but upon seeing inside any of the rooms with doors left open, beds looked more crammed together, and the people milling about were just a bit more disheveled and gaunt, like they had to ration their food.

They did. There were just too many of them.

The common rooms had activity spaces as well as TVs and other technologies, but the need for improvement was clear. They needed more space and to get more people out on their own instead of spending years here. That was never meant to be the intention of a Shelter, yet in some ways, it had become tribal slums.

People steered away from Jay and the others as they moved through, though out of respect to allow them passage, not to avoid their Alpha. In fact, many paused to nod or smile at Jay and cast Bari curious glances. There was some wariness, however. News of the murder must have spread.

A little boy saw Jay from the doorway of one of the rooms and called out, "Alpha! Wait!"

Jay stopped, but the boy disappeared inside the room. Assuming the boy meant to get something, Jay waited, and a few moments later, he came out, rushing up to Jay with a homemade doll in the shape of a black-and-white cat. The boy had black hair and big green eyes.

"Is this you?" Jay smiled, crouching beside the boy as he accepted the doll.

The boy nodded. "Momma says we're getting a home soon because of you. Is this your new mate?" the boy added in a not quite covert whisper.

Bari smiled down at him but left Jay to do the answering.

"For now, a friend," Jay said, holding Bari's eye a moment so he'd know he hoped more than a friend eventually. "You're... Jordan, right? Your mother's starting a job as a bank teller?"

Jordan nodded again.

"I wish you two well. And thank you for the doll. I get to keep it?"

Jordan nodded more frantically this time.

"Thank you. I'm going to put it on my dresser in the circle's den. Maybe after you and your mother get settled, you can come visit and make sure I'm taking good care of this little guy."

Now the boy nodded in unblinking wonder.

"Jordan," his mother called from the same doorway, smiling, but having used a tone of "Don't bother the Alpha."

Jordan rushed to her side, but Jay hadn't minded the interruption. He never minded encounters like that, because it was what he wanted from his Shelter—success stories of people moving on, moving out, and living their lives.

With an acknowledging nod at the mother and a wave at Jordan, Jay slipped the cat doll into his jacket pocket.

"Are you really going to put that on your dresser?" Bari asked once they were on their way again.

"Absolutely," Jay said without falter, and if he still had points to earn with Bari, that seemed to be worth a few.

"Alpha. Max. Bain," Anjali greeted them stiffly at the mouth of the central common area.

"I'm doing wonderful!" Bari replied cheerily. "Thanks for asking."

Anjali didn't look amused.

"So, this is the center of your Shelter," Bari said as he pivoted to take in the room, not keeping his voice low should any of the passersby be listening. "Correct me if I'm wrong, but is this like your parks? Each section segregated by tribe?"

Indeed, the central common area split into six different directions, and above the doorways to all but the main entrance they'd come from, which was a transition area, were runic signs to indicate which area lay beyond, such as Rat or Lizard and so on.

"The section marked Wolf doesn't look very populated with, well, wolves," Bari noted, since that area had various races moving in and out.

"There are never many wolves here," Jay admitted, "so that area tends to be more for spillover when the other sections are full."

"That must make some people angry," Bari said. "Hardly any wolves and everyone keeps to their race."

"Maybe because mixing is when trouble starts," Anjali grumbled. "I've been hearing that a lot lately."

"Because it's true, or we wouldn't have a murder to solve."

"Yes," a new voice responded, "how dare we mix. Oil and water and all that."

Jay turned toward the entrance marked Cat, which was nearest them, though it surprised him this was where Des was appearing from, since he was a lizard.

Des was a tall and very handsome Black man with hazel eyes and flawlessly trimmed hair and beard. He echoed Anjali's style in jeans, a T-shirt, and a leather jacket, with an equally confident swagger and an air of being in complete control of the room.

"And which would that make you?" Anjali asked, crossing her arms in challenge.

Des's answering smile was goading. "Obviously the oil, polluting our crystal-clear Councilor, who is, of course, beyond reproach. 'And what shoulder and what art could twist the sinews of thy heart?'"

Jay recognized the line from William Blake's "The Tyger."

"Cute," Anjali said, "but I'm not a tiger."

"That's the problem, isn't it? You think it matters."

"Goodness," Bari interrupted with a laugh. "Do you two need a room?"

Anjali and Des both startled and turned to Bari with uncharacteristic gapes.

"All right." Jay had to break this up. These two could have spectacular pissing contests, and Bari would only fan the fire. "Anji, Max, if you'll excuse us."

Maximus clearly didn't appreciate being left out any more than Anjali did. As Second, he usually went everywhere Jay did, but Des wanted to see Jay alone, and while he wasn't going to send Bari away unless asked to, Jay wanted to honor that.

"I think I like you already," Bari said to Des, extending a hand. "Bari Bain."

"Desmond Keyes," he said as he accepted it, "but everyone calls me Des."

"An absolute pleasure."

"From you, I might believe that, given what's said of your brother." Des gestured for them to follow him into the cat area.

"Are you going to tell me why you wanted to talk alone?" Jay asked.

"Seems we aren't alone," Des said with a friendly smile.

"I thought you'd appreciate Bari's presence."

"I do. He is an exception, but what I'm about to show you shouldn't be shared with your circle. Not yet."

The path they followed was suspiciously empty of occupants, even when they entered one of the living areas, where the cots had curtains for privacy, all currently open—save one, where Des was leading them.

"What are we doing back here, Des? This is cat territory, and these rooms are usually for panthers."

"They are. The panthers came to me, and I only want to share this with you. And your guest."

Bari squirmed like he wasn't sure he wanted to be included anymore.

"Whatever you show me," Jay said, "I will have to tell my circle eventually."

"I know. But this is bigger than one mixed-mated rat being murdered."

"What do you mean?" Bari asked.

Without ceremony, Des reached for the lone drawn curtain and pulled it back with one firm yank, revealing the corpse of an obviously pregnant woman. "Angus wasn't the only non-wolf killed yesterday."

BARI WAS trying very hard to not throw up, and being back in a car wasn't helping.

Maximus had offered to drive them, but Jay insisted on taking his own car, since not even Jay's Second was meant to know this yet.

"Pregnant. She was pregnant. How could someone do that just because of tribal differences?"

"Maybe because she was pregnant," Jay said. He was being impressively impassive, but then, that was an Alpha's duty.

"A panther pregnant with a child that would have been half wolf...." Bari considered, marveling at the wonder Des had shared with them, or at the wonder it might have been. "It's nearly impossible."

"Less than 1 percent."

Bari blinked back the tears forming, but his eyes still felt hot. "You know the saying, two's a coincidence, three's a pattern? I really don't want to wait for us to find number three."

"Agreed." Jay pulled into a parking spot in the heart of downtown. "Two deaths the same day, across town from each other, both shifters in mixed coupling. If there are more, I need to know."

"Are you going to tell Reggie about the panther?" Bari asked.

"Not yet. I know it's risky to wait on an autopsy, especially if anyone from the Cat area spreads news about the body, but Des said he can get it on ice until we're ready. I need to know if anything else has been reported."

"Are we going to the police?" Bari glanced at their surroundings, but there didn't appear to be a police station on this block.

"We don't need to. I have connections." Jay offered a subtle smile and got out of the car.

"Shifters on the force?" Bari followed him.

"Naturally, but not only that. My day job has its advantages."

"Day job?" Bari repeated, hurrying to keep up with Jay as he entered a building split into various offices spaces and continued to one of the doors. "Alphas don't have day jobs."

"Maybe Bashir doesn't or others you've met, but I never could have given up my job." Jay grinned wider and tapped the glass on the door, where a name was neatly etched.

Jeffrey Russell, Attorney at Law

Bari was still gaping after a solid minute of being inside Jay's small but polished law office. "You're a defense attorney? What is it with this pack and people not telling me their job!"

Jay chuckled, settling at his desk and immediately typing away at his computer, while Bari slumped into a chair opposite him like an inelegantly toppling cat. "I don't make much. I mostly do pro bono work."

"How… legitimate."

"I thought you liked legitimate. Bashir mentioned you didn't approve of packs having so many illegal practices."

"I know some of it's necessary, but an Alpha doesn't need to be a crime boss."

"Your brother doesn't seem so bad."

"He's not really a crime boss. I mean, maybe technically…." Bari trailed off enough that Jay laughed. "They do launder most of the money used to get by and to take care of the Shelter. How do you manage not to?"

"I'm not squeaky clean," Jay amended. "The previous Alpha made a lot of investments, though, which keeps a steady stream of income coming in. I just wish it was enough. Like I told you, despite the state of the den, fancy dinners like our date aren't common. With the way things are going, I might need to become a criminal mastermind after all."

Bari couldn't help teasing, "At least you could defend yourself in court."

"Ah, but you know what they say about that?"

Bari did: The man who represents himself has a fool for a client.

"I don't have any active cases, since I was on vacation the last few weeks," Jay continued, "but it's great cover for keeping tabs on what the pack is up to, and I get to help a lot of other people too. What we need right now are missing persons reports. We're assuming the two murders are connected, so what if there are more? What if there are humans? What if it is coincidence?"

"I get it," Bari agreed. "We don't know enough yet to be jumping to conclusions. You know, Ethan was a CSI who wants to become a PI. He might have a useful… eye." He grinned at the apropos rhyming.

Jay's smile twitched. It was difficult to not like Ethan after meeting him, vampire or no, but it was understandable why Jay didn't enjoy being around him. "You may be right, but if I'm not ready to share everything with my circle, I can't go behind their backs and share it with someone else. Not yet."

"All right. But since it ended up getting shared with me, how can I help?"

The printer in the corner sprang to life, and Jay gestured to it as he ceased his typing. "Help me sort through about two or three dozen police reports?"

"I'd be happy to. Not as different as you might think from my day job, just another type of research."

"We'll focus on similarities between cases. Any similarities, but particularly location, especially if they went missing near the den or the Shelter."

"What about John and Jane Doe cases? We're assuming we'd know if there were more shifter bodies found, but what if they were discovered by people who couldn't identify them?"

Jay glanced at the already growing stack of papers in his printer tray. "You're right. I'll pull those files too. It's going to take a while to cross-reference everything, but at least we'll find out more details before telling the circle we have another death." He turned in his roller chair to face Bari directly. "Thank you for this. Really."

"It's why I came here, isn't it?"

"I don't think you were planning on helping solve murders."

"Not quite on my bucket list, no." Bari chuckled and then held Jay's gaze for a long span of intimate beats, enjoying the genuine affection he found in those pale blue eyes.

The truth was, Bari was terrified, and part of him wanted to run like he always did, just pick a direction and go as quickly as possible, but even another body found and that awful call with Joseph couldn't convince him to abandon Jay now.

Maybe it was time to tell him about the prophecy….

But no. Not yet. Not until they had a lead.

"At least the company is good," Bari said and shared a smile with Jay as they readied themselves for a long afternoon.

Chapter 6

JAY WAS pleased with the amount of progress he and Bari made, but it was only a start, an initial organizing of case files that would take much longer to investigate than a few hours' work. He might need to bring in his circle sooner than he wanted, if only for the manpower.

Ethan Lambert was also an option, as well as Bashir and his circle, but Jay wasn't ready to bring them into this mess.

Since he and Bari needed a break, they headed back to the den around dinnertime, planning to dig deeper into the case files afterward, safely sequestered where the others wouldn't pry.

"Um… is she crying?" Bari whispered.

Jay glanced deeper into the foyer after depositing their jackets in the front closet. Anjali was half obscured in the doorway leading to the living room with her face in her hands and shoulders hunched. Everything else within the house was quiet.

Jay stepped toward her, unsure if he should call out or not, since it seemed like she was mumbling to herself. After the mind-control and magic he'd encountered in Centrus City, Jay was on high alert, flexing his fingers should he need to release claws. He could feel Bari shadowing close behind him as they moved cautiously, and when nothing changed about Anjali's condition and she didn't seem to have noticed them, Jay reached to grab her shoulder.

"Anji, are you—"

"Shh!" She whipped toward him with an angry hiss. Her face didn't look like she'd been crying. "I'm counting." Then, upon returning her face to her hands, Jay was able to better pick up on what she was mumbling. "Eighteen… nineteen… twenty! Ready or not, here I come!"

Bari erupted in a laugh behind Jay, and Jay couldn't help smiling as well. Playing some sort of game with William before dinnertime was customary, and Jay and Bari were late.

Anjali ducked into the living room, and Jay took hold of Bari's arm to drag him in after her, scanning for any telling signs of where the others might be hiding. Jay could smell something delicious wafting from the kitchen, so Daisy was probably ready with dinner and also playing. The fact that his circle members were all in their thirties and forties was beside the point—they still had a ten-year-old in the house.

Bari patted Jay's hand and nodded toward the door into the kitchen. It was swung open, but it had just moved about a half inch on its own, as if someone was hiding behind it. Anjali hadn't noticed. Then Jay patted Bari's arm in turn and winked toward the curtains. Visible beneath one of the panels was a pair of taupe-colored heels—definitely Clara.

Despite the tall, slender woman's ability to blend in without making a bulge, the heels Anjali did see.

"Aha!" She whipped the curtain aside, revealing Clara, stylishly dressed as always and pouting with a huff that upset one of her short auburn curls.

"Shoot. If I was allowed to use magic, I could have hidden my feet!"

"Rules are rules," Anjali said haughtily and spun back around to continue the hunt.

This was the side of the circle Jay wanted Bari to see. He could tell Bari was amused by the display as they stood back to hug the living room wall and stayed out of Anjali's way.

Next she checked behind furniture, finding nothing until she exclaimed, "Max! I can see your tail sticking out from under the love seat. No shifting."

Bari stifled another laugh as a beautiful black wolf crawled out in a humorous shuffle from beneath the love seat, woofing in dismay, and then ducked behind the love seat to transform.

A moment later, a nude Maximus stood from behind it. His nakedness was mostly hidden by the height of the furniture, and he turned to open a cabinet in the built-in behind him to retrieve his clothes. "No shifting? When did we make that rule?"

Anjali didn't bother answering, as she was already darting across the living room to enter the kitchen.

Jay pulled Bari forward with him to get a better view through the doorway, where the first place Anjali looked—the pantry—proved to be Daisy's hiding spot.

"Dang it!"

"Be more creative next time," Anjali scolded, and upon turning to head back into the living room, she must have seen the person hiding behind the door through the crack. "Gotcha, Reggie!"

A similarly affronted grumble preceded Reggie stepping out from behind the door. "Bollocks. I still vote magic and shifting optional next time."

Anjali tore her way out of the room to check the rest of the main floor. By the time she returned, Maximus was dressed, Reggie was lounging on the chaise with a drink Jay would swear he materialized out of nothing, and Clara was helping Daisy move items from the kitchen into the dining room, all while keeping an eye out and an ear open for signs that Anjali had finished her search.

Instead, Anjali came back with hands on her hips and announced, "I give up! You win!"

"Yes!" came a triumphant shout, and the top of the large ottoman they used as a coffee table burst upward as William jumped to his feet from inside.

Bari practically fell over with renewed laughter, something Jay and most of the others easily echoed. It was nice, since Bari toppling in glee meant him clinging tighter to Jay's arm, practically hugging him for support and leaning in close to his body.

He smelled like jasmine again, and Jay resisted the urge to sniff the crook of Bari's neck or nuzzle into his soft dark hair.

"What?" Anjali shouted in affront, though Jay could tell she was only acting upset and trying to hide a grin. "When did that become storage?"

This only rekindled everyone's laughter.

"Oh my!" Theresa said upon entering the scene, still wearing her jacket as she stood in the living room doorway, returned from work. She spotted Maximus and crossed to kiss him hello, to which he reciprocated with fervor. "Hide-and-seek again? Did you win, sweetheart?" She turned to William climbing out of the ottoman.

"I did this round!"

"I demand a rematch!" Anjali argued, still playing up her outrage. "I didn't even know that thing existed!"

Everyone tittered at her expense while William beamed.

"Hold on, lovelies," Reggie said, swinging his legs up off the chaise to stand and strolling toward the door that led to the basement. "Aren't we forgetting someone?" Upon reaching the door, he dramatically swung it open—to show Ursula waiting with a victorious grin.

"Hey!" William protested. "We said only first floor! That doesn't count!"

With smooth, sure steps, Ursula walked up to him. "Guess you shouldn't have played your hand so soon. Know when to bend but not break the rules, little one. I wasn't down the steps, so technically I was still on this floor. Better luck next time." She ran a hand across the top of his head in a familial pat.

Another round of chuckles flitted through the circle, while William sulked, but only for a moment before he smiled too.

"Dinnertime!" Daisy declared.

"And on that note, I shall see you gorgeous lot later," Reggie said, reclaiming his drink and heading through the open doorway into the basement.

When Bari looked to Jay in question, Jay shrugged.

"He never joins us. Don't take it personally." With a gesture forward where the others were headed, Jay kept hold of Bari's arm to lead him into the dining room.

DINNER WAS remarkably cordial—even if it was obvious to Bari that Ursula acted as though Theresa wasn't at the table. If it hadn't been for the two corpses Bari had encountered in the past two days and having to hang up on his ex earlier, he might have taken this for the vacation it had been intended to be.

After dinner, Jay wanted to discuss his itinerary for tomorrow with Maximus, so Bari milled about downstairs to wait for him. He'd found his way into a separate sitting room, which had obviously been a brandy-and-smoking lounge at some point, and maybe still was if the faint smell of cigars and alcohol was any indication. Bari loved that smell, even if he wasn't one for smoking. Something about the combination mixed further with leather from old books and wingback chairs eased his swirling thoughts.

Hopefully he and Jay would find something in those case files, but maybe only that there were more unexplained deaths. Bari still had no idea who the woman from his prophecy might be. Maybe he should—

"I love the smell in this room, don't you?"

Bari whirled toward the entrance. Ursula hadn't made a peep sneaking up on him.

She continued forward at a measured pace, waiting for an answer.

"Some of my favorites," Bari admitted, on guard and keeping her in his sights. He'd never seen her lose her cool the way Maximus could, or the way he'd seen from Anjali either. Wardens couldn't afford to be hotheads since they were meant to retain order, but her calmness set him on edge.

"Let me show you a secret," Ursula said with a smile Bari couldn't quite read, very different from the genuineness she'd displayed with William. There was a hutch against the wall, and through the glass of the top cabinets appeared to be more books, which Bari assumed were collectibles to be handled with care, but when Ursula opened one of the doors, that image proved to be a trick.

There was the brandy, along with an assortment of other liquors, some in crystal, as well as various pieces of glassware.

"I'm a Scotch girl myself," she said, taking out two tumblers and an unmarked decanter. She poured a couple of fingers into a glass and then looked at Bari, as if waiting for his say.

"Brandy?" Bari asked.

She nodded, exchanged her bottle for another, and poured two more fingers. She put the liquor away, closed the cabinet, approached, and handed Bari his glass. They clinked, and each took a sip.

Recent events made Bari want to play this close to the chest, but the brandy was so damn delicious, his knees sagged, and he couldn't resist closing his eyes and humming in approval.

"That's Jay's vintage. You have similar tastes."

Bari opened his eyes to stare at her, wondering at her game.

"Do you know the creation stories, Mr. Bain? From the tablets at the museum? I was told you got to see them while you were there."

By whom? Bari wondered, grateful for the brandy as he took another sip before answering. "Theresa showed me. And I'm very familiar with those stories. Once, if they are to be believed, every tribe had their own kingdom."

"With wolves at the top, overseeing all the others."

"Stories say that, but they might just be stories."

"Are you sure?" Ursula asked, taking a slow drink, as if to allow him time to process the question, but when Bari didn't say anything, she pushed on. "I've heard our new collection is the first to have every piece of the whole tale. There were others once, long since destroyed, a few copies of one tablet or another, but ours is the only set all intact."

"Not completely intact," Bari corrected. "There are some things on those tablets that have been worn away or may not be translatable."

Ursula took a step closer to Bari, and though he was taller, she made him feel instantly lesser. "Maybe you need to study the tablets more closely to be certain. I'd be fascinated to know what you find."

"History isn't a blueprint for the future," Bari said with a snap of anger that almost surprised him. He cleared his throat to collect himself. "Unless, usually, you're talking about things to avoid."

"I agree. There's constant fighting today. Cities aren't united. We run some things but are wholly outnumbered by humans. Many of our people live like lowlifes and vagabonds. And the choices of the past led us here. All I'm saying is that a stronger structure of leadership might help, when right now, everything is scattered."

Now Bari knew why he was angry, because this was twisted familiar logic that made him angry. "You make it seem very much like we want the same things, but I doubt your idea of achieving a better world for shifters would be all that nice for many of my friends. Deanna, Bash's Second, is a panther and like a sister to me, to both of us. She is a good Second without being a wolf."

"Yes, just think of what happened in Centrus. Such an example." Ursula took one more step closer. "Let me know what you discover about those tablets. I'd very much like to see them someday." She downed the rest of her Scotch without dropping her gaze from Bari's, smiled dangerously, and pivoted on her heels, taking her empty glass with her.

Bari gulped in a breath like he'd been facing down an executioner, which in some ways a Warden was. Part of him wondered if he should have tried to touch Ursula like he had Theresa, but right now, he doubted he could handle another prophecy, even if it was a nice one.

And to think he'd been starting to have such a nice evening.

Turning to the window, Bari swallowed down the last of his brandy. The warmth of the liquor wasn't helping the churning in his stomach. He could see the courtyard, and though it was dark, there were fairy lights strung about, making the garden terrace look ethereal and beautiful.

Until a shadow disturbed the twinkling.

Bari leaped closer to the glass, heightening his wolf eyes to cut through the night. There were three entrances into the courtyard: one from the dining room, one from a gated area, well warded, which eventually led to the street, and another from a secondary stairwell to the basement.

That door was open, with Reggie silhouetted before it closed. The shadow moving across the courtyard to leave was Des.

What the hell was going on in this place?

"Bari?"

Bari whirled toward the entrance.

Jay.

Taking another trembling breath, Bari held up his empty glass. "Ursula poured me some of your brandy. I think I might need a bit more."

Without questioning how shaken Bari must appear, Jay grabbed the bottle and a glass for himself, and they stole away upstairs to Jay's room.

It was even more beautiful than Bari's, also with its own balcony and bathroom. Besides the canopy bed and other furniture similar to the guest room, Jay's walls were covered in stylized photographs of the city that might have been taken by the Alpha himself, and he had a plush L-shaped sofa that Bari wished he could lie down on and just not think for a while.

He watched Jay set the black-and-white cat doll atop his dresser. He must have rescued it from his jacket before collecting Bari from the lounge. Jay was a good man, a good Alpha, but Bari had no idea who around him could be trusted.

"What's wrong?" Jay asked, seeing Bari still standing stock-still near the door. Jay had a briefcase full of the files he'd brought from his office and set it next to the coffee table. "Besides far too many things to count." He tried to smile, and Bari wished he could smile back.

"There's something I need to tell you."

"About?"

"A prophecy."

Bari told Jay everything, reciting the words and what he had seen. Afterward, as they sat on the sofa, Jay digested what he'd heard for some time before speaking.

"All this tells me is there's some dangerous woman who wants a return to the past," Jay said steadily. "If that's who committed the murders, there are far too many people in this city with traditional views to know who she might be."

"Unless it's Ursula."

"What?" Jay looked at Bari in shock.

"Or Anjali. Even Daisy—"

"Do you hear yourself? My circle? That would be pack mutiny."

"Have you been listening to some of the things they say?" Bari contended.

"Words, yes. But prejudice and bitter thinking are not the same as murder or a coup."

Bari sagged into the sofa and let his head tip back, exhausted and torn. "I know. Which is why I didn't want to tell you. I didn't want to cast doubt on anyone from your circle if I wasn't sure."

"Are you saying you're sure now?"

Bari lolled his head to look at Jay. "No. But I didn't want to keep it from you anymore. I'm sorry I did even for a day." Defeated, he sat up to fold his hands between his knees. "I told Bash. I've never had a prophecy before. He was always the Seer, not me. I was scared. Especially because I didn't want to lead you somewhere you couldn't come back from."

"For what it's worth, thank you for telling me now," Jay said sincerely. "Did your brother have any thoughts?"

"Not yet."

"I don't want to believe the woman in your vision is one of my people, but I understand why they are your prime suspects if this person is meant to be so influential. At the very least, I'll have to share this with Max."

"Jay—"

"Not everything. I won't admit you're a Seer. That's yours to tell. But I need to tell Max I'm concerned our list of suspects might include people in this house. If there is a traitor here, it's not him. He can be trusted."

"On that we can agree," Bari conceded. Even if his vision hadn't starred a woman, he'd never suspect Maximus of betrayal.

"I'm glad you told me this, Bari. At the very least so I can rule my circle out."

"I do still think you're too easy on them and the offhanded way many of them condemn humans and other tribes. I know you want to keep the traditionalists happy, but should you, if happy for them means being miserable for everyone else?"

A flicker of indignancy crossed Jay's expression but quickly faded to shame. Theresa was right—Bari needed to push, and Jay needed to listen.

"I have been too lenient, haven't I?" Jay said. "It's easier to turn a blind eye to keep some semblance of peace, but look where that's brought us. It has to stop."

Bari offered a somber smile. "If I see anything new, I promise I won't keep it to myself."

"Thank you. I suppose if you've already shared your prophecy with Bashir, you might as well share with him and whoever else you deem fit the rest of what's been going on."

"Are you sure?"

"Tomorrow. After we've gone through these files." Jay lifted his briefcase onto the coffee table. "Still up for that?"

Bari really wasn't, but he knew they had to.

He was about to say, "I'm all yours," when Jay spoke again first.

"You can be honest with me, you know. When I asked earlier, at the Shelter, if you were okay, I know you were only pretending to be."

The words were understanding and soft, yet they cut through Bari like glass, and when he took a breath, the sharpness stung his eyes, and everything rushed to the surface. The tears Bari had been able to hold back before streamed hot and fast down his face so suddenly, he gasped and touched a hand to his cheek.

"Oh my… what is wrong with me? It wasn't anything so terrible. My stupid ex called. And you know… bodies are dropping all around us. Oh, and my whole life changed with the flash of a fucking third eye, and… ugh," he groaned at the venom he hadn't intended, scrubbing at the tears that were falling faster than he could wipe away. "I'm sorry. I should not be this weak."

"Bari," Jay said with the same softness, reaching across the sofa to replace Bari's hands at wiping his tears away, "the last thing I think when I look at you, yes, even with tears down your face, is that you're weak."

Jay was so the opposite of Joseph, of most of the awful choices in partners Bari had made over the years, that his tears only streamed down faster, and he threw his arms around Jay's neck to bury his face in Jay's shoulder. Maybe everything would end in disaster with Jay someday too, but all Bari wanted in that moment was him.

"It's okay. I'm here," Jay said, like he knew that was what Bari needed.

Jay's arms encircled his back without hesitation, moving soothingly up and down, and Bari dug his face that much harder into the crook of Jay's neck, feeling his tears smudge away.

"S-sorry," he stuttered, forcing himself to be done, to be stronger than this.

Pulling back to look at Jay, the concerned look Bari found in those beautiful blue eyes captivated him—the affection bared so openly, the subtle part to Jay's lips as he shuddered from them being so close.

He had to see the hunger in Bari's eyes, the need for something to feed the beast that was haunting him. That's what Bari needed now, something to banish his fears of the future and pains from the past. Jay's lips looked as inviting as they had at breakfast.

Without overthinking, Bari sealed their mouths together, seeking Jay's smooth tongue, and rocked forward until Jay toppled back onto the sofa.

"Bari." Jay gasped as Bari climbed atop him, straddling him easily since Jay was knocked flat. "What are you doing?" He already looked flushed and wanton, the most delicious temptation.

There were still tears in Bari's eyes, down his cheeks, and his hands wouldn't stop trembling as he rested them on Jay's chest, breathing in the close scent of him, like cinnamon spice and crisp autumn air—Bari's favorite smells, like a true mate should be.

"Please," Bari said, feeling pathetic, but he didn't care. He needed something to ground him, and he wanted it to be Jay.

Jay placed his hands over Bari's, his eyes caring and concerned but pitying too. "You're upset. We should—"

"No. I mean, I am, but... but I don't want to think of all the bad when I finally have something good in my grasp." He tried to go for another kiss, but Jay held him back.

"Bari—"

"Please," Bari begged, which he knew was even more pathetic. He tried to smile, and because it was Jay beneath him, so powerful and capable and everything Bari doubted he was at times, the expression was genuine even through his lingering anguish. "It's not taking advantage if I'm asking."

Jay huffed a laugh, and though the smile it fell into was real, there was doubt in his eyes.

"I adore your sweet, uncertain side," Bari said, gently touching Jay's cheek, "but I want the dominant part now, because every time I see it, I quiver. Dominate me, Jay. Take me. Claim me. Get me hot and hard with nothing to interrupt us so we can forget the rest of the world for a while."

A menagerie of emotions flitted across Jay's face. Surprise. Delight. Desire. Then the deepest of longing, like Jay had never been wanted this much before. He didn't act yet, however, as if still doubting Bari was sure.

Pleading with another touch of their lips, Bari kissed Jay, but chastely this time. Bari's hands still shook as they curled into Jay's T-shirt, hips aligning over Jay's but waiting, beseeching silently for Jay to answer his advances by taking the initiative.

When Bari pulled up once more, that's exactly what Jay did.

He grasped the back of Bari's neck and claimed a kiss of his own.

Chapter 7

JAY HOPED this wasn't a bad idea. Everything about the past several months after first being introduced to Bashir Bain had felt like a bad idea, but in the moment, everything was worth it if all that heartache and disappointment led here.

It felt so good, pressed down into the sofa cushions by Bari's weight, the other man sitting atop Jay, knees on either side of Jay's thighs, as Jay clung to Bari's neck and kissed him.

Bari's hands, that had been braced on Jay's chest, started to drift downward as Bari let more of his weight settle onto Jay's hips. They were both fully dressed, but even through Jay's jeans and Bari's form-fitting slacks, very little was left to the imagination as they began to react.

Jay gasped when cool fingers found the hem of his T-shirt and pushed up underneath it, reaching as high as Jay's clavicle while the other hand clung to his hip. Jay didn't mean to grind up into Bari so tellingly, but the tease of heaviness growing between them as he thrust up, feeling how hard Bari was for him already, was maddening.

The hand up Jay's shirt slid slightly down and to the right, grazing dull fingernails over a nipple. Jay hissed.

Bari broke from their tangle of tongues to kiss across Jay's jaw and down his neck. The spot right beneath Jay's ear was particularly shiver-inducing, especially with how Bari snuffled like a wolf in the wild leaving a scent mark. When Jay whimpered and bucked up harder, Bari latched on hotly, sucking firm enough to leave a true mark. Jay didn't mind; it'd be gone by morning anyway, since they were shifters, which he almost lamented. Finally Jay was with someone who wanted him as desperately as he wanted them, and they couldn't even wear any badges of honor.

Jay wasn't doing what Bari had asked of him, though—taking charge. Dominating. Jay wanted to touch Bari in return and show him just how dominating he could be.

The barest shift in weight made Bari whine, tearing his mouth from where he'd started licking the rim of Jay's ear. Jay grinned, and with one swift roll and show of strength, their positions were reversed, with Bari lying back and Jay straddling him. A tighter press of their hips made both men moan.

Bari smiled up at Jay, sort of smirked, really, his tears forgotten and drying on his cheeks. He looked more like the confident, flirty man Jay was used to.

It was unfairly hot.

Jay took a moment to roll his hips, with Bari's hard length pressing lewdly against his own. He didn't want to undress them yet. He wanted this to go slowly.

Holding Bari's face in his hands, Jay let his thumbs wipe away the last traces of wetness. For a moment, Bari's heated expression faltered, becoming that somber, tragic desperation again. Nothing about this should be tragic.

Jay kept hold of Bari's face as he kissed him with a brief, deep lick of his tongue between teeth and a soft bite at Bari's lower lip. He rolled his hips again, and Bari shuddered. Jay dragged his nails through Bari's hair, pressed his fingers deep to pull Bari closer, and plunged his tongue deeper too, with long smooth strokes connecting them.

A gentle rocking began, the fabric between them dulling the sensation just enough while the wetness gathering at their tips and soaking through several telling spots made Jay feverish for more than just that awful tease.

He was tingling, trembling. In a surge of adrenaline and desire, he ripped Bari's button-down open, pulling it from being tucked into his slacks and sending at least two or three buttons clattering onto the coffee table. Jay would have feared Bari would be upset, but the flash of Bari's eyes and glint of sudden fangs told him he was forgiven.

Jay let his wolf surface too, growling low as he slid his hands down Bari's bare chest, around his back inside the shirt, hoisted him closer, and ground even harder against him.

"We… need these pants off," Bari pleaded.

"We'll get there."

The groan that fell from Bari's lips was deep in his own rough growl and settled into a long rumble. He pawed at Jay's T-shirt, sliding it up with his cool hands dragging along the skin and pulling at the fabric until Jay let him yank it over his head. Then Bari gripped Jay's back, his other hand twisting into Jay's hair and urging him down for another connection, wet and messy and frantic with a click of matching fangs.

The constant roll of their hips had Jay quaking. After minutes of sucking Bari's tongue into his mouth and feeling just how hard they both were within their feverish rocking, Jay pushed Bari away from him into the cushions and slipped down between Bari's legs. Bari's slacks were already tugged low enough to reveal the finely carved grooves of his hip bones. Feathering his hands down Bari's stomach, Jay lowered himself to press a kiss beneath Bari's navel.

Jay wanted to run his hands over every dip and curve, map everything out, and worship Bari a little. Bari needed to know he was worthy of that, and that Jay would never mistake him for Bashir again.

So, for a few minutes, that's what Jay did. He undid Bari's belt, opened his slacks, and ran his hands firm and wanting over Bari's chest, stomach, and down his hips, but never past the barrier of his underwear. Jay teased at the possibility, even let his thumbs slip beneath the elastic several times as if he'd finally pull everything down, but never followed through.

"Fuck," Bari huffed, his golden-brown eyes hooded as he lay back and watched each careful movement of Jay's hands. "Are you going to torture me all night... Alpha?"

Anyone else calling Jay that was business, but Bari saying it in that tone, in this situation, made a louder roar build in Jay's throat and more fur sprout along the edges of his body. This was his favorite line to ride when being intimate with someone, and he hadn't been with anyone in so long, but this—being human and the beast in perfect harmony—was where Jay felt most in control and his true self.

He licked his lips and flicked his eyes up to meet Bari's. Bari's legs were crooked up and spread open, with Jay nestled neatly between them, his face right there between Bari's thighs. The heady smell of Bari was all around Jay. It was easy, so easy to lower himself and latch on to the wet spot through Bari's underwear.

"Fuck!" Bari cried again, neck arching from the sofa and both hands digging into Jay's hair, tight, right at the edge of painful and hot as hell.

Jay liked to be teased, to have every moment drawn out until he was so wet, he soaked the sheets. He could feel the precum dribbling down his length now from offering his attentions to another. Bari's soft, shuddering whimpers were the best validation Jay had ever heard.

He slid his hands beneath Bari's thighs to brace himself, sucking harder through the fabric and getting it sopping from his eager mouth.

"Jay...." Bari's voice sounded wrecked, and when Jay looked up, Bari's pupils were so blown, the glowing gold of his eyes was a thin ring. Those eyes spoke of nothing but need in their depths, and it made Jay grin to be the cause.

He moved his hands up to Bari's waistband, teased his thumbs beneath the line of fabric again, but finally, this time, he slid the underwear and slacks down Bari's thighs. Jay purposely hadn't looked too closely when they were at the park, but this new, glorious view made him wish he had something to grind against. The couch cushions were not enough in this position, but he'd get what he wanted in time.

Bracing his hands at the curve of Bari's hips, Jay descended, lips parting, gaze locked with Bari's the entire time as he sucked him into his mouth, careful around his fangs but letting the barest hint of them graze the skin.

Bari's moan was long and loud and wonderfully deep. He only lasted a handful of moments like that before he was tugging Jay's hair. "It's too... I c-can't.... Jay...." And fuck, Jay's name had never sounded so lewd.

Jay broke away with a pop. He didn't want Bari to get too far ahead of him. He licked his lips again, grinning as he tugged Bari's underwear and slacks the rest of the way off, leaving him naked save for the open shirt, spread out before Jay.

Bari's chest heaved as he caught his breath, hips subtly arching at the loss of contact.

Jay snickered, husky and deep, with his wolf still very much present, keeping fur all along the edges of his body. "You knew what you were asking for. And it doesn't sound like you're complaining."

"Hardly," Bari said, only shifted as far as his eyes and fangs, maybe deliberately, as if to keep himself smaller and submissive by comparison. "I love this side of you."

"I can tell." Jay bent his head to lap at the bead of wetness at Bari's tip.

Bari pressed his head into the sofa.

Mercifully, Jay slithered up Bari's body until their faces were parallel, Jay's still-clothed erection dragging purposely along Bari's skin.

"Ugnn... take your jeans off... please," Bari begged, gruff and breathy, and fuck, it made Jay want to ravage him for hours.

First, Jay bent to nibble Bari's ear, the right one, pierced with a diamond, and tongued all around the stud and up the cartilage. He husked a growly, "I like hearing you say please."

"Ngnn...."

With a triumphant chuckle, Jay lifted as slowly as he could, keeping his eyes on Bari to ensure Bari's eyes were on him, and let his knees rest on the cushion between Bari's spread thighs so he could pull his jeans and underwear off. He half expected Bari to reach between his legs as soon as denim hit the floor, but instead, Bari ran his hands up Jay's stomach and across his pecs, down his shoulders, his sides, around his back, and then used that new grip to try to jerk him down into a harsher kiss.

Jay resisted, stronger than Bari and enjoying the strain and struggle, and how it made Bari's eyes darken even more with lust.

The moment Jay sank down into Bari and their slick, naked cocks slid past each other for the first time, Bari moaned, and Jay snarled with a snap of his teeth at Bari's parted lips before granting him the kiss he wanted.

Bari squirmed in delicious contentment.

Sliding a hand between their bodies to grasp their cocks, Jay wrapped his fingers around them, gentle with the curl of his claws, and stroked.

Another moan spilled from Bari, forcing their lips apart. He mewled and panted but also held Jay's gaze with want of more. Bari pulled his knees up so his feet were flush on the sofa and his thighs tight around Jay's hips. Then he reached down to nudge Jay's hand to move lower and replaced the grip Jay had on their cocks.

As Bari stroked them, Jay brought already precum-slickened fingers beneath Bari's sac and toyed at his entrance. He teased with the soft drag of a claw before shifting his hand human and prodding deeper. The first finger slid inside with wonderful ease.

"Yeah... yeah...," Bari praised.

"You like that?" Jay asked through a growl. He may have let his hand shift human, but the rest of him was all Alpha.

Bari nodded, biting his lip. It wasn't supposed to be this easy the first time with someone. It wasn't supposed to be this hot, this mind-blowing, but then nothing about this was anything Jay would have expected a week ago.

He was getting close from the frantic pumping of Bari's hand and his own rhythmic rocking into that grip, but the noises Bari was making while he fingered him were the pinnacle. Jay knew Bari was close too. There would be no true claiming tonight, they wouldn't last that long, but with the time they had, Jay planned to ruin Bari in every way he could.

Bari kept frantically nodding, no matter how fast or deeply Jay twisted, as if to say one finger wasn't enough.

"Tell me what you want, Bari."

"More...."

Bari keened when Jay added a second finger. Bari's hand had slowed on them, moving more languidly over their cocks in time with Jay's twisting. Now he picked up speed again, and Jay took that as his cue to do the same.

Faster. Faster. Jay teased the tip of a third finger—and Bari came with Jay's name on his lips and a rumble of pleased snarls following it. The tightening of Bari around Jay's fingers brought him over that last precipice too, and with the added wetness of Bari's release in the continued strokes Bari granted him, Jay came only moments later.

He collapsed forward onto Bari's chest, and Bari hugged him there, held him, until the stickiness between them demanded attention.

"I've got it," Jay said, though when he lifted his head, he captured Bari's lips in a deep kiss before moving any other part of him.

With his first step off the sofa, he was human, though when he glanced at Bari lying there stained and flushed, still with his arms in the sleeves of his ruined shirt, a flash of golden eyes made Jay flash his back at Bari like silent affection passing between them.

Jay wiped himself clean with a washcloth from the bathroom and returned to do the same for Bari. They dressed, though Bari's shirt was left open since it could no longer button completely, and he cast Jay a teasing glower.

"You owe me a shirt."

"I do. Maybe I can take you shopping sometime."

"Darling," Bari cooed, "enough with the dirty talk. I'm already spent."

Jay chuckled and then tapped the yet unopened briefcase on the coffee table. "Up for a return to the real world?"

"I think I can handle that."

Hours later, maybe the biggest pattern emerging was how little of a pattern there was. All those files, whether related to their actual case or not, were littered across the city. Jay and Bari did, however, find a few curious John and Jane Doe cases, including one that proved there might be at least a third shifter murder waiting to be solved.

Cause of death—animal attack.

Chapter 8

WHEN DEANNA first mentioned the idea of a round-robin each week between her, Bari, and fledgling vampire Ethan to discuss pack gossip, Bari had imagined a phone conversation or at most a small group video chat. Telling Bash that an address to the entire Centrus City circle was needed about progress in Brookdale, however, had resulted in a fascinating alternative.

"I feel like I'm looking at the opening of The Brady Bunch," Bari muttered.

"A lot of magic works off personal visualization, okay?" Preston said with a scowl. "So sue me."

"CBS might." Luke snickered, his blue eyes and ginger hair contrasting with Preston's East Asian features.

The entirety of the Centrus City circle was on display in the frame of Bari's guestroom vanity mirror, where he sat facing it. His own image reflected at him in the center of a block of nine total squares, each showing a different face. The top row was Deanna, Bash, and Ethan. Bari's centered image was framed by Preston and Luke. And finally, the bottom row was filled with Nell, Siobhan, and the newest member of the household, Rio.

Well, Rio was newest except for Jesse, a thirteen-year-old tiger who had been adopted by mated pair Preston and Luke and was currently peering over Preston's shoulder at what was no doubt a similar display in his mirror.

"Wicked," she said, as the several streaks of blue in her hair shimmered with the swivel of her head.

"It's the magical equivalent of a Zoom meeting," Siobhan droned, sporting her signature blond pixie cut, with eyes almost the same golden color and tattoos stretching up her neck. "Don't be so easily impressed."

"I beg to differ," Nell argued sagely, the epitome of a long-haired hippy, even more so than Reggie. Shamans often had that flower-child air about them. "The runes I cast over Preston's original signal ensure no one can intercept or overhear us, even if someone was standing right outside Bari's door. Zoom hasn't mastered that trick yet."

They were a mismatched crew to be sure. It was part of what Bari loved about them and the way his brother ran his pack. Bash was the only wolf, with Deanna, a panther, his Second, Ethan, a vampire, his mate (or at least close enough to one even if they hadn't made anything official yet), a Rat King Magister in Preston, alley cat Councilor in Luke, lizard Warden in Siobhan, and two humans rounding things out, with Nell as Shaman and Rio, a Focus and… well, hopefully future mate for Deanna, but that was also in the works. For now, Rio was simply too valuable to not live at the den.

They were everything most people in Brookdale hated—a mingling of species that worked, even if it did balk at tradition. Everyone had a unique backdrop too, obviously all at different locations when Bash had called them together.

"Young lady," Preston chastised a lingering Jesse with a purposeful nudge of his glasses up the bridge of his nose, "you have a bus to catch."

"Oh, come on! I'm part of the circle too!"

"No, you are part of the household. And if it wasn't a weekday, maybe I'd consider letting you listen in. As it stands, you need to get to school." Preston didn't nudge her as he had his specs, but he turned with an impressive parental glare for someone brand-new to fatherhood and not yet thirty.

Jesse pouted.

"I'll fill you in later, Jess," Luke said in a mock whisper, which didn't really need to be mocked, given all of them would have heard him regardless.

Jesse smirked and bounded off-screen.

"Luke," Preston growled once she had gone, "do you have to make me the bad guy every time?"

"I don't make you the bad guy," Luke defended. "You make you the bad guy."

"Because you give in to everything she asks for. You can't spoil her like this."

"I'm not spoiling—"

"Can we remember why we've gathered this morning?" Bash cut in, his voice like Bari's but far more severe, since he tended to take everything too seriously—including his wardrobe. Not that Bash didn't look smashing in black, gray, and navy, but there were other colors in the spectrum.

"Is everything all right, Bari?" Ethan asked once the other voices hushed. He was a beautiful redhead with brighter hair than Luke's and green eyes.

"You're a dear for asking," Bari answered. "Unfortunately... not really."

Bari relayed everything he'd told Jay last night and everything that had happened up until now—without mentioning he'd spent the night in Jay's bed. No one else needed to know about that yet, much as it was killing Bari keeping it to himself.

"Sorry, but... what are creation tablets?" Rio asked with a sweetly innocent raise of his hand, which made Deanna's usually brusque demeanor crumble into adoration toward his square. He had his long brown hair tied into a bun, and his dark eyes were ever wide.

Since Rio and Ethan were both newer to the world of shifters and magic and other myths proven real, Bari filled them in on the tablets' history and known meaning.

"And these are recent acquisitions by the museum?" Ethan recounted. "That feels a little too perfect. Something deeply coveted about shifter history ending up in that exact city right when you have a prophecy about some mystery woman hell-bent on a return to the past?"

"I agree," Bash said in his low, lilting rumble. "Bari, you need to find out where those tablets came from."

"Already on it, dear brother. I'll try to find out everything I can from Theresa and investigate the tablets more myself. I should be familiar enough with the language and runes to decipher everything, but there are pieces missing and some that just don't make sense to me."

"Can you take photographs?" Nell asked. "Without flash of course."

"I don't know if I should risk taking full photographs, but I'll confirm with Theresa if I can send you shots of the words and runes that are giving me trouble."

Nell might be human, but as a natural witch and Shaman, she had familiarized herself with shifter culture to the point of being more knowledgeable than most actual shifters. If there was a rune Bari didn't know, she'd be the best candidate to fill in the blanks.

"I don't suppose either of you had any helpful prophecies lately?" Bari asked Bash and Ethan. "I mean, you must be brimming with power, between your own boosted strengths and having both Ethan's father and Rio in the den. That's Focus power times four!"

"Sorry, but no," Ethan said. "Maybe we need to be in Brookdale. We'll be there next week."

"Right...." Bari all but bit his lip. "Be wary when you arrive, darling, and not just because of some villain in the woodwork. Jay's circle won't be too happy to see you, I'm afraid."

"That's to be expected," Bash said.

"Don't sweat it, Ethan," Luke added. "If you can win me and Pres over, you'll have those wolves lining up to be your friend in no time."

Whatever tension might exist between Luke and Preston as new fathers didn't deter the shared smiles they offered Ethan—that everyone offered Ethan—who ducked his head and laughed lightly, rubbing at the back of his neck.

"Thanks, guys. Pity we can't just enjoy William's science fair. You be careful until we see you, Bari."

"And don't get in any deeper than you already have," Bash ordered. "Jay may be trustworthy. Maximus too, I believe, and his family. But from what you've said, everyone else is fair game to be our enemy."

"Lucky us." Bari smiled soberly.

"We'll see you soon. Preston." Bash nodded at Preston to break the spell.

"Hang on!" Deanna cried with a bright flash of her violet eyes. "Pres, can you leave the spell running if everyone hops off but me, Bari, and Ethan? Gotta talk to these guys about something."

"Sure," Preston said. "I'll tweak it so that as soon as you all leave your mirrors, the spell will automatically end. And Luke," he spat the name with something akin to his stern parental tone, "meet me in the kitchen." With that, Preston stood, causing his image to vanish from the Brady Bunch display.

Luke looked a little alarmed before he did the same. "Bye, Bari!"

One by one, the others left, until it was only Bari, Ethan, Deanna—and Bash.

"You can go away too." Deanna waved a hand at Bash's image.

"Excuse me?"

"Trust me. You don't wanna hear about your brother getting laid last night."

"What?" Bari sputtered.

"Seriously?" Ethan asked.

"How did you—" Bari cut himself off as he tried to think of an answer. "I mean...."

"You did!" Deanna pointed an accusing finger.

"You were guessing?"

"Eh, I was 95 percent certain."

"Ugh." Bash sneered with an exaggerated eye roll. "You're right, Deanna. I do not need to hear this. Bari, promise me you're not on the road to unraveling ties with Brookdale even worse than I did?"

Sometimes Bari wondered about that, but Jay was too good a man to let that happen. "Even if things don't work out between us, and I am really hoping they do, it'll be amicable, brother. I promise."

"In that case... good luck," Bash said with an almost imperceptible smile and left.

"Now," Deanna said with a dramatic shake of her black bobbed hair. "I want to hear every dirty detail."

"You've been there two days!" Ethan scooted to the edge of his seat, equally as excited. "How did it happen?"

Bari supposed he did have fifteen minutes until Theresa would come knocking on his door. "Okay, first—" He leaned in closer to the mirror. "—let me tell you about our date."

BARI HONESTLY could have stayed in the hidden area of the museum forever and been content, organizing and cataloging secret artifacts. He'd prefer if the stakes weren't so high for solving the tablets' origin and lost meaning, but he was truly in his element.

He snapped a few photos of the runes and bits of language he didn't recognize, as well as the areas where it seemed like the words had been worn away, and texted them to Nell. Almost immediately, she answered that she didn't recognize them either or what they might be saying.

It's almost like pieces of a larger whole, she said.

Bari had thought that too, but they had the whole, spread out before him on an enormous table, and he still couldn't figure out what was missing.

He'd have to finish cataloging them all, everything they depicted, everything known about the tablets and their stories, and hope something came to him.

I'll send more photos if anything jumps out at me, Bari sent to Nell. It might be worth the risk of taking and sending full photographs, but usually, keeping traceable records of any shifter relics was dangerous. Even cataloging the items was done in code.

"I was able to learn where the donation came from," Theresa said as she breezed into the room carrying a printout, "just not exactly from whom. The person was anonymous." She set the paper on the table in front of Bari.

"Glenwood?" he read off the report. That was the third city from his prophecy, where Alpha Kate allowed Ethan's vampire "uncle" to live without incident. "Interesting. At least we have an origin. Is there any way to find out who the donor was?"

"Not without some serious investigation skills. The Glenwood Museum director is being very hush-hush."

"Good thing we know a few people who have investigation skills." Bari smirked. "Anything more you can share, can you bring it home to the den tonight?"

"Of course." She smiled and turned to leave.

Once Bari was alone again, he picked up the donation report and stared at the minimally offered location. There wasn't a full return address, but the original shipment had come from Glenwood—meaning all three nearby major cities were involved in this mess. Bari had already assumed as much given his prophecy, but knowing for sure meant nothing about the days ahead was going to be easy.

His phone buzzed again, and instead of Nell, this time it was Jay checking in. He and Maximus had been spending the day spying on Ursula and Anjali, which Maximus hadn't been too keen on, and now they were on their way to the museum to pick Bari up.

Anjali checked in with Alice Leer. Seems Angus was meeting with Des in secret, which Alice assumed was to help keep their marriage quiet, but she isn't certain.

Nothing too suspicious there, Bari texted back.

Ursula's visit to Angus's office was more interesting. His coworkers, all wolves, didn't know he and Alice were mated, just seeing each other, and they think he might have been having an affair.

An affair? Are you sure?

No, but the reason they think that is because another woman came to talk to him one day during lunch—a pregnant panther.

Bari's stomach dropped. The victims were connected.

That's not all, Jay continued. They overheard her say she was going to visit Des too. He's keeping something from us.

If possible, Bari's stomach dropped lower. Des had been at the den last night, and Bari had completely neglected to tell Jay about it.

"Oh! No, I'm sorry, sir, that's a private area. As is my office. Who let you in here?"

Theresa was talking very loudly if Bari could hear her all the way from inside her office—like she wanted him to hear.

A low-toned voice replied, but it was too faint for Bari to understand what was said, though something about the voice struck a chord deep inside him, familiar enough to draw him from the table, put his phone away, and hurry down the corridor to Theresa's aid.

"Would Mr. Bain be expecting you?" she asked next, just as loudly, hurrying Bari's feet faster. The bookshelf was ajar, which meant this man had been waiting when Theresa exited and could see the secret passageway.

"He'll talk to me. I know he's here."

Almost to the exit now, the clearer resonance of that voice stabbed icicles around Bari's heart. He turned that ice into burning fury and burst out of the passageway before Theresa had to answer.

"What the fuck are you doing here, Joseph?"

Chapter 9

BARI WAS seeing red all across his vision.

"My cellphone? You tracked my cellphone!" he bellowed.

He hadn't meant for the argument to spill out of Theresa's office, but his priority had been to lead Joseph away from the open passageway and any notions of getting involved in what lay beyond.

Telling Joseph to leave and leading him out of the office hadn't diminished the fire in Bari's belly, however, when instead of exiting the museum, Joseph had planted his feet in the middle of the punk, queer, and counterculture exhibit and said he tracked Bari's cellphone so they could talk.

"Aren't you the one who said you wanted a big gesture? Well, here I am." Joseph spread his arms to encompass himself.

He was older than Bari, rugged and roguishly good-looking, like a well-aged Adonis, with dark blond hair, deep brown eyes, and a firm, square jaw that had been so alluring for Bari in the beginning. He was beautiful as a lizard too, the same golden breed as Siobhan in Centrus City.

That didn't change that, right now, Bari seriously wanted to punch him.

"It's too late for big gestures, Joseph. I do not want to be with you. End of discussion."

"You did want me once," Joseph countered. "Remember? You loved me once."

"I thought I did," Bari said, recognizing that the otherwise empty exhibit was gaining onlookers peering in through the doorways, and nearly everyone smelled human. He should keep his voice low, but he couldn't help the way his volume kept increasing. "I wanted what we had to be real. I wanted you to be worth it, but I was chasing something that didn't exist because I wanted one part of my life to be a fairy tale. So, there you have it!" He laughed mirthlessly. "You were right. I do want a fairy tale. Everything else in my life is such a goddamn nightmare sometimes, I thought I deserved a happily ever after. But again and again, I chase the wrong person to find it, and now, when I've finally met someone who is everything I ever wanted, you have to show up to ruin it!"

"You think you're cut out to be with an Al—" Joseph stopped himself, also recognizing the crowd listening. "With someone like Jeffrey Russell? Don't make me laugh."

This was the reason Bari had left, because there was a snake hiding beneath Joseph's scales. "Fuck you. But you know what? At least I finally get why I stopped wanting you. I went looking for romance and found a shadow of my father instead. Go home, Joseph." Bari spun around to leave, since Joseph wasn't taking the hint, and through the entryway directly before him came Jay and Maximus.

Shit.

"There you go again," Joseph scoffed, catching Bari by the wrist before his stuttered steps could continue forward. "And why am I not surprised? All you know how to do is run."

Rage tinted Bari's vision with even more bloodred, and before he could stop to think, he felt his eyes begin to glow, his fangs start to extend, and he clenched an almost clawed fist that he intended to spin around with and punch Joseph hard enough to hurl him across the room.

He pivoted to swing—

But his arm was stopped after only a few inches, his hand caught and squeezed so tightly, the wolf drained right out of him from the pain.

Magic. A disembodied glowing blue hand had grabbed his other wrist to stop him.

Clara and Ursula had entered behind Jay and Maximus, and some sort of magical barrier was in front of the entryways now, while Ursula told the onlookers to disperse, none of whom looked even mildly disturbed.

A glamour, so that even looking right at Bari, no one outside the blue glow could see the magical hand or what Bari had almost allowed to happen.

"I...." He tried to think of something to defend himself with, but the cold stare from Ursula in particular let him know that the magical hand would break his arm if he took this any further. He wouldn't, and there was nothing more to say.

"Get your hands off me!" Joseph bit out angrily, and Bari turned to see that several larger wolves had entered from other doorways and were seizing Joseph's arms. No one seized Bari, but then, he wasn't fighting, and eventually, the magical hand dissipated.

"I would advise you to not struggle, Mr....?" Ursula trailed off, steadily walking toward Joseph after ensuring the crowd had left. The glamour over the entryways disappeared too.

"Cleary. Joseph Cleary. And I have every right—"

"You have no rights here, Mr. Cleary. I am Warden of Brookdale, and you do not have permission to be in my city. Or did I miss a memo?" Ursula glanced behind her, Bari thought for him to answer, but it was Jay who came forward.

"You did not," Jay answered gravely. "We haven't met, Mr. Cleary, but I am the Jeffrey Russell whose name you threw around so cavalierly, and I don't care what past you and Bari have, you do not make a scene like this, coming here without requesting passage into my city, and accost my guest in a public place."

"Your guest," Joseph scoffed again, struggling once more against the hold of Ursula's agents. "More like your—"

A growl rumbled from Jay, echoing low throughout the room as a warning for Joseph to not finish that sentence. No humans were near enough anymore to hear it—save Theresa, who had flown to Maximus's side—but although that was all Jay risked displaying in public, he made it clear how quickly that could change.

Joseph looked cowed, more than Bari had ever seen from him.

"You are going to leave Bari alone," Jay said with superior threat and malice than Ursula had displayed, and for that, Bari would have been grateful, if he didn't feel nauseated from having acted so recklessly. "I do not want to see you or hear about you contacting Bari ever again. Do we understand each other?"

Once more, Joseph shrank beneath Jay's commanding presence, and his answering nod was small.

"We have this under control, Alpha." Ursula stepped between Jay and Joseph, standing tall where Joseph had shriveled. "We are going to escort Mr. Cleary out of the city. And you aren't going to return, are you?" she snarled over her shoulder. "Or we might not be as hospitable next time."

When Joseph made no plea in his defense, Ursula nodded at her agents, and they began to lead him from the room. He didn't even glance in Bari's direction, which was a small mercy.

"Thank you, Urs," Jay said in a lighter tone. "I'm glad—"

"Did you see what your guest almost did?" Ursula whirled on Jay with her own menacing glower. "I should be escorting him out of our borders too."

"Bari was only defending—"

"He nearly outed himself to a building full of humans."

"We arrived in time, and Clara was able to—"

"I don't care. I have every right to supersede your orders if pack safety is compromised. Keep him leashed," Ursula warned with controlled but audible venom in her words, "or I will."

She left without fear of reprimand, because there was no risk of one when she had spoken only the truth.

Clara, standing separate from the others and straining to muster a smile, added, "At least humans are easy to fool. I'll make sure we didn't miss anyone."

Bari couldn't look at Jay when he came up to him. "I'm so sorry. I wasn't thinking—"

"It's all right," Jay said with infinite understanding Bari didn't deserve. "Let's go home."

JAY FELT like he was trapped at the exact moment when a pot of hot water was on the brink of starting to boil. It would have been nice overhearing that he was everything Bari ever wanted in a partner, if those words hadn't been spat at Bari's ex with an audience of humans and an almost catastrophic incident having occurred.

Bari was so obviously riddled with guilt that he barely spoke on the way back to the den. Upon arriving, Jay lost track of Bari while discussing a few things with Maximus, but the sweet smell of jasmine eventually led him to the dining room, where dinner was not yet being laid out and Bari stood staring out the glass of the courtyard doors.

Slowly, Jay moved up behind him.

"You remain indelibly sweet," Bari spoke without turning, "even when I should have repercussions for what happened."

"Bari, you were provoked—"

"That's no excuse and you know it. It's the first lesson we learn— never in public."

Jay finished his approach and came up parallel with Bari in front of the doors.

"If anyone had seen me…." Bari closed his eyes in deeper shame.

"If anyone had, it happened too fast for them to believe it. If you think you deserve punishment, I think we can agree on extenuating circumstances. It was… a really bad breakup, I take it?"

"Joseph's an asshole." Bari's eyes fluttered open, damp and shimmering, yet through the wetness, he smiled. "Honestly, I wouldn't mind if Ursula's muscle roughed him up a little on their way kicking him to the curb. Although, given he's lizard tribe, that might be considered a hate crime these days."

Jay snorted.

"Sorry, inappropriate jokes in an uncomfortable situation are sort of my forte."

"I wouldn't have thought you could lose your temper like that." Jay turned to lean his shoulder against the glass. "I almost didn't believe it when Theresa called to warn us what was happening. What he said really got to you. You don't have to explain why," he amended when Bari looked uncomfortable all over again.

"I think I do. Joseph wasn't wrong. I run when things get difficult.

"When my father sent me away after Bash's prophecy about one of us being his undoing, I didn't argue. I left Bash to that abusive bastard for a decade. After Bash killed him, I went home, but only briefly. Bash asked me to join his circle, and I said no, because I couldn't stand to be there and be reminded of what I let happen by leaving willingly.

"And while I realize I am a marvelous catch—" Bari smiled less convincingly this time, since a few stubborn tears streaked down his cheeks like last night. "—there's a reason I'm still single. I fall for the wrong types of men, and when I finally realize it, all I have left is to run."

"Do you think I'm the wrong type of man?" Jay asked.

"No," Bari said with passion that finally drew his eyes upward, "but that makes it worse. Because if I run from you, then I will truly prove how pathetic I am." Another tear slipped free, and Bari furiously wiped at it.

Jay wished they could return to inappropriate jokes, but in lieu of that, he said, "Come here."

Bari blinked uncertainty.

"Come here," Jay said again and opened his arms to pull Bari to him.

The Alpha tone made Bari shiver in that wonderful way Jay loved as he relaxed into Jay's embrace.

"I hope I never give you reason to run from me, Bari. Though I realize your welcome to this city has been less than ideal."

Bari huffed muffled laughter into Jay's shoulder.

"I promise, if I think you run for the wrong reasons, I will follow and fight for you, and if I don't live up to what you deserve, I will let you go. But you are not pathetic. You are so much stronger than you think and, if it's not too forward or sentimental to admit this... everything I ever wanted too."

"You heard that part, huh?"

"You sort of screamed it."

Bari muffled another laugh into Jay's skin and then pulled up with such radiance in his damp eyes, his beautiful brown features smoothed into something like painted marble not even the museum could have displayed as flawlessly.

One success deserved another, Jay figured, so he took Bari's face in his hands and kissed him.

Bari leaned into it, into Jay, with the most delicious hum.

When they parted, something dark flitting across the light in the courtyard caught Jay's attention, and he glanced over—to see Des slipping in through the gate and heading swiftly for Reggie's door.

Pulling Bari with him, Jay flattened himself to the wall to keep them from being spotted. What on earth was Des doing here, just as the sun was starting to set, and why did he have access through the wards?

"What is it?" Bari asked in a whisper.

"I just saw Des sneaking in to meet Reggie," Jay said in an equally low hiss. When he glanced out the glass again, Reggie's door was already closed. No—slightly ajar, which might give them an advantage. "Max and I learned he might be hiding things, remember?" When Jay turned back, Bari had gone far more pallid than should be possible for someone with such a dark complexion. "Bari?"

"I saw Des leaving Reggie's door last night. It completely slipped my mind to tell you. I'm sorry!"

Two nights in a row? The plot was thickening in far too many terrible ways, but right now all that mattered was acting before anything new caught them by surprise. "It just means we need to figure out what they're doing. Now." He grasped Bari's hand and pulled him out into the courtyard.

They moved swiftly to the partially open door leading to Reggie's basement level. Once they'd opened it farther to slip inside, the voices below were still too faint even for wolf ears to pick up on. They needed to go deeper.

Jay kept hold of Bari's hand, descending one slow step at a time until they reached low enough into the basement to hear the hushed conversation clearly.

"All missing?" Reggie asked.

"And we know for sure Angus and Serena are dead," Des said.

Serena was the name of the panther woman.

"I think we're going to start finding more bodies," Des continued, "and it's going to look very much like I had a hand in it."

"Well, hopefully the fact that we have an audience," Reggie said in a suddenly louder voice, "will help clear your name. JJ! Is that you, love? Really, you know I have alert wards on those stairs."

The tension heightened and then fled from Jay at being revealed, though he doubted much could quell the roiling in his stomach tonight. With a weak smile thrown at Bari, who still looked ashen and tightened his grip on Jay's hand almost enough to bruise, Jay led them down the rest of the way into Reggie's chambers.

Reggie and Des stood not far away, with Reggie smiling as benignly as ever to contrast the startled expression on Des.

"More bodies?" Jay repeated. "And you'll look at fault? Why don't you explain to me why that is."

Chapter 10

"HAVE A seat, boyos," Reggie declared, grandly sweeping his arm toward the lounge area.

The basement was finished and mostly an open floor plan, save for a bathroom and Reggie's bedroom on the far side beside the second staircase leading to the floor above. Since the basement spanned almost the entire square footage of the manor, it was large but mostly taken up by a small library, an area where Reggie could look over patients, and space for experiments.

A portion of the library was glamoured, hiding half a dozen cold storage lockers, where Angus's body was being kept until they could turn it over to the family. The rest of the basement was the lounge, often used as a waiting area, complete with several chairs and a sofa.

Reggie was his usual undaunted self, but Jay had never seen Des look so nervous. He was a collected man who stood up to Anjali on the regular—he didn't spook.

"What glum faces!" Bari tried to break the tension, showing no sign that he'd been near tears only minutes prior, as he and Jay moved to the sofa as requested. Reggie and Des took chairs across from each other, bookending them. "Thank goodness for you, Reggie darling, ever the host. Nothing to hide, I hope?"

Reggie also kept his chipper tone, as if he and Des hadn't been caught discussing multiple murders. "Depends, what all did you loves hear?"

"Enough to be wary," Jay said, less cordial. "You know things are pointing toward you," he threw at Des, "because you had a closer relationship with the dead than you told me. You also expect there to be more bodies and know full well who's missing. So you understand my concern that you brought this to Reggie—and were also here last night— instead of bringing anything to your Alpha.

"What is going on?" Jay looked back and forth between them. "I was starting to think Angus and Serena were having an affair, that Angus was the father of that mixed panther child, but this is bigger than some love triangle, isn't it?"

"Angus would never cheat on Alice," Des affirmed. "And Serena was just as loyal to her husband. Her child would have been half panther, half wolf, like I told you."

"You never gave us the wolf father's name," Bari noted, reminding Jay that Des had not, but Jay had been too preoccupied with another death to care. "Where is he in all this?"

Des glanced furtively at Reggie before answering, "One of the missing. Crispin Jahns."

"A wolf is one of the missing?" Jay asked in surprise.

"If you doubt this is racially driven, consider that someone like Alice, who merely stooped below her station—" Des spat in disdain. "—can still recover her honor and mate with another wolf. Crispin, however, dared sully the bloodline by creating spawn with a panther. It's not hard to believe he'd become another target."

"While that makes sense," Bari spoke up again, "it doesn't explain why you know who's missing. Are you protecting the killer?"

"No!" Des said with a flash of his eyes. "We don't know who the killer is. Everyone missing has been…." He trailed off, but when Reggie didn't try to stop him, he continued. "They were all seeing Reggie to help with procreation between tribes. He's been experimenting on ways to increase the chances, and obviously with Serena it worked. I was helping keep things secret, but someone must have found out what was going on and chose those people to target."

The magnitude of this felt like that pot of boiling water Jay's life had become had upturned over his head. "If that's true, why did Alice sound surprised to learn Angus was seeing you? Wouldn't they both have been coming here?"

"Angus, dear boy that he was," Reggie answered, "didn't want to get poor Alice's hopes up if nothing could be done. After all, a rat and a wolf have never been known to successfully reproduce, but he knew how much she'd always wanted a child of her own, so he wanted to be certain before he told her."

Jay hated having to be so paranoid of people he trusted, but he knew something was being left unspoken. Reggie continued to smile, but Jay could see through his sunglasses the faint flitting of his eyes back and forth that proved he was as nervous as Des. "I expect to be given the list of people who are missing—"

"Of course, love. I'll—"

"I'm not finished," Jay said with the tinge of a growl in his words, causing Reggie and Des to flinch, and Bari to squirm in his seat. "You're withholding something. If what you're not saying has any bearing on these murders—"

"It doesn't," Des spoke for Reggie, which made Reggie drop his head back, almost certainly rolling his eyes behind his shades.

"Oh, you beautiful bastard, could you try being less of a martyr?" he muttered. "Yes, JJ, there are things we're not saying, but it's necessary, I assure you. Consider it… doctor/patient confidentiality."

Bari snorted, and Jay took the pause that followed to gauge Reggie and Des very carefully. He still had that annoying paranoia clawing at the back of his brain, but there was no reason to not trust them, and when Jay considered the words he'd overheard, it did seem like this explanation was the truth, even if secrets remained.

"I'll accept that. For now," Jay said and then pointedly focused on Des. "If you're being honest with me, then even if your name does continue to pop up should more bodies be found, there's no real evidence pointing toward you having committed the murders. You're simply someone the victims knew, and you know everyone. I'll vouch for you if it comes to that."

"Thank you, Alpha." Des smiled at the concession.

"Now, who all do you believe is missing?"

"I'll make a list!" Reggie announced, hopping up from his seat to retrieve a pen and pad of paper, as well as a previously forgotten drink he reclaimed.

When Reggie was finished writing, he slapped the pad on the coffee table between them and plopped back down in his chair to take a long draw from his drink.

Jay glanced at the pad, noting the names. While he didn't know any of them well, he recognized most of them. Reggie had made two columns, one for "Missing/Dead," with Serena and Angus's names crossed out, and another for "Mixed Couple Patients," indicating possible future missing persons. The very idea made Jay's stomach twist. There were dozens of them.

Something else Jay noted was that among those missing or dead was a lizard shifter who matched the description of the Jane Doe that had died from an animal attack—Linda Bouchard.

Even stranger was that in that smaller column was exactly one of each type of shifter.

DINNER WAS much quieter than the previous night, but Bari couldn't shake that he might be sitting at a table with a murderer.

After William left the table, Jay finally told everyone about Serena, the pregnant panther, who it turned out was also in their morgue, since bringing the body to Reggie was how Des had put it on ice. There was some contention then since most of the circle had been kept in the dark, but Jay explained it as having wanted to wait until after he had a list of missing persons. Now he did, which pointed to a third body.

He didn't mention Reggie or Des's involvement, nor anything about Bari's prophecy, but three murders and a list of who to look for next was plenty for the circle to work from—assuming none of them were involved.

What Bari wanted now was to relax. He'd hoped that might be possible with Jay, but as Alpha, Jay vanished after dinner, barely having the chance to whisper in Bari's ear that he'd update him later if he learned anything new.

That left Bari to decompress in a hot bath alone—in the gorgeous clawfoot tub in his private bathroom that made him want to call his super right that moment and have everything from his old apartment shipped to Brookdale so he could move in tonight, murderer on the loose or no.

The den truly was spectacular, but Bari would have taken a Motel 6 over having to empty his apartment in person, where Joseph might be lying in wait.

Bari sank lower in the still soothingly warm bathwater, scented lavender from the bubbles he hadn't been able to resist using. He didn't want to think about Joseph, or how angry he'd been earlier, or how foolishly he'd acted. It was the stress of his prophecy. It was having to see Joseph again. It was the murders, targeting happy couples who simply wanted children together.

It was knowing that being a Seer, being the one person who'd seen what was to come, meant Bari was destined to play a role, and he was terrified of screwing it up like he'd screwed up so many other things in his life.

Because he couldn't stop running.

"Oh, get a hold of yourself, Bari Bain," Bari chastised himself, sniffling back the fresh tears threatening to fall. "What would Bash say? He'd say… you stop that, Bari. Crying never accomplished anything," he muttered in approximation of his brother's more serious voice. "And I'd say… don't be ridiculous, brother. Crying got me the last cookie plenty when we were little." Bari chuckled and then sank a little lower to let his hair dip fully into the water. "Too bad cookies aren't the prize this time. Or crumpets."

That made Bari think of the real prize—besides the ultimate goal of stopping a murderer and saving countless lives throughout three major cities—and it was far sweeter than any baked good.

Jay could have penalized Bari for nearly shifting in public, but instead, he'd been understanding again and endlessly sweet. He even kissed Bari and kept hold of his hand all the way down Reggie's basement steps. The chaos of the day couldn't spoil what had grown from last night or overshadow the way Jay's hands had felt on Bari's skin, running over every inch of him, bold and claiming, and eventually prodding deep inside—

Okay, that train of thought wasn't going anywhere but… well, up, and Bari wanted to save any upward momentum for the real thing. Few activities banished troublesome thoughts like being in the throes of worthwhile passion.

If Jay ever managed to escape his duties.

Bari could have stuck to Jay's side, but along with Anjali and Ursula giving off an even stronger air of "you're not welcome here," he'd almost been relieved to have a little time alone. Well, now he'd had his time alone, and he was pruney and horny and couldn't keep being useless when everyone else was pulling their weight.

After tugging on the stopper to drain the tub, Bari got out to dry off. Maybe he'd seek Theresa before it got too late and confirm whether she'd neglected to mention anything about the origin of the creation tablets. He doubted it, but their involvement had been plaguing him ever since he first saw them, especially after Ethan confirmed his own thinking that the timing was far too apt.

Rather than get completely redressed, Bari pulled on a fresh pair of shorts and donned his favorite paisley robe. Maximus and Theresa's room was directly across from Jay's at the end of the hall. As Bari approached, he noted that Jay's door was closed, but the opposite was open—where Maximus was lounging atop the bed, reading from a very "Fabio and scantily clad woman" sort of paperback.

"My, my." Bari leaned against the doorframe, watching Maximus jump and then attempt and fail to hide the paperback beneath his pillow. "I was going to ask if Theresa was off with young William somewhere, maybe helping with homework, but I'm afraid I may be hallucinating because that very much looks like a dirty book, Mr. Thornton."

"Do you mind—"

"If you're about to ask why I didn't knock, um…." Bari knocked on the door now to remind Maximus that it had been left open. "Don't be embarrassed. What do you think makes my bags so heavy? Bricks?" He entered, brazenly crossing to the bed and sitting on the edge with an outstretched hand.

As annoyed as Maximus looked, he retrieved the book to slap into Bari's palm. "It's Theresa's."

"Oh, I'm sure." Bari flipped the book over to read the back.

"It is. I only grabbed it because I see her and Jay reading that sort of trash constantly and wondered what the fuss was about."

"Mm-hm," Bari hummed in mockery. "And I'm sure this particular title being about a single father falling for a new woman in his life is just… coincidence? Or are you man enough to admit you might be looking for tips on re-wooing your scorned love?"

"She's not—" Maximus cut off his usual angry outburst and snatched the book back from Bari. "Not that my love life is any of your business, but why should she be scorned? Also, you better be wearing underwear beneath that robe."

Bari snorted, half tempted to say he wasn't. "Do you really not notice the way some of the people in this house treat your wife?"

"I… notice."

"Yet you do nothing to defend her. Please don't bite my head off for saying this, but… I think she deserves better. And what sort of example do you want to set for your son? Unless you truly believe those prejudices."

"Of course I don't," Maximus growled.

"Then act like it, or my joke about stealing your wife away from you won't be the problem. You might lose her all on your own. I'd wager you can tell she's been more upset lately and have no idea how to make it up to her. Defending her on occasion would be a good start, but a little wooing never hurt anyone."

Rather than admit Bari had guessed right, Maximus fell back onto his pillows. "What's it matter? This drivel isn't going to help me."

"Drivel? Really?"

"Maybe it isn't all terribly written."

Bari grinned and scooted farther up the bed. "What's your favorite part so far? And it's okay, you can admit if it's the sexy bits."

Whatever thin ice Bari might be walking with the large, muscled Second, it hadn't started to crack yet, because Maximus answered, "Maybe... how the female lead is the aggressor their first time."

"Darling," Bari gushed. "You don't need to explain the allure of someone being dominating to me."

Maximus sneered.

"Now, now, I'm honestly trying to help you here. I realize I can be a bit... much, one might say?"

Maximus averted his eyes, obviously getting the reference.

"But it's only because I adore Theresa and William. You are an acquired taste, but then, so am I." Bari grinned wider, waiting to say more until Maximus met his gaze and didn't look entirely homicidal. "Is Theresa going to be back any time soon?"

"Not yet. She's helping William with schoolwork like you guessed. Why?"

"Be honest: it's not really such a terrible chore reading that?" Bari nodded at the book.

"It has its moments."

"Any that have been inspiring for your lady love, such as that strong aggressive woman bit? I could help."

"I am not taking sex advice from you."

"Purely on the romantic side, I swear! Besides, with women, I'd be a bit lacking with the hands-on experience."

Maximus laughed—more like huffed, but it was definitely amusement. Then his eyes drifted, and he worried his bottom lip.

"What is it?" Bari asked, scooting close enough that their hips bumped. "Come on. Spill."

With a sigh and shift onto his elbows, Maximus said, "Our anniversary is coming up."

Bari practically toppled onto his elbows to frame his face in his hands. "Tell me everything."

IT WAS so late when Jay retired to his room that he didn't think it right to knock on Bari's door. He was admittedly disappointed to not find Bari waiting in his bed, but then they hadn't made any promises about that.

Only, before Jay could dejectedly strip out of his clothing to crawl under the covers alone, he realized his balcony doors were open and a shadowed but distinct figure sat at his terrace table looking down at the courtyard.

"Isn't it a bit chilly to be sitting out here in a robe?" Jay asked, enchanted as ever with Bari Bain, legs crossed and feet bare as he sat in a gold-and-blue paisley robe that complemented his tall, dark, and handsome figure.

It turned out he wasn't looking at the courtyard with its fairy lights, but reading, his eyes glowing with wolf precision to beat the low illumination. Resting on the small table was the brandy bottle with a clean glass awaiting Jay and one clearly being sipped from by Bari. Most of the balconies didn't have a table and chairs, but Jay's was the largest.

"Nonsense," Bari said with a radiant smile, as Jay took the seat beside him. "The cold never bothered me anyway," he added with a chuckle. "Besides, the brandy helps. If I was going to nick more from you, I felt it only right to do so in your room. I hope you don't mind." He stole a slow sip, watching Jay all the while, with his golden eyes still glittering a Stage One glow.

"I could use a taste myself," Jay said.

"Well, then, shall I pour you—" Bari didn't get to finish the thought, because Jay hadn't meant from a glass.

He grasped the curve of Bari's cheek and pulled him in to lick between his lips. "Mm… my favorite vintage to be sure."

Bari hummed back at him.

Maybe it was because they'd gotten their first time out of the way, maybe because it was late, maybe because Bari felt comfortable enough to simply be here, waiting for Jay, after crying in his arms more than once, but Jay didn't feel like a flustered teenager anymore, other than the part who would have been amazed he'd grow up to have someone this beautiful want him.

"Enjoying some light reading?" Jay teased about the book that had nearly dropped from Bari's fingers. At least the glass made it to the table.

"This? Research."

Jay faltered for a response, since it was clearly a straight romance.

"Not for me!" Bari laughed. "Well, not that this hasn't been motivating." He waggled an eyebrow and marked his place with a vintage-looking bronze bookmark before setting the paperback next to his brandy. "Let's say… Maximus and I have been bonding. Not to worry, though. I was wearing underwear when I was with him."

Jay laughed. Then, upon registering Bari's words, had to clarify, "When you were with him? Meaning…."

That brilliant mischievousness that made Jay want to shrug off all sense of decorum with the same bold abandon resulted in Bari uncrossing his legs and parting them just slightly to let the edges of his robe fall between them, revealing flashes of bare thigh. "Care to find out if I still am?"

Heat throbbed into Jay immediately.

He claimed Bari's glass to down what little remained. There hadn't been ice in it, but it was still cold from the crisp night air, and a wicked idea struck him. He brought the glass down and pressed it against the hot interior of Bari's thigh.

Bari hissed, his legs falling open wider, parting the robe too much for anything to be left to the imagination. The romance novel must have been motivating indeed, because Bari was at full mast with a bud of wetness glistening at his tip.

Jay pressed the glass against Bari's shaft next, awarded another hiss, and then let his warm fingers contrast the cold, feeling along Bari's velvety veins. The faint sparkling lights from below and the bright waning moon above made Bari look like a flushed prince about to be debauched on his palace balcony.

That sounded marvelous, Jay decided, and dropped to his knees. He set the glass aside, spread Bari's thighs as wide as he could, and dove down between the part in the robe's shimmering fabric.

"Jay!" a cry sounded from the door, followed by several loud knocks.

For fuck's sake! He'd just left Anjali!

"Is it important?" Jay called back.

"Would I be here if it wasn't?"

Jay sagged against Bari's knees, hating how appealing the scent of him was this close. There was that ever-present smell of jasmine, with lavender tonight and musk.

"One second!" Jay answered.

Bari laughed, fluttery and breathless, closing his legs for the robe to cover him as he dug his fingers into Jay's hair. "Better luck next time."

"There will be a next time," Jay promised and leaned up for another kiss—

"We don't have seconds! This is serious!" Anjali gave a few more insistent knocks.

Jay irritably leaped to his feet, spared Bari one last apologetic glance, and raced across the room to answer. "What?"

"Something's happening at the Shelter." Anjali shouldered inside. As soon as she saw Bari coming in from the balcony, she paused but didn't comment. "Ursula already has agents there and is headed there now, but it's pandemonium."

"What? Why?" Jay demanded.

"Wolves are descending as we speak. They found a fourth body." She paused only long enough to take a breath. "It's Crispin Jahns, and his family is blaming the Shelter."

Chapter 11

"I DON'T understand," Bari was saying as they drove near break-neck speeds for the Shelter. He'd only had time to change from his robe into real clothing because Jay and Anjali had needed to round up the others. "We think a wolf might be behind the murders, but local wolves are avenging a wolf we think the murderer killed?"

Bari might not have been so forthcoming if they weren't alone with Maximus. Ursula should already be at the Shelter, Anjali was driving Reggie and Clara, and Daisy, Theresa, and William had been left at the den to wait and fret.

"Not everyone knew Crispin and Serena were mated," Jay said from the passenger seat, as Maximus drove. "If what Anjali reported is true, Crispin's family and the other wolves they've gathered think the killer is from the Shelter and likely a lizard, trying to undermine the pack."

"Conspiracy nonsense," Maximus muttered. "The claw marks on the bodies were from a wolf."

"We think. Still more than enough speculation to incite an angry mob."

Bari collapsed against the back seat. "Anjali knew about Angus and Alice. Did she know about Crispin and Serena?"

"She made it sound like she did," Jay said.

"She's Councilor," Maximus countered. "She's supposed to know those things. You got this idea in your head that someone here is a traitor, but do you really think Anjali would want something like this to happen?"

"I don't know why anyone would want this to happen," Bari said plainly. "Maybe they didn't plan for this level of panic and retaliation. Maybe they did. But someone is behind it all, and we still don't know who."

Jay's tone was just as severe as he said, "For now, what matters is keeping the people safe—even from themselves."

Pandemonium wasn't an exaggeration when they arrived, parked behind Anjali, and leaped out onto the sidewalk. People were already spilling from the main doors, rattled, some partially shifted, hurrying to escape whatever was happening inside.

"Get to the parks!" Ursula directed them, having waited for everyone else before entering.

"And get a hold of yourselves!" Anjali added. "No shifting in the streets! We can't afford to draw attention from the police!"

"We'll handle this," Jay assured anyone who caught sight of him and paused to pay the Alpha homage, "and we'll let everyone know once it's safe to return. Go, now!"

Bari felt like such a fraud, like an even worse interloper than he'd been so far, watching the circle members control the chaos, quickly working to make their way inside. He should have been left behind with the others at the den, but it had seemed so natural to follow Jay, especially when Bari was caught up in this, knowing by the awful mercy of fate how bad things could become if they didn't fix this and find the real killer.

The people pouring out of the doors parted left and right like dancers in a stage play, giving leave for the circle to push inside. No one waited for Bari, but he couldn't sit on the sidewalk, twiddling his thumbs.

He followed—and inside was so much worse.

The noise was deafening, too many voices talking and arguing and screaming, with sounds of fighting echoing down the hall from the main common area and people running every which way like the building was on fire. The sparks of magic in the distance meant it might be on fire soon.

Two of Ursula's agents were left to guard the door and continue to usher people outside. Bari wouldn't have recognized any of the agents in a lineup; most looked so similar—big and burly and menacing. Several others must already be in the fray, and several more joined Anjali at the forefront of the circle members racing down the hall. All Bari could do was bring up the rear.

They were as awe-inspiring as Bash's circle, none looking afraid or even hesitant as they ran to do their duty. Circle members weren't only adept at their chosen position. They had to be warriors.

That wasn't Bari. What was he even doing here? He'd been next to useless during the fight in Centrus City.

"Please!" A strong hand gripped Bari's forearm midstride, yanking him back from keeping up with the others. He almost whirled about to take a swing, when he saw it was the mother of the little boy who'd given Jay that cat doll. "Jordan. I can't find him. Have you seen him?"

"I… I don't know," Bari stuttered to answer, shaky from adrenaline. "We only just arrived and—"

"Please." She clung with her other hand. "He's so young. I don't know what to do. I'm no fighter."

Again, Bari thought neither was he, but as he looked at the distraught mother's face, he knew why his feet had carried him forward despite his doubts. He could fight, he had to, and he wasn't about to run if a little boy was in danger.

"I'll find him," he promised and turned to hurry after the others, who'd already reached the mouth of the main room.

It was sobering, almost nauseating, to see shifters fighting shifters simply because of hate, and not only wolves fighting others, but any and every type of contrasting shifter race using this as an excuse to lash out. At least in Centrus, the shifters fighting each other had been under a vampire's thrall, wild and unthinking. This was mob mentality driven by something real.

Bari ducked, unsure exactly why he'd known he had to, just as a Stage Three tiger swiped at his head. Somehow, he'd seen the blow coming.

He pivoted, weaving as the tiger swiped at him again, expertly dodging like a boxer avoiding blows, which afforded Bari the chance he needed to shift. So many others were Stage Three and monstrously large, but Bari kept to Stage Two with sharpened eyes, fangs, and claws, and only the barest sprouting of fur. He needed to be sure the boy recognized him when he found him, and a werewolf barreling after a child would not be taken kindly in this frenzy.

"I'm not with them!" Bari snarled in the face of the tiger snapping sabretooth jaws. She would have been beautiful, perfectly orange-and-black tabby-striped, if she wasn't trying to eat Bari's face off. "I'm with the Alpha!"

A fireball struck the tiger in the chest just as she'd been about to leap from taut hind legs, causing an instant smell of burning fur as she was thrown into a wall from the impact.

Bari's head whipped toward the source.

Clara.

She waved, also at Stage Two, with a sprouting of reddish-brown-colored fur. Then she spun back around and leaped into a melee of five other shifters, summoning a violet rune Bari couldn't quite make out before sweeping her arms outward like a grand conductor and exploding the fighters in separate directions with something like concentrated wind or maybe just telekinesis.

Magisters didn't have to be masters of offensive magic, but Clara was something else.

They all were, Bari saw as he glanced more closely around the room. None of the circle members had gone to Stage Three, keeping themselves contained to avoid hurting anyone too badly. It was still a vicious display, the way Maximus didn't hesitate to pull limbs from lizards, knowing that tribe could regenerate, or how Ursula and her agents slammed people to the floor, rendering many of them instantly unconscious, only to move on to another and then another.

Reggie was somehow not even touching people, casting weakening runes that drained others of their strength and stamina. That's when Bari noticed Des in the fray too, almost back-to-back with Anjali, taking down those Reggie weakened. In the thick of things, it was hard to believe the pair would usually be bickering.

If it wasn't for the sheer numbers of those fighting, the circle might have already had this contained, but they needed to incapacitate before they could calm, and that's exactly what they were doing.

In the center of it all, Jay climbed atop a table with claws flexed and eyes gleaming as he threw his head back and roared. The power in it made Bari shudder, immediately brought to attention and captivated.

But he was one of only a few. The others weren't listening to their Alpha, least of all the wolves who'd started this. They merely took the hesitation Jay's roar caused in others as their chance to fight harder.

Bari had to find that little boy.

Taking a calming breath, he tried to decide which area to search first—

Only to be assaulted with clearer images of Jordan in one of the rooms, cornered by older children closing in on him.

Bari gasped. A vision? No, not a full prophecy or enough for his eyes to change and let others witness that he was a Seer, but enough to be certain of where he had to go.

Left—the rat area.

Darting that direction, Bari weaved and ducked between flying fists, claws, and offensive spells. It was thrilling to be able to avoid it all so easily, like second nature, like some Jedi Knight calling on the Force.

He would have laughed as the reference struck him if his momentary glee didn't make him nearly trip over a fallen Stage Three werewolf. He leaped, landing just on the other side of the massive downed body, and continued into the corridor quickly emptying of anyone else.

He knew someone was still in there, and he didn't hesitate on which room to enter, beelining straight for the third door on the right, where Jordan was surrounded by a half dozen rat children sniping at him.

"You think you're better than us?" one shouted.

"We saw you give the Alpha a gift," another accused.

"Is that how you're getting out of here so soon?" added another. "Your mama paying the Alpha off? Is that it? Getting all cozy, learning just what he likes?"

"I'll tell you what he doesn't like!" Bari rushed over with a snap of his jaws, grabbing on to shoulders in his path to yank the children away from Jordan. "And it's rude little shits like you who'd gang up on someone smaller. Get out of here!" he snarled, whirling around with a flash of his eyes in warning as he stood guard in front of the boy and dared the others to defy him.

Naturally, they scattered.

"Don't repeat bad words, dear," Bari said once the children were gone, and he turned to check on Jordan behind him.

The sweet little thing had tried to shift, his eyes slitted, with whiskers on his catlike nose and the barest bit of black fur on his lengthened ears. He was hugging another stuffed cat doll, this one larger but still black-and-white like the one he'd given Jay.

He shrank back when Bari approached him.

"It's all right. I'm a friend, remember?" Bari shifted fully human, stopping his advance to crouch at the boy's level. "I was with the Alpha the other day, when you gave him the doll."

The boy blinked large green eyes, studying Bari's face. "The Alpha's new mate?"

Warmth filled Bari's cheeks, like when the boy had asked that the first time. "If he decides he likes me enough."

With a surge of dampness in Jordan's eyes, the boy flew forward to wrap his arms around Bari's neck. Mission accomplished.

"Hey!" an adult voice called from behind Bari. At least an adult he could reason with.

Bari released Jordan to stand and turn around, only it wasn't one adult headed his way, but five, all partially shifted, all rats, and likely those little shits' parents, since the children were gathered in the doorway to watch.

Fuck.

"Damn wolves, always sticking your noses in our business," an impressively large woman said as she clicked elongated rat teeth at him, which, regardless of the fodder traditionalists told themselves, were just as formidable as those of a wolf.

"If by business you mean teaching your children to pick on a boy much younger—"

They rushed him, no warning, just full-on sprinted with a chorus of hissing and guttural snarls.

"Not in the mood to talk, I see!" Bari pushed Jordan back toward the wall as hard as he dared to give himself room, only just managing to square his stance when the first clawed hand swiped at him with more speed than the tiger.

Then another swipe came, and another, and... and none of them were hitting him! Screw Jedi reflexes! Bari was freaking Neo from The Matrix, and no one could land a punch!

It was almost like they were moving in slow motion, because Bari knew instinctually, every time, where the next swipe or lunge would come from and exactly how he needed to move to avoid it. Being a somewhat skilled dancer wasn't hurting him either, since he was pivoting and spinning with no small amount of grace.

As one of the men pulled back a fist for a harsher punch, Bari dodged and then grabbed on to the man to swing him forward, using his own momentum to aim that punch right into the face of the large woman. She staggered, and the man shouted an apology, rushing to aid her.

Someone else was coming up behind Bari, but he could feel it, practically see it in his mind's eye, and he twirled out of the way for the man to barrel into the others before the punched woman could recover.

That left two more, another man and woman, who grabbed on to Bari's arms, but he let them, because he knew exactly when to go limp, and the claws aiming for his face gouged at each other instead, allowing him to slip free.

The children watching had vanished, apparently not liking how the show was turning out.

"Now! Will you try listening—"

"We're not taking shit from some wolf!" the punched woman cried, and they all came rushing at Bari again.

"I thought you people liked Jay, for fuck's sake!" He cringed when his next bob and weave brought him in line of sight of Jordan. "Sorry, darling! Don't repeat that!"

"Don't pretend you're not with the others trying to rule us!"

"I'm not! I came with—oof!" Bari had been weaving and twirling closer to a wall this time, and that last duck caused a flying fist to plow through the plaster. "Listen to me!" He kicked up into the closest attacker's stomach and dove out from the others with a roll, springing back up onto his feet. "I just—"

One of them jumped at him, going to Stage Three midleap, and Bari growled and punched the bastard right out of the air.

Fuck it!

Tripping the feet out from under another, Bari dodged a hit from a third and then punched back in retaliation. Now he was angry, and for once, he didn't have to worry about landing a hit—he knew he could. He had this. He could take them. After a few more strikes at those still standing, the only one remaining was the punched woman again, and Bari was more than ready to—

To take a fist to the face so fiercely and suddenly swung at him, he hadn't predicted it, and he dropped like a bundle of lead pipes as the world around him blackened.

THEY WEREN'T listening. Almost none of them were listening to Jay, their Alpha, and in that moment, he was so incensed by their defiance, he leaped from the table into the fray, throwing shifters at every stage to the floor with enough force to stun them. Some, once they realized who he was, stayed down, but others lunged right back at him, uncaring to their mutiny.

Pandemonium didn't say it well enough. This was anarchy, and Jay would not stand for it. Although he didn't know the reason Bari had fled into the rat area, he was grateful to have one less witness of how spectacularly he was failing. There were still too many people part of the brawl, and despite the work the circle was doing to stop the fighters, more and more seemed to be appearing.

"Alpha!"

Jay's head whipped toward the voice, a child's voice, calling to him in the chaos.

At the entryway into the rat section was the boy he'd met the other day, waving frantically at him while clinging to a doll, looking far too fragile and vulnerable to be anywhere near this vicious melee.

"Get back!" Jay called to him, fighting his way to reach the boy and throwing anyone who dared try to stop him out of his path. He dropped in front of the child as soon as he reached him. "You need to hide! Get away from here—"

"Your mate! He's in trouble!"

"What?"

The boy tugged on Jay's still-clawed hand, not waiting to explain.

Jay's mate?

Bari.

Gripping the boy's hand harder, Jay took the lead, hurrying with him down the corridor. When it opened into a larger hall with different doors and Bari wasn't immediately visible, Jay let the boy pull him toward the third room on the right, where five rat shifters were circling a body on the floor.

"That fucker broke my nose," a woman grumbled. "Let's break a few things of his."

"Get away from him!" Jay growled, leaving the boy at the door so he could race forward. He was ready to transform fully into a hulking werewolf should they so much as look at him wrong when they turned toward him, but as soon as they saw who was giving them orders, they fell back and lowered their heads.

At least someone still remembered who Jay was.

"Alpha," the woman with the broken nose began, "we were just defending ourselves—"

"Like hell they were," the weak, muffled voice of Bari filtered up from the floor. He groaned and started to sit up, holding the bridge of his nose. "I was trying to tell you, I'm not with those other wolves. I came here with Jay."

"Bari." Jay crouched beside him, shifting human so he could reach for his face without claws. "Are you all right?"

When Bari pulled his hand from his face, there was a cut across his nose like the punch had come from someone wearing a ring. "I will be."

"Bari?" one of the men said. "This is Bain? Alpha, we didn't know—"

"I was here the other day!" Bari spat up at him. "Not that I expect everyone to know this gorgeous mug on sight, but still. Assuming it still is gorgeous…." He gingerly tapped near the cut on his nose again.

"You punched me first!" the woman with the broken nose cried as Jay helped Bari to his feet.

"Technically, your friend did the punching," Bari countered. "I just moved the target."

"He attacked our children!" someone else defended.

"I yanked on a few shoulders to get a bunch of brats off a younger boy. Did you even notice poor Jordan over there?" He gestured toward Jordan, still waiting in the doorway.

It was obvious by the group's wary expressions they had not.

"This is over with," Jay commanded. "Or am I not your Alpha?"

He took small comfort in how no one questioned him.

"I only want peace. Why can't the rest of you want that too? Do you really hate the other races so much that you'd gang up on a single defenseless target?"

"More like UFC fighter," someone grumbled.

Jay glanced at Bari in surprise. The other five people did look more beat up than he was, which Jay hadn't noticed at first.

"Must have been the adrenaline." Bari shrugged but held Jay's gaze long enough to convey something unspoken.

More like Seer senses. Thank goodness that had kept Bari from getting hurt worse.

The sounds of angry voices in the common area swelled in volume, reminding Jay this wasn't over everywhere. "We have to get back. And I better not see any of you rejoin the fight," he warned the rats, and then turned with a nod at Bari to hurry back out of the room.

Bari scooped up Jordan along the way, who snuggled into his hold.

Jay was about to tell Bari to stay with Jordan out of harm's way while he rejoined the battle, but as they reached the end of the corridor back into the common area, he had to stutter his own steps too. The loud outcry they'd heard hadn't been new fighters adding to the fray but complaints from the ones already there.

Clara and Reggie were together near the center of the room, guarded by Des, Anjali, Maximus, and Ursula with her agents. They were keeping the fighting from reaching the spellcasters to allow for a powerful combined spell summoning mass runes on everyone outside their close huddle. Anyone with a rune manifesting over them had been slowed and were one by one being halted completely.

Jay outstretched an arm to ensure Bari didn't go out there or he'd be halted too.

The many shifters weren't calming but fighting against the binding spell, still snarling, still mostly transformed, and Jay was done, ready to roar once more and remind them all who their leader was—when Ursula leaped up onto the table as Jay had before and beat him to the punch.

When she roared, the din calmed.

"You will yield!" she commanded, and silence descended like a wave of magic being cast all its own. "Your circle is investigating these murders. We do not need more! We have no suspects yet, and therefore, require no assistance in apprehending one. You will stop, retreat, and calm yourselves, or everyone currently entrapped in this room will be exiled immediately. Do we understand each other?"

Jay should have been happy the fighting was over, especially since everyone appeared to be listening to Ursula with no dissenting voices rising from those captured. He should have been happy, but he felt hollow.

The runes snuffed to nothing, like candles blown out by a strong wind, and although many of the shifters remained restless, everyone returned to human and began to shuffle away from each other. The circle members dispersed into the crowd, aiding wounded and keeping people calm now that the fight was over.

"Some Alpha," one of the departing wolves muttered.

Jay couldn't even argue. Some Alpha indeed. He hadn't been able to prevent this, and he hadn't been the one to stop it.

"Let's get you out of here," Maximus said as he came over, his clothing stained and torn in places, though like the rest of the circle, he'd been careful to never fully shift to Stage Three. "The others got things handled."

Jay should have been happy. He should have been happy. But this didn't feel like a victory.

They headed down the main corridor, where people, despite shooting wary glances at the retreating wolves, were starting to clean up the damage.

"Jordan!" a woman called out.

Bari set the boy down, who turned and ran into his mother's arms.

She was in tears as she hugged her son. "If anything had happened when we're only days from leaving this place...." She squeezed him tightly and looked up at Bari and then at Jay with boundless gratitude. "Thank you."

"Stay safe," Jay said.

"We'll see you again, hm?" Bari added with a soft smile, booping the boy on the nose and then booping the nose of his stuffed cat too.

The boy giggled.

It made Jay feel even more ineffectual because he'd done the least of the saving there too.

"Is everything all right?" Bari whispered to him in the back of the car on their way home. Jay hadn't even considered sitting up front with Max, and the coiling of Bari's hands around Jay's arm was nice. "Sorry. Stupid question."

"I need to fix this," Jay said.

"We will."

Jay looked at him, surprised but thankful for that we.

After they arrived at the den and Maximus took on the task of explaining what had happened to Daisy and Theresa, with William begrudgingly sent to bed, Jay pulled Bari upstairs.

"I could use another body in the bed tonight."

"My pleasure." Bari continued to hug Jay's arm. "Though I'm exhausted, darling, so if you decide to get frisky, you might lose a limb."

Jay couldn't laugh, but he did manage a smile. "For you, it would be worth it."

Neither of them was actually in the mood for any of that anymore. Not tonight. There would be a next time, but for now, they slept.

Chapter 12

FOUR BODIES. They had four confirmed deaths and more to watch for. Jay almost would have been relieved if they'd just found a fifth body right away. They didn't. There was still one name left in the missing-or-dead column of Reggie's list, and another column filled with others who might be in danger.

While the entire circle knew about column one, Jay was wary of telling them about those not yet missing before they had a lead, because if he did, he'd have to explain where those names came from, and the truth was, he still didn't know who he could trust. It was day after day of failing his pack, and he didn't know what to do.

His one consolation was Bari.

And it was maddening how every time they tried to steal another intimate moment, they were interrupted or too damn exhausted to be in the mood.

Bari slept in Jay's bed, but even trying to fool around in the early hours of the morning got cut off by knocks on Jay's door. There was too much unrest. The wolf tribe was being more vocal about their demands for justice for Crispin's killer, putting even more pressure on Jay to solve this, and every day that passed without a suspect made him look weaker.

During the day, Bari continued to work at the museum, cataloging and trying to decipher meaning from the creation tablets, though he hadn't yet found a connection to the murders, outside of a Seer's gut feeling. That feeling was more than enough for Jay, but they needed answers and quickly.

Then, before Jay knew it, more days had passed. There seemed to be a constant stream of people needing to talk to him, of all races, concerned and wanting reassurance. Jay could offer little. As almost exactly a week neared since the first murder had been discovered, Jay felt like a swinging axe was being lowered over his head.

That night, Bari came to bed later than Jay, having stayed up helping Maximus with plans for his and Theresa's anniversary. Jay couldn't even be upset. He liked that they were getting along, and if that meant he once again accepted Bari into his bed only for them to immediately drift to sleep, it was enough.

It didn't change that he awoke with the most painfully persistent erection yet, and in his initially groggy state, almost started grinding against Bari's hip.

Jay blinked awake to darkness. The sun wasn't up yet, but something sure was.

Bari was asleep, curled against Jay's side. Jay couldn't tell if Bari was in the same state he was, but there was no denying Jay's condition. He rolled away to stop stabbing Bari's hip, and a quick reach between his legs to palm himself through his sleep pants proved he was rock solid and weeping.

Fuck. Jay gave himself another firm squeeze and nearly moaned at how much the pressure needed to be released, casting a furtive, longing glance at the beautiful man beside him. Jay couldn't wake Bari for sex. Could he? That felt… rude and ridiculous somehow, and he couldn't bring himself to do it, much as he nearly lifted a hand on reflex to shake Bari's shoulder. He needed to take care of his problem, though. Maybe an early shower was in order.

Jay was careful as he climbed out of bed, though not too careful in case a small jostle might be enough to wake Bari on its own, and then, whose fault would it be, really? But Bari slept on soundly. Just as well.

Jay traipsed into the bathroom, closed the door almost completely before turning on the light, and stripped out of his pants. His cock bobbed in relief but wanted much more than freedom. After a few tentative strokes with Jay allowing the soft moans that left him, he hurried to turn on the taps and finish this where the drain could wash away the evidence.

The hot water from the shower was welcome, though not nearly as welcome as the continued strokes he granted himself, trying to keep the spray from striking his cock directly, since the natural lube budding at his tip was far silkier than anything water could provide. Although Jay could always grab some shampoo….

The shower curtain tore aside, letting a rush of cold air in to contrast the hot water. Jay jumped, hand locked on his hard dick, as he turned to see Bari staring with sleepy-eyed amusement that quickly turned to wide-awake want.

"Mr. Russell, now this is just a plain waste of resources." Bari licked his lips, eyeing Jay head to toe. "Or are you not in the mood to utilize everything at your disposal?" He lifted his eyes to meet Jay's and bobbed both eyebrows suggestively.

Jay laughed, releasing his cock and not trying to hide how sprung it was. "I didn't want to wake you."

"For this? Darling." Bari stripped his own sleep pants off without awaiting an invitation. "You can wake me any time. And at this rate, if not before your alarm goes off, when else are we going to get the chance?"

Bari climbed in after Jay, reaching immediately for Jay's hips, which kept Jay facing the showerhead, while Bari moved in behind him. Bari ran his hands down Jay's sides and over the curve of his ass before encircling Jay's waist with both arms and reaching down between his legs to palm his cock. The position pulled Bari flush against Jay, and he kissed Jay's neck, his own cock twitching to attention between Jay's cheeks.

Jay moaned as the water struck his front and rolled down his back between them. Having Bari hold him like this felt too good, too fulfilling, like everything Jay had ever been missing from his life for far too long, especially after the week they'd had with nearly everything going from bad to worse.

BARI COULD have held a wet, naked Jay Russell for hours, stroking his thick cock and pressing up against him. Mouthing along Jay's neck was such an easy thing, such a comfortable act, even after only a week together and only one other time getting to be this close, this connected.

Bari wouldn't mind being more connected.

"I'm sorry you've had to go through so much since coming here," Jay said, his words almost lost to the sound of the water.

He turned in Bari's hold, moving his hands around Bari's waist to pull them back flush but facing each other this time, and the slick collision of their cocks made Bari suck in a sharp breath.

Jay wasn't to blame for any of it, but Bari didn't think he was looking to be told that or that everything would be okay, so Bari answered the only way he knew how.

"Thank you," he said and leaned forward to claim a kiss.

The thing about sharing a shower was that, although everything rubbed a little smoother and the heat from the water could be tantalizing,

Bari found it desensitized him a little, making him last longer. Of course, if Jay kept rocking his hips like that, there were no guarantees.

While they were still kissing and holding each other and canting their hips relentlessly forward, Jay backed them under the spray of water.

"Hey!" Bari coughed, laughing out of their kiss.

"Sorry," Jay said, clearly not having intended that. He moved them forward again, blinking the water from his eyes, and let one of the hands holding Bari's waist slide down his ass between his cheeks.

Bari's eyes fluttered as Jay fingered the skin around his entrance. The water flowed down Jay's back as he bent toward Bari's neck and sucked on a spot beneath Bari's ear that made him whine, simultaneously slipping a finger inside him and starting a gentle thrust, a knowing curl as if gesturing Bari closer.

Water was a terrible lubricant, but one finger slid in as easily as the first time, and Bari sagged into Jay even at risk of moving them back under the water. He moaned, rocked his hips forward, and let his head fall back, the water seemingly cooler as their skin heated up. Bari could have enjoyed just that for hours too, Jay fingering him and kissing him and holding him close, but when he was about to beg for more, Jay suddenly pulled away. He pivoted to push Bari closer to the wall and rinsed off under the spray of water by himself.

Bari panted, flushed and disoriented as he leaned into the wall for support. "Tease."

Jay grinned, turning his face into the water and letting it cascade over him, and then turned beneath the spray to rinse down his back, peering at Bari, who was now at his left. "I thought you liked being teased."

There wasn't much space for two grown men to fully stand without touching, so when Jay glanced at him, Bari leaned forward to catch his lips, not kissing so much as nipping at Jay's bottom lip and then lapping at it with his tongue. He snuck a hand around to Jay's cock and took hold.

"I like a little teasing," Bari whispered between them, "but you should know… I can give just as good back." He squeezed Jay just shy of too tight, forcing a gasp Jay couldn't contain. "I've been thinking about you fucking me ever since our first night together. Before then. In fact, more than once this week, I fingered myself thinking about you, imagining it was you and all the different ways—"

"Oh God, stop." Jay kissed Bari to silence him and then rumbled against his lips, "I could come just from hearing you talk like that. A real shower can come later." He turned from Bari to step out of the shower, almost forgetting to turn off the taps.

Bari did it for him and eagerly followed, but before he'd even set both feet on the bath mat, Jay seized him about the waist, surprising him with a harsher kiss, and hauled Bari out of the bathroom. Bari only caught his breath when he felt a hard surface at his back, slammed up against the wall beside the bathroom door.

Oh, how Bari loved this side of Jay, the part that was rough and dominating and all over him. Bari no longer had any scratches or bruises to be careful of from the fight. The cut on his nose had healed after a day. Jay could be as rough as he wanted.

Jay's natural smell, freshly showered but without any soap to spoil it, was as intoxicating as ever. That spiced autumn crispness never seemed to leave Jay's natural aroma. Bari would have happily drowned in it and loved being surrounded by it now as Jay held him in place with his body.

They kissed and rocked, precum forming quickly despite what had washed clean in the shower, making the slide of their cocks slicker, tantalizing with how much it promised of what was to come. It was difficult to do anything but thrust against Jay's hip. Bari was caged by the door, wanton beneath Jay's power, and loved every minute of it.

"Okay, big boy," Bari gasped from the deep probing of Jay's tongue, "if we're going to do this, we better get to it, because I am going to burst in seconds if you keep on like that." He held Jay's gaze and kissed him once more, briefly, before pushing him with a hard shove. "How do you want me... Alpha?"

A bright flash of Jay's eyes was the response, and there was the peek of fangs forming as he looked Bari over. "On your back. I want to see your face when I give you what you asked for."

Mm, Bari could get used to this. But as he'd warned, he could give just as good back.

As he moved past Jay, he shifted one hand into silvery claws and grazed them light and teasing across Jay's chest, and then even more teasingly down and back up his own hips, drawing Jay's attention there as he turned and backed the final few feet to the bed. He spread himself out atop it, propped up a little on his elbows in wait, with his legs spread to welcome Jay in.

Jay crawled after him, letting more of his own wolf free with that lovely brown fur sprouting along his curves and edges like the final lines of a work of art being filled in. Bari growled out a contented purr as he did the same, trimming himself in silver.

As Jay crawled closer, he slid his hands up Bari's legs and the inside of his thighs, spreading them farther apart to settle in between them. He hooked Bari under the knees and rolled him backward, no restraint at all as he bent to lick a wet stripe up Bari's length.

"Ah!" Bari moaned, so easily folded, his eyesight sharp but already growing hazy with lust as he said, "Yes… get me wet for you, darling…."

Jay's brain seemed to short circuit. "It is infuriatingly hot when you talk like that."

"Oh? Then you better fuck me good and hard to put me in my place, Alpha dear."

Jay growled and nipped at Bari's thigh, making Bari squirm in heightened bliss. Then Bari moaned again, because Jay bent his head, licked up Bari's cock once more, but didn't linger, didn't give him the satisfaction of direct attention just yet. He licked down between Bari's balls instead, and the closer he got to Bari's entrance, the more Bari's cock twitched and hardened.

When Jay finally flicked his tongue where he'd already lightly stretched in the shower, Bari spread his arms and pressed his head into the mattress with a loud keen. There was hardly any resistance as Jay plunged inside, just the tip of his tongue to start, with Bari already so open that he nearly begged for Jay's cock—but oh, then he wouldn't be experiencing this.

"Oh God… oh fuck…," Bari muttered, his panting more labored with every closer, deeper thrust of Jay's tongue, until Jay licked his way in unabashedly and Bari stammered a stream of gibberish and bit his fist.

Jay pulled out and thrust his tongue in again.

Bari whimpered.

Again.

Bari pounded the mattress.

Again.

"I want your cock!" he pleaded, self-restraint be damned. "Now... right now. I want to sit on your cock, take you in so deep and ride until the bed buckles."

Jay pulled his tongue away and moaned just from hearing Bari say that. He lifted Bari's leg over him so he could go for the top drawer of the nightstand, quickly finding what he wanted and pulling out a bottle of lube. Condoms weren't needed between shifters other than to prevent pregnancy, impervious as they were to normal illness. Bari still used them with partners who didn't know what he was, but with Jay, it could be all slickness and skin.

"You want to ride me, Bari?" Jay asked in his growly Stage Two rumble.

"Can't imagine a better seat in all the land," Bari growled in kind, eyes hungrily raking over Jay's body as it lifted to hover over him.

"Then I think you need to earn it. You fingered yourself thinking of me, you said? Did you really?"

Bari was already flushed, but he felt his cheeks heat further, admitting, "It got lonely, waiting for you some nights. A man has needs."

With a sinful grin and the points of Jay's werewolf teeth glinting sharply, he leaned toward Bari's ear, and their cocks dragged along each other as he whispered, "If you'd told me... finding you wet and waiting like that... I might have slid right in."

"Oh, don't say that...."

"Then show me, Bari. Show me how you'd think of me while opening yourself up."

The request was almost cruel but pulsed a fresh heat into Bari's belly, imagining doing so with Jay watching.

He nodded.

Jay moved out from between Bari's legs, up on his knees to the side, higher on the bed than Bari expected, near his head, close enough for Bari to smell the musk of Jay's leaking cock. Close enough that he could have tasted it if only Jay moved the smallest bit closer.

Bari ran his tongue across his fangs and slightly over his lips. He looked at Jay's cock and then up into his eyes, those beautiful pale blue eyes, and crooked his legs up to raise his hips. His breathing picked up instantly, seeing the glow of Jay's eyes on him, moving to Bari's hand as soon as it started straying downward.

Bari kept his claws at first, starting by tracing his fingers along his cock, dancing around the heated skin, not yet searching for the wetness at his tip, just feeling the way it budded and pooled and was dribbling down his shaft. A whimper left him, but he gasped much louder when he finally swiped his hand through the precum and coated his length with it.

He lashed out to snatch the bottle of lube, popped open the cap, and poured a liberal amount down his shaft and over his balls toward his entrance. It was too much, enough to stain the sheets, but he didn't care, and Jay certainly didn't seem to.

Finally shifting his hand human, Bari imagined it was Jay's hand sliding through the slick mess and gripping tightly as he stroked Bari— Jay's thumb that passed over his slit and ran down the base—Jay's fingers that trailed between his legs.

As if in answer to what Bari had wanted before, maybe having planned it this way, Jay moved his hips closer, the thick heaviness of him bobbing near Bari's lips, descending in time with Bari pressing a finger inside himself. The breach occurred at the same moment as Jay's cock touched Bari's lips, and he sucked him in, tasting him at last while stretching himself.

So open already from Jay's previous teasing and tongue, Bari slipped in a second finger without waiting. He moaned around Jay's cock, spurred on by how good being stretched open felt, and sucked harder, took Jay in deeper, all the way into the back of his throat until his eyes watered.

"Bari," Jay husked, one of his hands human now too as he reached down, not replacing Bari's hand but joining it. He guided Bari initially, a gentle touch to direct his thrusting, but it wasn't long before he added to the stretch, sliding in a finger to join both of Bari's.

The burn of three fingers opening him made Bari want a fourth, a fucking fist, he was so turned on from feeling Jay's finger with his own, while sucking Jay's cock and knowing exactly where he wanted it next.

"Please," Bari sputtered away to speak since Jay's cock had started a rhythmic rocking between his lips. "Now… right now, please."

"If you want to ride me, Bari, you're going to have to get up. Think you can manage?"

Dominant Jay was Bari's catnip—or whatever it was for wolves— but he needed Jay inside him, and he needed it right the fuck now.

Bari doubted Jay managed to take a full breath in the time it took him to yank Jay down to take his spot, splayed out on the bed, and scrambled on top of his hips to straddle him. Bari's swollen cock twitched on Jay's stomach, while Jay let out a laugh at Bari's exuberance.

Gathering some of the excess lube from himself, Bari used it to reach behind him and take Jay in hand, coating him with the silky substance and making Jay hiss, already so sensitive. Bari pumped him a few times, his strokes tight, and then lifted himself to sit back, guiding Jay inside with a steady hand.

Bari took him in slow, and it was sweet, sweet agony for them both. He could see the ecstasy on Jay's face along with the strain of trying to hold back and not pound relentlessly into him. Once Bari had finally seated himself, his hands returned to eager claws that he scratched into Jay's chest.

Jay squeezed the sides of Bari's hips, and when Bari first rocked forward and back again, Jay sighed like an exclamation of finally that Bari absolutely felt too. The heat, the deep connection. Making a mess of the sofa had been one thing, but this was what Bari wanted, and having it now, here, in the dark wee hours of morning, made everything else fall away and seem so much less important.

Bari rocked harder, and the litany of obscene noises he produced drowned out any moans of Jay's. He gave a few more slow motions forward and back, forward and back, taking Jay in as deep as he'd said he would, before his speed started to increase.

"You feel so good…," Bari muttered. "I knew you would… like you were made to be inside me."

Jay reached for Bari's cock and pumped it rapidly. He didn't bother losing his claws but was careful not to catch the skin.

"Fuck, yes… yes…," Bari continued. "I couldn't even look at your hands all week without picturing how they looked wrapped around our cocks."

"Shit, Bari… that mouth."

"You can make use of my mouth anytime you want."

Jay laughed again, growly and low and so wonderfully sexy.

Bari launched himself downward to capture Jay's lips, and then sprang up again, moving with purpose and timing his motion to match Jay's strokes on his cock.

Jay roared—and fuck, nothing was sexier than that.

Bari felt his orgasm building from a long way off, rocking Jay in and out of himself so deeply that a flutter of his fingers across his stomach might have been able to feel that gorgeous massiveness moving. Nothing could have prepared him for the choked whine that left Jay before he was squeezing tightly at Bari's hip with his free hand and spilling hot and continuous inside him. It seemed to go on for so long, Bari felt it leaking out of him, and the sensation of Jay's cum dribbling down his thighs pushed him to pump his hips faster.

He was so close. Jay hadn't fully softened yet, so Bari didn't cease his rocking. Jay's strokes on Bari's cock had halted when he came, but now he renewed his grip. Instead of the fast pumps Bari might have expected, however, Jay went slow... so slow... passing his thumb over Bari's slit languidly and feathering his fingers down the shaft.

"J-Jay...," Bari complained.

"I thought you liked being teased." Jay gave another slow but tight pass of his hand over Bari's cock, said, "Next time, you're fucking me," and then stroked at the fastest speed he could manage until Bari came with a sharp cry.

Jay collapsed back with a deep chuckle as Bari shuddered atop him and then slumped forward onto Jay's chest.

"Did... did you mean that?" Bari asked, glancing up at Jay coyly. "Because absolutely yes, please. I just didn't realize Big Bad Alpha Jay was vers."

Jay chuckled, squeezing Bari's hips again and scratching lightly with his claws. "With the right partner, sometimes Big Bad Alpha Jay... likes to forget he's Alpha."

It seemed an unfairly sad comment after what they'd shared, but when Bari lifted his head to question it, Jay had banished whatever melancholy snuck into his words. "Besides, when I think of your cock inside me, Bari, I'm hard-pressed not to beg you to bend me over every flat surface in this house."

The renewed moan Bari released came out more like an elongated whine, and he smacked Jay's chest. "Meany."

"You started it."

"And you loved every second of it."

"I did," Jay said, looking at Bari tenderly now, and his wolf slowly faded as he gathered Bari closer atop him for a kiss.

It wasn't heated or deep the way they'd kissed leading up to now, but soft and sweet and affectionate. Bari could say with certainty he had never kissed anyone else like this, with emotion this deep, wanting nothing more than for this man beneath him to be happy for as long as he could make him.

And that was an equally sobering and promising thought.

Eventually Bari started to feel the mess between them a little more acutely, and the sun filtering in through the balcony reminded him that it was time to get up.

"Back to the shower?" Bari asked.

Jay laughed.

They managed to not fool around too much in the shower, but although Jay immediately got dressed afterward, Bari lounged a little in his robe. It wasn't technically time for them to be awake yet and—

A knock at the door nearly made Bari bark a laugh.

"And that is why I took advantage while we had the chance."

Jay shook his head with a fond smile, heading over to answer the door. Just as he opened it, Bari decided to be cheeky and called out a little louder.

"If it's Max, tell him he already missed the free sex show!"

A familiar voice that was not Maximus said, "I did not need to hear that," causing Bari to instinctually tighten the tie on his robe as he saw his brother, Bash, at the door with adorable vampire redhead Ethan.

Ethan waved. "Hi, guys! Sorry we're so early. It's science fair day, remember?"

Chapter 13

JAY DIDN'T mean to have an instant drop in his stomach at the sight of Bashir and Ethan. He'd come to terms with what happened between them, and he was glad for it, but the pain was still fresh, because that level of betrayal hurt, even if he had just finished some rather intensely gratifying sex with Bashir's brother.

"And how are things going with your father?" Bari was asking, having changed into actual clothing and currently working on choosing accessories. Since he'd been sleeping in Jay's room, he'd long since moved most of his things in here too.

"Slow," Ethan said with a tinge of sorrow. "It's a little like he's not all there. Not all the time. Some days, he's just my dad again, and I'll tell him things about my life. Other days...." He cringed, and Jay imagined those other days were a return to homicidal megalomania. It couldn't be easy, getting someone back who you'd thought was gone forever, only to not really have them back at all.

"I'm so sorry, dear," Bari said. "It'll get better. I'm sure of it. Who could possibly resist your charming company, least of all your own father?"

Ethan smiled sunnily, which would never not catch Jay off guard, seeing that jubilant disposition when he could smell vampire coming off Ethan in waves. Then Ethan directed his smile at Bashir, who also hadn't been able to resist him. There was a twist in Jay's stomach at seeing that, and when Ethan's gaze shifted to him, the young vampire looked immediately guilty.

Jay hadn't meant to cause that.

"Seems things here are going... well," Bashir said, scanning Jay's room and how Bari had very obviously moved himself in. The scent of what they'd been up to minutes before Bashir and Ethan arrived had to be obvious too, which really was déjà vu, since once upon a time, Jay had knocked on Bashir's door to find a similarly post-coitus pair, which had solidified the cancelling of their engagement.

But Jay didn't want to focus on the recently painful past. He caught Bari's eye across the room, and that sunny and gorgeous disposition was all his.

"Some things," Jay answered with a creeping smile of his own.

"I'm glad," Bashir said, and for as secretive and guiling as the Alpha of Centrus City could be at times, Jay knew those words were genuine.

"Thank you."

"So, did you already meet everyone downstairs?" Bari asked, giving a final fluff to his longish dark hair as he deemed himself "ready," a complete contrast to Bashir's all-dark ensemble, since Bari was wearing a bright lime-green shirt with floral-patterned slacks.

"Only Theresa," Ethan said. "She answered the door and ushered us right up here. We barely had time to gape at how gorgeous this place is. I think she was worried about us meeting anyone else without you two to chaperone. Are things really that bad?" he asked in a softer hush. "Any progress on the murders?"

"Still only four bodies," Jay answered.

"And nothing to point at a perpetrator?" asked Bashir.

He and Ethan knew most of what Jay and Bari did, about the lists, Reggie and Des, how the missing and so far dead had all been trying to have mixed-race children with Reggie's help, but while that tied the victims together, there was still no suspect.

"No, but we'll talk on all that later. Away from the den. For now—" Jay stood from where he'd been sitting on the sofa with Bashir. "—I think we have a fourth-grader to go support."

Enough time had passed that the rest of the household was up and bustling when they headed to the first floor. Anjali was the first to stop them, almost at the base of the stairs, with a whiff at the air and obvious sneer toward Ethan, followed by an unimpressed look at Bashir.

"I have a card for you from Charlee Young and her son, Jordan," she said by way of greeting, placing the card in Jay's hand. "I saw them off yesterday."

"That's wonderful, Anji, thank you. This is Centrus City's Alpha, Bashir Bain, and—"

"His pet vampire, I remember."

Jay sighed. "Anjali…."

"That's where you're mistaken—Councilor, if I recall?" Bashir stepped forward but didn't guard Ethan behind him so much as stand closer beside him. "I don't keep pets. I only have allies and enemies, and I'm sure you can imagine what those two groups usually do to each other."

There seemed to be an unspoken implication that Ethan was supposed to look menacing then, but he must not have been getting the message and merely glanced back and forth between Bashir and Anjali like a lost puppy.

At least Ethan wasn't another instigator.

"I'll keep that in mind," Anjali said and spun about to head into the living room, where the rest of the morning commotion seemed to be coming from.

Jay opened the card as they followed her.

New job. New apartment. New start. Thank you for everything.

Beneath the message was another handwritten thank-you, less neatly scrawled, and on the empty side of the interior of the card was a drawing of a black-and-white kitten accompanied by what Jay took for both a brown wolf and a silver one.

He showed the card to Bari, who beamed brightly and said to the others, "We'll tell you about it later."

William was bouncing with excitement in the other room, prattling something or another to Ursula, who was soon joined by Anjali. Theresa and Maximus were chatting off to the side. They all turned at roughly the same time to see Jay entering with Bari and their new guests, but it was William who exclaimed in jubilation.

"You came!"

Racing over to them, William launched himself at Ethan first, throwing his arms around the redhead's legs, just as Clara and Daisy entered from the kitchen carrying trays of food.

"Surpri—" They cut off before finishing the obvious "Surprise!" upon seeing who William was hugging, sniffing the air with the same immediate disdain Anjali had displayed.

"Hey, buddy!" Ethan hugged William back, not noticing the growing distaste for his presence. "Of course we came! We promised, didn't we?"

"Still, I'm so glad! This is, like, the biggest project of the semester, and everyone's families are going to be there, and all the teachers. You too, Alpha!" William launched himself at Bashir next, hugging him just as vigorously, though in contrast to Ethan, Bashir looked a little startled by the contact. "Thank you for coming!"

"Our pleasure, William," Bashir said with a tentative squeeze in return. "Pack relations need to go from top to bottom, and I am well aware of who keeps the bottom around here in line," he teased as though William was Alpha.

Bari snorted, trying and failing to hide it afterward, which Jay didn't understand....

Until he did, and then he jabbed Bari with an elbow.

Wrong top and bottom.

"Um, Daisy made muffins," Clara called, since the rest of the room had gone deathly silent. She and Daisy had set the trays on the ottoman which, when placed side by side, were color-coded into half red frosting and half blue.

"Pretty sure when they're frosted, they're cupcakes," Anjali said.

"Oh pish. It's William's big day!" Daisy waved a hand. "He can have a cupcake for breakfast."

"It's DNA!" Clara declared. "I know that's not related to your project, but it's still sciency, and well... ta-da!" She clapped, and all at once, the cupcakes lifted into the air. The color-coding made more sense as they began to form a cohesive shape and became a spiral, with the red cupcakes forming the outer lines of DNA and the blue making the connections between them.

William rushed over excitedly and snatched a blue cupcake out of the air.

"That is so cool!" Ethan dashed forward too. "I've been wanting to study shifter DNA. And my own for that matter. Did you know—" He tried to reach for a cupcake as he rambled, bringing him closer to Daisy, who growled with a flash of her eyes and glimmer of sharp teeth.

Ethan flinched, and Daisy immediately shifted human.

"Sorry! Instinct." She shrugged. "Usually, we'd never invite a vampire inside, you understand."

"Sure...," Ethan said, though the mar to his smile said a part of him really didn't. Then he gallantly stretched it wide again. "That's a myth, though. I don't actually need an invitation." When a blank stare and silence responded, he rocked back on his heels. "And… that wasn't a comforting observation, sorry. All this for William, huh? It's really sweet of you guys."

With a graceful spiral of her hands, Clara lowered the cupcakes back onto the trays. "Science is his favorite subject, and this fair is something he's been looking forward to for a long time. Right, honey?"

William nodded around a mouthful of cupcake, and Theresa giggled.

"I'll grab napkins," she offered and headed into the kitchen.

"We don't want you thinking you need to be nervous, though," Clara continued with a kind squeeze of William's shoulder. "I'm sure it'll go great."

He swallowed his bite, licking the frosting from his now blue-stained lips. "You'll all be there later, right?"

"We have a lot of work to do, kiddo," Anjali said, but her stern expression turned to a ready smile as she went over to rustle a hand across his head, "but we wouldn't miss it. Now, if you'll excuse me." She looked up again with a spike of displeasure at Ethan. "There's a particular smell in the air today I can't stomach enough to want cupcakes. I'll see you all later."

Jay shared a commiserating glance with Bari. He had really hoped someone could manage to be cordial—

"Ah! Our esteemed guests!" Reggie entered from his basement door, bringing him closest to Bashir initially, whose hand he grabbed on to to shake in welcome with both of his. "Reginald 'Reggie' Lancaster. And my… identical twins." He bobbed his eyebrows enough for them to be seen above his sunglasses as he looked between Bashir and Bari, and then pulled Bashir just a tad bit closer, whispering, "If no one's ever put the idea of a Bain sandwich on the table—"

"Reggie!" Jay shouldered closer, dislodging Bashir from Reggie's grasp and glancing back to be sure William was too occupied with finishing his cupcake and eyeing a second to have heard that. "Please ignore him."

"You can try." Reggie winked.

Bashir looked rightly scandalized, but Bari was holding back another snort.

"And you must be Ethan." Reggie grasped one of Ethan's hands in both of his the same way. "What a lovely face to have forever. I'm almost jealous. I hope the firing squad—I mean welcoming committee—hasn't been too terrible to you?"

Ethan stared at him, no response, not even a blink or mouth dropping open to indicate he'd try to say something.

"Helloooo?" Reggie pulled up one of his hands so he could tap the center of Ethan's forehead. "Bats in the belfry, love?"

"S-sorry!" Ethan stammered, as if having been lost in a very vivid daydream. "You just… remind me of someone. Have we met before? Ever been in Glenwood or—"

"I don't think so, poppet. I've lived in Brookdale for ages now. Maybe I just have one of those faces." Reggie grinned.

Again, Bari snickered, and since Jay was thoroughly lost on why this time, he raised an eyebrow at him.

Bari leaned close to whisper, "The Dude abides."

Jay had to fight not to snicker too. How had he never noticed?

Maximus wandered over, and Ethan turned to him with a hesitant smile.

"It's good to see you again, Max," Ethan said, holding out a hand. "I hope?"

Maximus sighed and said, "Try to keep from causing any pack-wide panic and it might be." But he accepted Ethan's hand and shook it firmly.

"No promises," Ethan said with a chuckle.

No one else laughed.

"Joke. That was… meant to be a joke." Ethan scratched the back of his neck with nervous tension. "I'm gonna need someone with me at all times or I might get killed on sight, won't I?"

"Yes," Ursula spoke for the first time, arms crossed, with her gaze never once having left Ethan since the moment they all entered the room.

Ethan chuckled again, until he realized she wasn't kidding.

Bashir looked ready to jump to Ethan's defense with another thinly veiled threat, when Clara glanced around like she expected to find an exposed wire somewhere.

"Does anyone else feel that… buzzing?"

"I do!" Daisy announced with a hand thrust into the air. "What is that?"

Jay hadn't realized until someone said it, but he'd been feeling it too—ever since Bashir and Ethan came into his bedroom.

"That would be these two." Reggie bowed toward Ethan and Bashir with a sweep of his arms, and then brought one hand up to fan himself as if overheated. "What massive auras you have."

"Please don't finish that with 'or are we just happy to see you,'" Bashir countered.

"Ha!" Reggie laughed. "I knew there was a funny bone in you somewhere. Speaking of bones—"

Theresa had come back with the napkins, claimed a cupcake for herself, and immediately smashed it into Reggie's face. "Oops. How on earth did that happen? Napkin?" She handed him one, which he used to slowly wipe the smear of frosting from his nose, and then folded up the ruined cupcake into it and set it back on the tray.

"Now, love, no sugar for me before ten, unless it's in my coffee."

"As if you drink coffee," Theresa refuted.

"That's right," Clara said more seriously, adjusting her glasses as she crossed to Bashir and Ethan, like she might be able to see their auras upon closer inspection, though that was impossible without a spell. "Two Focus-Seer hybrids. How... bracing!"

Three, Jay thought, glancing at Bari. He supposed they didn't have any proof of the Focus part manifesting, but it was still part of him. With all three of them in one room, the power was palpable, but not decipherable unless someone knew what was causing it.

Bracing was a good way to put it. The feeling would make most people naturally gravitate toward the three of them—assuming they could get past the vampire part for Ethan. Unfortunately, it didn't work quite as well when people knew what it was.

"I forget what being around you two feels like," Maximus said. "It's even stronger now than back in Centrus."

"I like it!" William rejoined the conversation, having polished off his second cupcake—a red one this time. "Kinda makes me feel invincible. Not that that's why I wanted you to come! I just hope the report came out okay."

"Did you want to show me anything before the big event?" Ethan asked. "I know my way around an eyewitness report. I'm happy to give feedback."

"Really?" William grabbed on to Ethan's hand, already tugging him toward the door. "That would be so cool! It's up in my room."

Several of the others looked startled at the thought of William and Ethan leaving together.

"We're not letting them be alone, are we?" Daisy asked quietly.

"Ethan is perfectly—" Theresa tried, but Clara spoke up before she could finish.

"How about I come too?" She hurried after the pair. "I'd love to see everything, William. Maybe give another opinion?"

"Totally!"

Ethan didn't look like he minded the extra company, and it helped the others relax as the three headed upstairs.

Well, it helped a little, but Ursula's stern stare shifted to Jay.

"Is this really the best time to allow him at a school function?" she asked pointedly. "William won't be the only shifter there, and a lot of them will remember the last time this city had a vampire infestation." She glanced at Maximus, who frowned at the reminder of his first wife, William's birth mother, and how her entire extended family had been slaughtered.

The former Alpha had sent every resource available after the vampires at fault, and a posse of shifters had torn them limb from limb.

"I'm aware," Jay said, "but at this point, I don't know how any of this can get worse. They'll know who he is, and if people want to be wary of Ethan, fine. He's not the enemy."

Ursula's expression didn't change as she stalked forward. "And here I thought you didn't know who the enemy was," she said and continued out of the room.

"Uh… there's still cupcakes!" Daisy announced.

Maximus finally claimed one, and Theresa pointed out to Reggie that he hadn't gotten all the frosting off his nose.

Bari took a cupcake too, just as Bashir grabbed Jay by the elbow and started leading him into the dining room.

"Excuse us."

The dining room was empty, and Bashir pulled Jay nearly to the other side of the room.

"I'm going to be selfish for a moment if I may," Bashir said. "You promised to support my pack if I have any reason to fear reprisals from other cities."

"And I still plan to," Jay confirmed.

"Bit difficult to do that if your own circle doesn't have any confidence in you."

"Bash!" Bari exclaimed, having followed them, cupcake in hand as he rushed over.

"He's right," Jay intervened. "And it's not just the circle."

"You think they'll call for a vote?" Bashir asked. "Push you out?"

"The thought has been weighing on me."

"That's ridiculous!" Bari said. "You're doing everything you can. The pack can't blame you alone."

"Of course they can. That's part of being Alpha." Jay smiled somberly at Bari and then returned to Bashir. "I understand your concerns. If that were to happen, I doubt it would be long before a new regime here would take up arms with other cities against you. At least the wolves and most of my circle aren't pleased with your… relationship."

"That's why this fair is a good thing," Bari broke in again. "Big function. Two Alphas showing support of a vampire that no one has reason to fear. We have to show these people that differences don't define us, they simply make for more interesting friendships."

"Maybe," Bashir said, "but that's a lofty hope, brother."

"So what? If hope is all we have, best to embrace it." Bari took another bite of his cupcake, leaving very little room for pessimism.

Not for the first time, Jay was glad to have Bari there.

BARI MIGHT have been acting bigger than his beliefs, but someone had to be the optimistic one! And while sometimes that could be Jay, it was rarely, if ever, Bash.

William's timeslot for presenting his project to the judges at the science fair was midmorning. The fourth-graders didn't have a normal day of classes but were to use their first hour to put any finishing touches on their projects and set them up in the gymnasium. Other grades had the chance to see the projects during some of their classes, and afterward, the fourth-graders would get to end their day early.

Once William left for school but before they were expected to join him, they had a little time to themselves, and Ethan asked if they could visit the Shelter.

"I think I need to see it."

"I was about to suggest the same thing," said Bash.

"Me too!" chorused Bari. Moments before Ethan had mentioned it, the same idea had dawned on him. "This sixth sense is kind of fun when I can tell where it's pointing me."

"If only it could draw us a forensic sketch of the perp." Ethan snickered.

Bari hoped that proximity to his brother and Ethan meant their abilities might continue to expand until they simply knew who the enemy was, though he doubted it would be that easy.

"I was hoping to talk to Des anyway," said Jay. "Let's go."

They decided to enjoy a brisk autumn walk rather than drive, filling Bash and Ethan in along the way on anything else they didn't yet know.

"I'm sorry, you were dating your boss, who threatened to fire you when you broke up, which is the real reason you came home—"

"And he stalked me, followed me here, made a big to-do at the museum, and was escorted out of the city, yes," Bari cut Bash off. "Please no big-brother speeches. I'm the big brother anyway."

Bash scowled at him. "Fine. He's lucky, I suppose."

"Lucky?"

"If it had been my city he showed up in, being escorted out would have been the least of his problems."

Bari smiled at the intended sentiment and leaned over to peck his brother's cheek. They were taking up a good portion of the sidewalk with all four of them in a line—Ethan, wearing his fetching sunglasses to shield his vampire eyes from the sun, followed by Bash, Bari, and Jay. "Thank you. Please don't tell Deanna, though. She always says I have terrible taste in partners. I hate when she's right."

"Oh?" Jay nudged him.

Bari leaned over to kiss Jay's cheek next and clung to his arm. "Even a broken watch gets the time right once in a while, darling."

The display prompted Ethan to discreetly take Bash's hand, as if looking for his own added intimacy, which was adorable, especially since Bash didn't shy from it.

"Speaking of the museum," Ethan started, "still no leads on those tablets coming from Glenwood?"

"I was hoping you might be able to help with that, actually, Mr. Former CSI," Bari said. "At least as far as how to find leads on where it came from when a donor requests anonymity."

"There are ways. There's always a record somewhere. Depends on how it was procured."

"There's a sister museum in Glenwood. Supposedly, they were gifted the tablets under the explicit request to send them to Brookdale first, and after an undisclosed amount of time in this museum, they're meant to be sent back. Theresa and I have both tried talking to the director in Glenwood, but he won't budge on giving up the name. If things get any worse around here, we may need to consider sending someone to investigate. I know the tablets are involved somehow. I can feel it."

"I don't think any of us want to be away from our cities for too long of a stretch right now," Bash said, "but maybe we could ask Preston and Luke to make the trip. They've been planning to take Jesse. Seems Glenwood is where her family came from."

"Perfect!" Bari declared. "Of course I'd rather it was simpler than that and this all got resolved in a few days." He snuggled Jay's arm, which he had no intention of releasing.

"There's really no evidence from the murders, no leads?" Ethan asked. "That just seems so… hard to believe. There's always something left behind."

"Claws marks," Jay put forth, "and by a wolf, but that's about it. We can't very well ask for DNA samples from everyone in the wolf tribe to compare."

"No shifter database somewhere?"

"I'm afraid not. What we know is that the victims were all alone before they were discovered, and they were all found by different people. Angus, the first body, was the only one in the company of others before he was killed."

"The one who tried to get into the den?"

"And succeeded, poor bastard," Bari lamented, "not that it saved him."

"Witnesses said he got a message on his cellphone and left," Jay continued, "but they didn't think he seemed concerned by it."

"What was the message?" Ethan asked.

"Um… I don't remember a report on that from Ursula." Jay's steps nearly stuttered in their trek. "She must have looked into it, though. I'll ask her."

"Even though she might be the culprit?" Bash reminded him.

"Until we have proof of who the woman in Bari's vision might be, I refuse to point fingers at anyone."

Bari sort of hated how sensible that was.

They rounded the last corner to reach the Shelter's main entrance. When they went in, the reactions from people were about what they expected, only Bari couldn't help noticing the initial startled expressions became more curious as they went. After all, a vampire was being escorted by two Alphas and, well… him.

The visit continued almost uneventfully as they showed Bash and Ethan the entry hall and onward into the main common area that had so recently been a battlefield, but once again had people watching TV, playing board games, and acting normal.

It was as they were nearing the rat area that a group of children exited from it, looking particularly stunned at the sight of them. It was the ones who had been bullying Jordan.

"Well, here are some familiar faces," Bari addressed them with a hand on his hip. "Are you all behaving yourselves?"

"We're sorry, Mr. Bain," one of the kids muttered softly. "You too, Alpha."

"We just want out of this place, you know?" one of the others said.

That simple admission seemed to sting Jay deeply, and he went toward them, crouching to their level. "Please believe me, it was never my intention for this place to stay so crowded for so long. There'll be more homes available soon. I'm working on it." He cringed after he said that, because he really hadn't been, since lately he'd been too focused on the murders.

The kids looked appeased by the promise at least, though they cowered a little closer together when they looked at Ethan.

"Are the rumors true?" one of them asked. "You're a… good vampire?"

Ethan smiled, coming forward to take Jay's place crouched in front of them, and to their credit, none of them flinched. "Yep. So's my uncle. Maybe there are more good vampires out there than you'd think. We don't have to be so different. You know, in Centrus, the Magister is a Rat King and a good friend of mine. He has these two little rat pets who sit with me sometimes when I'm reading or watching TV. For whatever reason, they really like me, and it was them trusting I was a good person that helped the Magister trust me too."

"Because animals have a good sense of things and people," Bari added. "Too bad shifters don't always, hm? But Ethan doesn't seem so bad, does he?"

The children nodded timidly before scurrying off. It was simple but also more rewarding than most of their encounters here.

Bari was about to comment on how his initial idea, made seemingly so long ago now, to simply toss Ethan into the Shelter to shake things up, hadn't turned out so bad—until the expressions on both Bash and Ethan's faces mirrored the sinking feeling Bari felt himself, and he barely had time to notice both their eyes changing color before he knew his own did too.

The whites went black, the irises glowed blue, and with a third eye appearing on their foreheads and the sign that they were Seers displayed for everyone nearby to see, Bari expected mystic words to pour from each of their mouths next. When nothing did, when all he got for his troubles was a far bloodier vision than his first, and a blink brought him back to himself with nothing new having been said, he didn't know what to expect.

Only he knew something awful was about to happen, and his attention whipped to Ethan as he shouted, "Ethan, get down!" too late, because in that same breath, a gunshot rang out, blaringly loud throughout the Shelter, and Ethan looked down at the blood seeping from a hole in his chest before he crumbled.

Chapter 14

"ETHAN!" BASH roared.

He dove down beside Ethan, catching him as he fell.

Bari had seen plenty of blood and vicious fighting lately, but he'd never seen someone shot before. Even as a vampire, if Ethan was struck in the heart, he could still bleed out and die like any human, and already the blood was gushing over Bash's hands as he held them to Ethan's chest, trying to stop the flow.

Chaos erupted with an outward ripple from where Ethan had gone down, with people running every which way as Bari stood frozen and Bash held Ethan on the floor, trying to keep him focused and his eyes open.

"Where did it come from?" Jay was making himself larger by sheer presence alone, not yet shifting any further than his eyes glowing, as he stood guard in front of them and scanned the room.

Bari looked too, and he couldn't see anyone with a gun, but with the madness of people scrambling, it could have been any of them.

"Ethan," Bash said more insistently, and when Bari whirled back around, Ethan's eyes were fluttering like he was losing consciousness. "Stay with me! You need to feed, do you understand? Ethan! I am going to rip whoever did this into pieces," he finished in a growl.

Pulling one hand from holding pressure to Ethan's wound, Bash lifted the wrist to his mouth, wolf fangs elongating as he readied to tear into his own veins to give Ethan what he needed.

"Wait!" Bari dropped down beside them. He didn't have time to freeze, not now. "I'll do it. You and Jay need to find the shooter and keep everyone calm."

Bash looked at him with uncertainty.

"They'll listen to two Alphas. Please. I can do it."

Possessive indignation tore across Bash's expression, but at the last moment, he passed Ethan's body into Bari's arms and leaped to his feet, finishing his shift to Stage Two, and looked to Jay for confirmation.

Jay shot a worried look down at Bari, even as he shifted in kind.

"Go!" Bari shouted at them and didn't bother looking up again as he extended his own fangs, bit deeply into his wrist, and pulled Ethan into his lap. With Ethan's back against Bari's chest, he lifted his wrist to Ethan's slackening mouth to make him drink.

He didn't at first, barely awake now, with so much blood soaking his shirt, but after another insistent press of Bari's wrist to his mouth, Ethan's tongue darted out to taste it.

Ethan's hands came up so quickly to grab Bari's wrist and forearm, the sudden vise of it made Bari lose his breath. He hadn't even seen Ethan move, but he felt him drinking now, the surprisingly swift extraction of blood leaving Bari dizzy. Or maybe that wasn't blood loss quite yet but Ethan's thrall, telling every part of Bari that this didn't hurt, it wasn't bad—it was a fucking ecstasy high, and he moaned as euphoria thrummed through him.

"E-Ethan…." Bari tried to warn him that it was too much. Nice, but way more than was necessary. He assumed Ethan couldn't control himself as well when he'd almost dropped dead on the floor. "St-stay focused, darling. Wouldn't want Bash getting the wrong idea." He moaned again the moment the words left him, unable to suppress how good this felt.

Though he was also feeling light-headed.

Shit.

Bari needed to stop Ethan, but he also needed to be sure Ethan had taken enough to heal himself. He tried to open his mouth to speak, but the room was spinning and he was succumbing to such a wonderful floating, fuzzy feeling, like the perfect contentment of taking a nap….

A gasp left Ethan as he pulled Bari's wrist from his mouth, and all at once, the world returned. Bari expected pain in the aftermath, with Ethan's thrall fading, but the bite on his wrist carried only the barest sting.

"Bari!" Ethan cried, turning in Bari's lap. He looked quite cute with his glowing yellow eyes, fangs still present, smaller than any shifter's, while licking the blood from his lips. His shirt was awash in crimson, but at least the wound wasn't gushing anymore.

"I'm fine, dear," Bari said, even as he felt the strongest urge to lie down and close his eyes. "I might need to… rest a bit. But well done. Even at death's door, you controlled yourself."

Ethan's brow pinched, like he didn't believe his control had been enough, but Bari reached up to lovingly pat Ethan's cheek. Ethan was part of the family now, after all. Bari would gladly do anything to keep him safe. He'd always felt that way about those closest to him, but he supposed he'd rarely had much chance to be a martyr about it.

It was then Ethan took Bari's hand from his cheek, since it attached to the wrist he had bitten, and brought it to his mouth to lick the wound. It wasn't only to get another taste but to heal the torn skin with the kiss of his saliva, which Bari felt with a tingle traveling up his arm.

He shuddered.

"One thing I need to ask," Bari said when Ethan released him. "You'd tell me, wouldn't you... if I had a very inopportune boner right now?"

Ethan laughed, but then, with a sobering expression, furtively glanced at Bari's lap. "You're fine. Are you fine?"

"Just woozy. I'll be okay."

A roar made Bari's adrenaline spike again, not at all helping his light-headedness. He and Ethan looked around, and it wasn't only one roar, but two overlapping—Jay and Bash together, causing the still scattering shifters to freeze in place. It was a bit thrilling to see everyone listening this time, when they hadn't heeded Jay the other day, though two Alphas for the price of one certainly helped.

It didn't seem like a shooter had been pointed out, but there were other shifters who must have stopped scrambling before Jay and Bash's roar, because they were staring at Bari and Ethan. A vampire getting shot and then feeding from someone in the middle of the Shelter was a spectacle, not to mention their earlier Seer display. Bari assumed, however, that their gawking had more to do with how Ethan had stopped himself, and even after being fed from, Bari was fine and wide-awake.

"Let me move you so you can rest," Ethan said, getting to his feet and hauling Bari quite impressively to the nearest wall to lean his back against it. His strength was incredible, maybe more so because he'd freshly fed.

Being able to relax into the wall made Bari very much want to sleep, but he knew he shouldn't. "Help them," he said instead, nodding at Jay and Bash, who had split to begin questioning people. "I'm fine. Just need a cookie or something."

Ethan seemed skeptical, but eventually he squeezed Bari's knee and jumped up to join Bash.

Bari could really use a cookie. Or a sandwich. Or anything. He just had to keep conscious. And dammit, glancing down and seeing the bloodstains on his shirt helped. That was never going to come out.

"Mr. Bain?" a small voice whispered, and when Bari turned toward it, he realized how close he was to the rat entrance, because it was one of those children—no, all of them, he saw, as more heads peeked around the corner. The one who'd spoken was passing him a box of crackers and a bottle of water, scared as they all seemed about venturing any deeper into the common area. "You need food and something to drink after donating blood, right?"

Bari smiled weakly as he accepted the items. "Indeed I do. Thank you." Bari tore into the box first with a lurch of hunger. He should have had two cupcakes that morning instead of one, but the salty, cheesy crackers tasted better than crème brûlée in that moment. After washing them down with water, Bari hummed relief.

"Was it scary?" another child whispered. His head seemed to float with the way he peeked around the corner barely enough for his neck to show.

Bari had no intention of telling the children that being drained by a vampire had actually felt quite erotic. He certainly wasn't going to tell Bash or Jay that, though he suspected they both knew from firsthand experience. "Not at all. Ethan is my friend. I knew I had nothing to worry about. All that mattered was saving him."

It wasn't much later when Jay, Bash, and Ethan returned to check on Bari, causing the children to scatter. Bari had almost emptied the box of crackers and was feeling a bit better.

"Are you all right?" Jay asked as he crouched beside him.

"Well enough. Annoyed, though." He looked at Bash and Ethan. "Why would these abilities tell us to be here if it only led to Ethan getting shot? I can't even picture who did it. I just knew something was about to happen."

"We're here because this was where the enemy was," Bash said, "even if we don't know their face. If we're unable to see them clearly, they must be veiled somehow, either with magic or... I don't know what." He was standing close to Ethan, almost leaning into him, so clearly shaken by what had happened. It was actually very sweet.

"What did you find out?" Bari asked.

Apparently, it was like the worst version of an eyewitness study, because almost everyone reported having seen something different. They all had a distinct description of seeing someone run away, but then so many people had run when the gunshot rang out, who was to say any of them had been the perpetrator?

There were also different whispers and glances being cast on Bari and the others now, and not only because Ethan was a vampire.

"They know you're Seers, can't help that," Jay said as he noticed the glances too. "What did you see anyway? Just Ethan about to get shot?"

Bari's stomach dropped at the reminder. He'd almost forgotten in the haze of what happened afterward—the blood, destruction, and chaos like a horror movie playing in his head. He was thankful Bash and Ethan handled the brunt of explaining. The main lingering point was that if they didn't solve this soon, there was going to be a lot more death.

"Why weren't there words, like before?" Jay asked. "Or do you only hear the words in your head?"

"We would have spoken them aloud," Bash said. "Our mother never had words, though. It's a product of not being as adept with our abilities. It's like trying to solve a dream, like our subconscious is trying to sift through something it can't fully understand so it gives us riddles."

"Then, if there were no words this time, you're getting stronger?"

"Fat lot of good it does us if it shows the what but not the who or how," Bari grumbled.

"One thing was clear, brother." Bash looked at him seriously. "In the midst of all that carnage, I saw you as the main force holding it back."

Bari's stomach dropped through him to the floor. He'd seen that too, but... it couldn't be. "That just as easily might have been you."

"You know it wasn't me, Bari. You feel the truth just as we do."

Bash and Ethan had such stoic faces, Bari sort of wished he could scream at them, but he knew none of this was their fault.

A fresh eruption of movement and activity alerted them toward the lizard area, as Ursula and several of her agents finally arrived on the scene.

Two of those agents dragged Des along with them, while Ursula held a rifle she dropped at Jay's feet.

"WHAT IS the meaning of this?" Jay demanded, standing to his full height.

"We found that in Des's bunk," Ursula said, "freshly fired."

"What?" Bari sputtered from the floor.

"That isn't mine," Des insisted, though he wasn't trying to fight the hold on his arms.

Jay glanced between them all, trying to assess what was happening. "You just got here," he said to Ursula. "Why would you even think to look in Des's bunk?"

"Because the reason I'm late isn't because I was at the science fair. Our last missing person was just found in an apartment he owns."

"What?" Jay spouted in surprise. "I didn't even know Des owned an apartment."

"An apartment building, turns out."

"I'd been working up to own it for years," Des broke in. "It was meant to be an offering to the pack for more housing."

"I'm sure." Ursula glanced back at him. "Unfortunately, we can't keep things from the police this time because your name is on the lease, and the body was found in your original unit. They're looking for you." She turned back to Jay. "Meaning we need to turn him over first."

Jay couldn't believe this, but he knew, if the situation involved anyone else, he'd agree with her.

"Alpha, you know I didn't do this," Des asserted. "All the evidence points to the killing blows being made by a wolf."

"Which we have no reason to believe couldn't be faked," Ursula rebuked. "We need to turn him over to keep the heat off the pack. If they track him to the Shelter...."

"I know," Jay said. They couldn't risk that.

Ursula would contact shifter officers to take Des in, but that was a small comfort. This would become much more complicated with humans involved, because Jay, however many connections he had, would have to solve this through legal means.

And there was still something he hadn't had the chance to ask.

"I need to speak with you alone." Jay gestured for Ursula to move off to the side, leaving Bashir and Ethan to stay with Bari.

He had to be careful how he worded what he asked next, because the only reason he knew this was because he and Maximus had spied on her.

"Were there any recent messages of note on any of the victim's cellphones?"

"None of the victims were found carrying cellphones."

"Not even Angus?"

"No," Ursula answered curtly. "Witnesses mentioned Angus should have had one, but he must have dropped it between his office and the den."

That was a very long stretch of distance to find a single phone, especially after a week's time. "Thank you," Jay said, though it didn't help any.

None of the victims having their phones couldn't be coincidence.

"Give me a moment with Des," Jay requested next, and Ursula complied.

"I'm being framed," Des hissed once he reached Jay. "You know that."

"I want to believe you, but that means I need a way to prove it. I'll be in touch. No need to hire a lawyer," Jay added with a small smile. "You have one. Do not say anything once you're in custody until I join you."

Seeing Des carted away didn't leave anyone looking like they believed the shooter—or murderer—had been caught.

Jay and the others called for a shifter driver to return them to the den, given several of them were covered in blood. No one was home when they arrived since everyone else should be at the science fair. They used what time they had to clean up and change.

"What if the people are right?" Ethan ventured, once they were seated in the living room. "From the shooting. Maybe they're not remembering wrong or confused by the chaos. What if they're all right?"

"You mean accomplices caused chaos on purpose so no one would be able to point at who had the gun?" Jay queried. "I've been wondering that too. It would have made it easier to plant the gun in Des's bunk. We can't pinpoint time of death close enough to know if the murders happened exactly at the same time, but even so, it makes sense for it to be more than one person."

"In my first vision, the woman was like a puppet master pulling strings." Bari leaned back to settle against Jay's shoulder, which eased a little of Jay's anxiety, if only because it felt nice to wrap his arms around Bari's waist.

"I know we're missing something important," Jay said, "but what's been bothering me most is that each victim was from a different tribe, and they all happened at the same time."

"Rat, cat, wolf, lizard…." Ethan trailed off with a blink. "What's the fifth?"

"A raptor," Jay confirmed.

"A… what?" Ethan's eyes bugged out at the mention.

"Wrong kind of raptor, darling," Bari assuaged him. "Has no one told you about the fifth shifter tribe yet? Raptors as in birds. Hawks, falcons, and the like. They're rare in this part of the country, but there are several in Brookdale."

"Guess I'm still learning. Are there shifters for every kind of animal?"

"Mostly. Foxes fall under wolf tribe. Other rodents under rat."

"What about, like… bears?"

"There are exceptions," Bari said, and then winked at Ethan. "Although I did date a lion once who was definitely more of a bear."

Ethan laughed, but Jay couldn't find the humor, much as he appreciated Bari trying to keep the mood light.

"We need to leave," Bashir said without warning.

"What?" Bari lurched up in Jay's lap. "You can't just—"

The front door opened with an eruption of voices as the others returned, cutting off Bari's protest, and they hurried to right themselves, assuming word of what happened at the Shelter had spread.

As soon as they peeked into the foyer, William spotted them and raced over to hug Ethan even more fervently than that morning.

"You got shot!" he cried as he squeezed Ethan. "Are you okay?"

"I'm fine, buddy," Ethan said. "Real tough to kill. I'm sorry we missed the science fair. Is that a blue ribbon?"

Clutched in William's hand was a first-place ribbon. "Yep!" he said excitedly. "And it's okay you missed it. I mean, you got shot."

Ursula came in with the others, having delivered Des to police custody. Anjali wasn't with them, since after the incident, she'd been called to the Shelter to clean up. It was only now Jay learned that Reggie hadn't attended the fair either and would have been downstairs this entire time. Before he could question that, there was a knock at the front door.

Theresa answered it, revealing a girl William's age. She was a gem of a little thing, in a pink dress, rainbow-colored sweater, and with two dark puff-ball pigtails atop her head.

"Hi, ma'am! Is Will home? He left the fair before I could say hi."

"He's inside, honey," Theresa said, permitting her to enter.

She lit up when she saw William and dashed over, carrying her own blue ribbon. "Will! You got blue too? Great job!" She looked as though she would have happily hugged him but stopped with a bashful smile.

"Thanks, Em!" William smiled back.

She seemed about to say more when she sniffed the air and looked at Ethan, causing her to scuttle back a step. "Whoa… you're…."

"It's okay," William said in quiet reassurance. "He's my friend. Ethan, this is Emily Lestari. She's my friend too."

"Hi there." Ethan waved politely.

Emily blinked at him in owlish astonishment.

A tiger, Jay could smell now.

The pair talked in hushed whispers, probably mostly about William having a vampire for a friend. The others moved into the living room to give them space, and Daisy and Clara scuttled into the kitchen to make coffee.

"Young love," Bari cooed with a glance at the foyer.

"I should hope not," Ursula scoffed.

The usual tension rippled through the group.

"Thankfully, that's never going to be your decision to make," Theresa spat.

"Maybe not, but you can't blame me for noticing when people around me keep making poor decisions." She stared at Theresa pointedly.

"That's enough." Maximus stepped between them, and Jay couldn't help the internal cheer that sprang in him. Max kept his voice low, but it still carried plenty of venom. "If we simply had differences of opinion, that would be acceptable, but this is my wife and child you keep bringing into your prejudices. I can't make exceptions when they're the ones who might get hurt."

"Max—" Ursula tried, and there came that awful pandering tone Jay kept hearing from his circle, but Maximus didn't let her speak.

"You're my friend, Urs. You were Carolyn's best friend. I couldn't have moved on from losing her without you there, and William couldn't have either. I will always love you for that, and I hope one day you change your thinking, because the way you think now isn't a difference of opinion—it's wrong—and I am not going to stand by and let you voice it in front of my family anymore."

Maximus pulled back, as if surprised by his own visceral reaction, though not looking ready to apologize. Instead, he took Theresa's arm and headed back to William.

"Hey, kiddo, how about ice cream to celebrate that ribbon? Maybe Emily can join us."

Theresa had never looked so proud.

Jay didn't miss the way Ursula's cold stare found Bari, as if he was to blame for this. He looked like he'd happily take the credit and beamed right back at her.

Then Bari's attention shifted to his brother, who'd grabbed Ethan's hand and was pulling him back into the foyer to lead him upstairs. They'd set their bags in one of the guest rooms—Bari's actually, since he didn't intend to use it again himself. If Bashir was set on leaving, he'd need their things, and honestly, Jay couldn't blame him for wanting to go.

Bari shot Jay a rueful look before racing off in pursuit.

"BASH!" BARI chastised, finally catching up to him and Ethan inside the guest room, where they were hurriedly stuffing what little they'd unpacked back into their bags. "You can't seriously be leaving—"

"We're only giving the enemy extra targets," Bash cut him off without turning to look at Bari. "They were never this bold before Ethan and I arrived."

"But our abilities are stronger when it's the three of us—"

"Yes, and they're telling me that we are not supposed to be here."

Bari wanted to throttle him, he was so mad that for once Bash was the one running, but when he looked to Ethan for support, it wasn't uncertainty he saw in the young vampire's face but apology.

"He's right, Bari. You're the one who's supposed to stop this. We're only in the way."

"That isn't fair." Bari clenched his fists, feeling heat fill his eyes.

"You feel it too. Don't deny it," Bash said, finishing up the packing with a harsh crack of a zipper closing.

"I can't do this alone," Bari said, closing his eyes to steel nervous, fearful tears.

Before he could open them, he felt warm hands take his, and it was Bash, carrying just as much apology in his expression as Ethan but with more resolve. "You're not alone. You just have to decide if you're going to listen to what this power tells you and trust yourself or fight it."

A tear spilled down Bari's cheek despite his best efforts. "See, that is why you're an Alpha, and I'm—"

"You are just as strong as I am. This could be your city someday, Bari," Bash said more earnestly. "Maybe that's why it's calling on you to save it."

Bari sniffled. "All right, but if I screw this up, I am coming straight home to haunt you." He jerked Bash forward into a tight hug.

When Ethan crept over, Bari hugged him just as fiercely. Then Ethan offered to take the bags downstairs and call a cab so Bari and Bash could be alone.

"He's going to make a fabulous PI someday," Bari said, scrubbing his tears with the sleeve of his shirt.

"Sooner than someday," Bash said with a grin.

"You already got him a license?"

"More than a license."

Bari smiled at seeing this domesticated side to his brother that he'd honestly wondered could ever exist. "He is going to make a fabulous Alpha's mate someday too." He tapped Bash firmly in the chest, right over his heart.

"Don't get ahead of things," Bash countered. "Especially when you're likely to get there first. But listen, I don't know why this is yours to shoulder alone—"

"I do. I need to stop running someday."

Bash didn't seem to know what to say to that, so Bari hugged him again, tight as ever.

"I love you, baby brother."

"Ugh," Bash groused at the name.

"And yes, I know you love me too."

No one looked sad to see Bash and Ethan go, other than William and Theresa, and maybe Maximus the tiniest bit, and Jay didn't try to stop them, merely said they'd keep them in the loop.

When Bari and Jay finally had a moment alone, Bari asked, "What do we do now?"

Jay answered without an ounce of hesitation, "We're going to prove Des is innocent."

Chapter 15

JAY WASN'T a tie man, but when he was working, out in the field around police or in a courtroom, he wore a blazer and vest over his button-down.

He sat across from Des in his changed attire in the little interrogation room, where they would soon be joined by detectives. They didn't have much time to be alone since the police were itching to get Des's statement.

Jay kept a calm face as he explained where they stood.

"Official charges haven't been filed yet. They don't have sufficient evidence that you were aware of the murder or present when it occurred, since there are no witnesses."

"So they'll let me go?" Des asked.

"Not yet. They can hold you a while longer, given the victim was found in your apartment. They're still investigating, and you're still under suspicion. If anything else, even the smallest link, shows up, it'll be enough to charge you."

Des was also a master at keeping a calm face, but Jay could see, just like he had in Reggie's basement, that Des was worried. "What next?"

"I need your alibi. The body they found was killed roughly the same time as the others. You're lucky they only know about this one, but they have Linda Bouchard's body as a Jane Doe, and if they have any reason to see a connection, there's enough wiggle room with time of death that they could pin them both on you. So, where were you?"

"At the den seeing Reggie."

"Again?"

"Yes."

Jay tapped his fingers on the table between them. "It might not be enough to only have Reggie corroborate. What about afterward? Did anyone else see you who could verify your whereabouts?"

The way Des wouldn't look at Jay as he answered wasn't reassuring. "I can't say."

"Can't?" Jay sat forward. "Des, you realize this is—"

"I can't."

Like before, Jay had a hard time believing that Des, who he'd known for years as always being willing to stick his neck out for others, would be this concerned with his own safety.

Which was why Jay knew it wasn't Des's own safety he was worried about.

"Who are you protecting?" Jay demanded.

Des's eyes drifted up slowly. "Everyone."

A chill tore through Jay, which was par for the course lately, and he hated it. "Des, this has to be by the book or we risk the entire pack, and I don't know if by the book will be enough to save you."

"If it's not, it'll be worth it, but you have to solve the rest." Des leaned closer too, keeping his voice low. "Find the shooter from the Shelter. It wasn't me. Figure that out and the rest might finally start falling into place. That's all I can tell you."

He sat back after that, and try as Jay might, Des wouldn't say more, giving Jay very little to work with when detectives finally came into the room. The one thing they had going for them was that there was too little evidence to book Des, but that could easily change, even if there was no way they'd get a confession.

Eventually Des was taken back to holding, and Jay had to figure out where he'd go next. He decided on his office and almost immediately hung his jacket and vest on the back of his chair.

They had reports from everyone at the Shelter who'd witnessed the shooting, but they were almost all different, and some might simply be innocent people who'd run. Yet the more Jay looked over the descriptions, he started to see a connecting thread he hadn't noticed at first. These were descriptions of what people looked like, but with no guesses at their names, meaning no one had seen these people and thought, that's someone I know.

They were different descriptions, but all of larger, well-built people, whether men or women, and fit very well the appearances of several of Ursula's agents.

Jay needed to check in with Bari.

WHEN JAY left to join Des, Bari asked to be dropped off at the museum. It was the first time he'd been there without Theresa present, but she'd already gifted him an extra set of keys. He slipped into the hidden passageway and shifter artifact room beyond without anyone noticing.

The cataloging was finished, what little good it had done him, but the tablets remained on the table, beckoning him to figure them out. For a long while, all he did was look at them. He'd examined each of them so many times, but that had done little to illuminate the truth. There were still worn-away places and runes that didn't make sense.

In fact, a couple of the tablets had worn areas that looked nearly identical to each other, like the erosion had occurred in the exact same way, perfectly dipped like a painter's brush stroke, like it was on purpose instead of natural, like....

Bari's intuition had been working on overdrive, and even with Bash and Ethan headed out of the city, he could feel them still, feel the power that radiated between the three of them when they were close.

He needed a higher view.

Grabbing a stool, Bari placed it at the edge of the table and climbed atop it to stand. Not just some but all the worn-away places looked the same, with the same strange dip. He didn't know why he hadn't noticed before, but the positioning of each when compared to the positioning of others could connect several of the tablets together in a specific order.

Bari leaped back off the stool and grabbed a pair of disposable gloves. There was a cart nearby that he used to rest certain tablets on while he shifted others around like a child's sliding puzzle. A few times he had the order wrong—he knew it the moment he placed the tablets incorrectly—but in very little time, he had it solved, with each tablet laid out exactly as intended.

He almost expected them to glow with his achievement, but nothing quite so magical occurred. Instead, he stood back on the stool to observe the whole picture.

He and Nell had been right. Half right. Some of the tablets had language that seemed cut off or half formed, because it was meant to be read with its neighbors. There were no areas worn away. Those dips that looked like erosion connected with other dips to form what looked like oversized thumbprints, the key to how the tablets were meant to interlock. The ones without dips could be included in any order, but the connecting tablets told a specific story.

And now, with everything in the correct order for the first time, Bari could read exactly how the past had unfolded.

"Fuck."

His phone rang, and Bari nearly toppled off the stool. He was still woozy from Ethan feeding off him, though he'd been sure to eat a hearty lunch before they departed from the den. After carefully lowering himself from the stool and seeing that the caller was Jay, he spoke as soon as he answered, nearly overlapping with Jay's equal eagerness.

"We need to talk—"

"We need to get back to the den."

Bari chuckled.

"I'll pick you up," Jay said.

They were together in Jay's car in mere minutes, and Bari let Jay explain his side first.

"So you believe Des is innocent?" Bari asked.

"I want to."

"Anything else?"

"I was looking over our witness reports and realized something. Each of them could be taken as describing several of Ursula's agents, which explains why no one at the Shelter mentioned names. They don't know them well enough because they're not residents. Even stranger is I don't remember seeing any of them before the gunshot."

"You think they were hiding, blended in after the chaos started, and fled to plant the gun in Des's bunk. When some of them came back in with Ursula later, no one thought to question it, because they'd only gotten partial looks at the runners. I knew Ursula was involved," Bari finished with a growl.

"I didn't say that," Jay countered, "but some of her agents might be. We can't rule anything out yet. What about you? What did you discover?"

"Oh, darling." Bari passed Jay a forlorn look as they pulled into the den's driveway. "I hate to have to say this, but… things are actually far more complicated than we thought."

They didn't see any of the others when they went inside, though Maximus, Theresa, and William might still be out, as might Anjali. Not wanting to risk anyone overhearing them, they closed themselves in Jay's bedroom before Bari started to explain the tablets.

"Vampires?" Jay sputtered with an openmouthed gape. "Whoever is behind all this is a vampire?"

Really, once Bari realized it, he wasn't surprised.

"Likely a very old one too." He pulled out his phone as they sat on Jay's sofa so he could retell the translation properly. "Pardon my paraphrasing, but the real story tells of figureheads 'made from the first men.' Basically, a fancy way of saying, humans came first, and then some of them started manipulating magic and known sciences to achieve immortality—making them vampires.

"It wasn't a curse, like most of the stories say, but a choice, and shifters were merely a byproduct of the experiments. Once the first vampires were powerful enough, they enthralled shifters and humans alike to serve under them."

He showed Jay several of the photos he'd taken that displayed this, as well as the figure he'd originally thought was a shifter at Stage Two.

"I didn't make the connection before, but this image is clearly a vampire. It has to be. It's the only non-human image not transformed into an animal-like state."

He moved on to the tablets ordered in a way to show wolves above the other tribes.

"Then we get our usual hierarchy of wolves as the first shifter kingdom and the other tribes beneath them, but that might only be because wolves were one of the first experiments. They didn't like being forced into this way of life. They started resisting the vampires' thrall after intermingling with humans and across tribes.

"It was the vampires who put a stop to it, because they didn't want to risk mixed births producing something more powerful than them, something they couldn't control—and it did. That was how we got the first Focuses, Seers, and Nulls."

Jay's eyes widened further at the implication. No one knew where people like that came from, assuming it was a rare byproduct of magic, but another thing Bari hadn't understood until the tablets were in the right order was that, while some of the humans on the tablets were shown as just humans, others had a halo about them like an extra aura—just like the humanlike baby born of a wolf and lizard.

"The vampires tried to stop the cross-breeding by using magic and science again to prevent mixed births, which is why people with unique abilities are so rare today. When shifters and humans realized what was happening, that they were no longer able to have children together, they revolted against the vampires, led by the very Focuses, Seers, and Nulls vampires wanted to eradicate, who were the only ones powerful enough to take them on and win.

"The vampires who weren't destroyed went into hiding and started purposely altering the narrative. That's why the tablets were separated, so we'd be told a different story and never learn the whole truth. Other tablets discovered over the centuries never had the full picture because they were incomplete. Without all the tablets, you'd never know how to order them correctly.

"Eventually, different stories were being told, some tribes held on to what they'd been taught by vampires, and over time, it all got twisted. Now, what whoever is behind this has been waiting for is finally happening. A time has come when they can try taking over again."

"Wait." Jay held up a hand to halt Bari. "While all that does fit the depictions in the tablets, there are so few vampires now. We've been killing them for decades on sight, longer."

"But we don't truly know how many there are, and honestly, it might only take one. We know it's possible for them to hide, like Ethan's father and uncle did for years. If there are any older ones, ancient ones, like I believe of whoever was in my vision, she knows what she's doing and how to manipulate us. I think she's been waiting for people like me and Bash and Ethan to exist, and that's why she's making her play now."

"I don't understand. Why? Wasn't it people like you who beat the vampires in the first place?"

"Exactly. So even diluted over time and with so few of us in existence, what better way to win the second time around than to get people like us on her side? Think of what she tried to do in Centrus."

"Bari, that was Ethan's father—"

"Was it? How do we know everything hasn't been set in motion for much longer than we've been aware of?" Bari hated to say it, hated all of this, but he knew he was right. "I can feel this, Jay—it's the truth, and she's playing us right into her hands."

Jay paused to digest everything Bari was saying before he asked, "Why the murders? What does that accomplish if she wants to take over the city? And for that matter, why let us get our hands on the tablets? Why let us figure this out?"

"I don't think she's the one who sent them," Bari said. "The only people with access to the tablets are you and Theresa. And now me. I think this mystery person in Glenwood was trying to warn us. I don't know why the murders are part of this, but I don't think any of our big bad's accomplices are aware of what she truly is."

"You think she's enthralling people?"

"Maybe, but she can't be a Focus or anyone with that sort of power or she'd already have won. She is powerful, though, maybe enough to enthrall a shifter, even if not enough to enthrall more than one at a time."

"How are we supposed to fight a vampire that ancient? We can't even know who she might be controlling. Unless...." Jay's eyes danced with sudden epiphany. "Nell, Bashir's Shaman, used that rune on Ethan to know when he was accidentally using his thrall. What if Reggie reverse engineered the idea?"

"To help us see if anyone is being enthralled." Bari hopped in his seat. "Brilliant!"

"The others said he never attended the science fair, so he should be downstairs. Come on." Jay sprang up from the sofa, and Bari leaped after him, feeling a surge of optimism for the first time since Ethan got shot.

They had real leads and real options for being pointed toward the enemy. The excitement made even two flights of stairs feel like too long a trek.

"Reggie!" Jay called, as soon as they were in the basement. He wasn't visible in the main area, but after a moment's pause, a muffled reply came from the bedroom.

"Is it pressing, love? I'm resting my eyes."

"It is very pressing," Bari called back. "It's about the murders."

It was impossible to hear Reggie sigh through a closed door, but Bari was fairly certain he did. "All right. Give me a minute."

They moved farther into the lower level to wait for him. Bari was too anxious to sit on the sofa, so he paced into the lab area, never quite landing his eyes on anything. He needed to calm down. There was still so much they didn't know, and they didn't yet have their sights on a target. They were getting there, though. He could feel it.

When Bari reached the edge of the lab, he turned around to lean back on a neatly organized counter. Jay was walking toward him, and Bari realized he hadn't been paying much attention before, because Jay was wearing a blazer. And a vest! He was very buttoned-up lawyer at the moment, and it was exceedingly sexy.

"What?" Jay commented on Bari's staring.

"Aren't you all prim and proper."

Jay glanced down at himself, like he'd forgotten what he was wearing too. "I took some of this off earlier, but I didn't want to leave it at the office."

"Took it off? It looks good on you. Unless you absolutely hate it?"

"I don't hate it. Certainly not if it gets you to look at me like that." Jay reached Bari with an easy lean forward, and Bari parted his legs enough for one of Jay's to slot between them. Jay's hands found Bari's waist, and Bari's arms wrapped around Jay's neck. A simple kiss felt like the best injection of Prozac that Bari could imagine.

Jay was an exceptional kisser and didn't skimp on the tongue.

"Mm," Bari hummed when they parted, still clinging to Jay. "You know the worst part of all this? Okay, maybe not the worst, but... if I'd had my way, this past week would have seen us having at least our fifth date by now. Fun as it's been solving a murder spree together, I'd prefer more dinners and wine than homicide."

Jay chuckled, letting his forehead drop to meet Bari's. "Me too. Especially since we have our next date planned."

"We do?"

"Of course we do. Don't you remember what I said this morning about how our next time should go?"

Bari felt a bit dumbfounded at the reminder that their last time together, starting with a shower and ending with a marathon display of hotness in Jay's bed, had been this morning, only to remember exactly what Jay was talking about.

Next time, you're fucking me.

"Mm," Bari hummed again, feeling warm all over and maybe half-hard from the mere mention. "Well...." He trailed off, honestly trying to think of the right comeback, which was why his eyes strayed to the bookshelves.

As the day had worn on, Bari had been seeing things differently, like the shared prophecy with Bash and Ethan, knowing Ethan was about to get shot, figuring out the tablets, and all that surge of added power was stronger than ever—which was probably why he noticed something wrong with the shelves.

Not meaning to push Jay away quite as firmly as he did, Bari walked closer to the shelving with a softly uttered, "There's a glamour here."

"That's to hide the morgue drawers if the den was ever searched," Jay said.

"I can see that, the part making them look like shelves." Bari could see through the glamour, see the drawers behind the faked rows of books with an aura of gold, but that wasn't all he saw. "There's a secondary glamour on one of the drawers itself."

"Secondary?" Jay followed Bari to the area he was talking about. "Hiding what?"

Bari grabbed the handle on the farthest morgue drawer and pulled it open, breaking the glamour that covered what lay inside.

There was a body, but it wasn't one of the ones they expected.

"Joseph...."

It was Bari's ex, who should have been escorted out of the city but instead was rotting inside a cold metal box. Bari was too stunned to feel remorse.

In the small bit of space around the body were five cellphones.

The victims' phones....

"Reggie," Jay growled in an angry hiss.

"No," Bari refuted.

"No?"

"The extra glamour doesn't feel like his magic. I don't know how I know, but this wasn't Reggie."

"What the hell is all that?" Reggie's voice boomed from across the room. When they turned to him, he was racing toward them but skittered to a stop once he saw everything more clearly. "Who is that? And how did they get into my morgue?"

Bari stared. The second glamour magic had a blue tinge to it, but the first, the glamour put in place by Reggie, was gold.

And that same golden aura was all over Reggie.

"You're glamoured too."

Reggie lurched backward. He seemed far more disheveled than usual, in a tunic and yoga pants but without the kimono cardigan, like he'd forgotten to grab one. His sunglasses were different too, darker. "You can see that?"

"What's going on here?" Jay demanded. "We don't believe you're responsible for this, Reggie, but we don't have time for secrets. While you've been in the basement, what, napping? Ethan was shot at the Shelter, he and Bashir returned to Centrus, and Anjali brought Des to the police as a suspect for the murders."

Reggie gaped at that slew of information. "Des? That's why he never came…."

"Came for what?" Jay pressed.

A deep sigh left Reggie like succumbing to the great weight of defeat. "No hiding it now, I suppose. I'm too low on time. That's why I couldn't go to young William's science fair. I hope he wasn't too upset." With a nonchalant clap of his hands together as if in prayer, Reggie swept his arms down and outward, causing the glimmering light of the golden glamour to fizzle.

Instantly, Bari smelled the difference, and he knew Jay could smell it too, as Reggie removed his sunglasses to show the amber-colored eyes of a vampire needing to feed.

"I'm getting hungry."

Chapter 16

JAY LET his fangs and claws grow and his eyes flash as he growled at Reggie in warning, pulling Bari behind him.

"It's not what you think!" Reggie held up his hands and then slowly slipped one of the bows of his sunglasses into the collar of his shirt.

A vampire's eyes were yellow when normal, amber when hungry, and red when frenzied, and Reggie's were far too orange. Jay couldn't believe how close they'd come to having a frenzied vampire in their basement without ever knowing, but even hungry and weak-looking, Reggie didn't make any aggressive moves.

"I wasn't worried this morning when I saw you all because I had a date with Des," Reggie explained. "Not a real date, mind you, lucky as that would make me, more a… date with his neck. We have an arrangement."

"That's the other part of Des coming here you couldn't share with us?" Bari balked from behind Jay.

"But you're a wolf. Shifters can't become vampires," Jay snarled, not willing to reel back his own shifting just yet. When Reggie looked at him with a telling tilt of his head, Jay had to admit the truth. "You're not a wolf. You were never a wolf."

"But I am fantastic at making people see what I want them to. It's why I'm such a good Shaman." Reggie spread his arms with a grin he clearly struggled to muster. "Before Des came along, I had an arrangement with the previous Councilor, the one before you."

He would have had to have an arrangement to hide for so long. Jay had never even questioned anything, because although Reggie had been part of the circle before him, his seeming agelessness wasn't strange. Shifters aged slower as they neared middle age, maintaining an appearance like being in their thirties and forties for decades longer than humans.

"I only need to feed every six weeks," Reggie continued. "That time was right upon us when these damn murders started, and it seemed risky to act as normal. Then, since we were down to the wire, Des volunteered, and well….” He waved a dismissive hand.

“Six weeks?” Bari questioned. “How old are you?”

A twitch at Reggie's smile told Jay exactly what he was about to say, and Jay was not in the mood. “Don't you dare joke with 'a lady never tells.' Not now!”

That squashed whatever remaining humor Reggie had tried to fabricate. “JJ, love, we've known each other for years now, haven't we? You trust me.”

“I thought I did. The only person in this circle I trusted more was Max, but it's comparable. I always thought you meant well by this pack.”

“I do, and partially because this pack has always done well by me. Des wouldn't normally be who I fed from. He was my… handler, if you will. He brokered arrangements with willing donors from the Shelter.”

“The other column….” Bari came up beside Jay now, not appearing to fear Reggie in the slightest. “All the people on that list you gave us, the couples you were helping, those are your donors?”

“Not that I wouldn't have helped them anyway,” Reggie insisted, “but keeping something that big a secret was still a heavy ask of me. I was keeping it from the entire circle. Serena was actually slated to be my previous donor, but that's when we discovered her pregnancy, so Crispin took her place. Angus was up this time. When he was dying, I think he tried to get into the den to reach me.”

“Are you the one who messaged him the day he died?” Jay asked.

“No. He wasn't scheduled to see me for a few days. After the murders, I couldn't risk any of the others coming here and painting targets on their backs. Des and I planned to wait it out, see if everything got resolved. Eventually, he was my only option and graciously offered. Obviously, he never made it.”

Jay clenched his fists to keep from lashing out like part of him wanted to. “All those people, both sides of that list, many of whom are or were at the Shelter, know about you?”

“Of course,” Bari said with far less ire than Jay. “It wasn't only Ethan's charisma that had people at the Shelter acting more receptive. Some of them already know a trustworthy vampire.”

“Just your friendly neighborhood fanger,” Reggie added with a grin. “I swear.”

As angry as Jay was, he couldn't keep his shifter form after that and shook it off with a bristle of his shoulders. "We don't have time for this. I am going to need much more of an explanation and several favors from you today, Reggie, but first we need to get you fed before you endanger everyone in this house. If Des isn't an option, you'll have to take me."

"What?" Bari flailed before Reggie could answer.

"And you," Jay said to Bari, "can keep watch to make sure he is a friendly vampire and doesn't try tearing my throat out or taking too much while I'm vulnerable." Jay couldn't very well ask Bari to volunteer; he'd already fed a vampire today.

"JJ… are you sure?" Reggie ventured cautiously.

"If you're being honest with us, then you are still my friend, even if you didn't trust me enough to tell me this."

"It wasn't about trust—"

"I don't care." Jay unbuttoned his blazer, shrugged it off, and tossed it onto a nearby table. Then he dropped his vest there too and unbuttoned the top few buttons on his shirt.

"Um, Jay…," Bari began, "just to warn you…."

"I was fed on by Ethan once too, you'll recall."

"Sure, but he was under his father's influence and not trying to be nice about it."

"Meaning it'll only hurt for a moment?" Jay tried to smile but doubted it came across.

"That… and you're probably really going to like it."

That wasn't what Jay expected to hear, but then, none of this was as expected, not anything from the past week.

And damn, Bari wasn't kidding, as delicate fangs lengthened in Reggie's mouth and he pulled Jay to him to bite sharply into his neck. Admittedly, Jay didn't remember much from when Ethan bit him, because he'd been forced into a complacent stupor. Unlike Ethan as a newborn, however, Reggie had clearly been a vampire longer and never pushed his thrall too far.

When it was over, Jay didn't even sway, though he did swallow deeply to tamp down how good that had felt.

Reggie's eyes became blessedly yellow, and then faded to banal brown. He clung to Jay like he didn't want to let go, and it was almost more unsettling that he hadn't said anything truly inappropriate for the past several minutes. "You really are one of my dearest friends, JJ. I'm sorry I couldn't tell you the truth."

The part of Jay that remained upset might have pushed Reggie away from him, but he didn't truly want that. "At least now I know what's actually in those drinks of yours."

"Guilty," Reggie said with a chuckle, finally releasing Jay. "An extra pint to tide me over in the interim keeps the cravings down, but having something fresh is still necessary.

"As for more explanation…. Des and I fibbed a little before, about the murders. Okay, a lot. We're not protecting the killer! We don't know who it is. We know who it likely is, but we need to be sure we've figured out everything before the last secret gets spilled. You need to be sure. I can't tell you more than that until you are, or it could compromise weeks' worth of investigating."

"Weeks?" Jay sputtered.

"It had to be need-to-know. Please understand."

When need-to-know didn't include the Alpha, it was hard to not take it personally. "Fine, but then help us with the body." Jay gestured back at the open drawer of the morgue. "We need to know who set up the added glamour, how that man died, and what is on those cellphones. Then we have another task for you involving a rune."

They set to work. Jay examined the phones, Reggie the body, and Bari looked over the residual magic left from the glamour only he could see.

"The extra glamour magic looks blue? You can see that?" Reggie questioned, even as he was hunched over Bari's ex. "Incredible."

"You missed the show before," Bari said, "but since most everyone else knows the Seer part… I've been manifesting my brother's abilities since coming here."

He explained to Reggie about his prophecy, their hunt for a woman behind everything, the hidden truth in the creation tablets, and how Bari's powers seemed to be increasing exponentially ever since Bashir and Ethan's arrival.

"Your brother can see auras too?" Reggie asked.

"Actually, he's never mentioned that power. Maybe our abilities are manifesting differently."

"Unfortunately," Reggie went on, "while I was obviously a natural witch before I became a vampire, I'm not so powerful that I can see auras without a spell. Feel them, certainly, but seeing the colors by blind sight? I'd have to cast a spell on the person we suspect, which would hardly be covert, but if you can see the color, you should know the second they cast something in front of you."

"Wouldn't it have to be Clara?" Bari asked.

"Seems Daisy is a contender too." Reggie waved them over. "Because while this poor soul had his throat cut with claws, before that, he was poisoned to weaken him, probably to make killing him easier. Daisy is well-versed in poisons. I'm the one who made sure of it, since certain plants can be toxic to different tribes. I needed to be sure she wouldn't accidentally kill someone if we had visitors! There's also this."

On a pull-out shelf beside the drawer, Reggie had placed what looked like a small carrying case containing five vials of something dark, thick, and red.

"Not anything of my stash, mind you. I found the case tucked beneath the body."

"Five vials, five victims." Bari grimaced.

"Six now."

"True, but I think Joseph was simply wrong place, wrong time." Bari rested a hand on the drawer where his ex's body lay. He had no love for him, Jay knew, but that couldn't make this easier. When Bari pulled his hand back, he looked at Jay. "What about the phones?"

"No luck. They're all wiped. No messages on any of them. If the victims all received texts before they died, maybe luring them to meet someone, there's no way to know who it was."

"Anyone would respond to a circle member calling them out," Bari noted.

"Or Ursula's agents. We can't know anything for sure. After seeing how easily Reggie fooled us, anyone could be this vampire in disguise, or under her thrall. What if the accomplices don't even know what they're doing?"

"Anjali can't be ruled out either," Bari said, rather than admit any of the women in the circle might be innocent. "She's too close to this."

Jay wished he could blame the awful buzzing in his brain on loss of blood. "Reggie, could an ancient vampire enthrall more than one person at a time?"

"Maybe." Reggie pushed the drawer back into the wall. "I'd have a hard time managing two myself, and certainly no shifter. But if you really believe this woman from Bari's prophecy is from the beginning, a time when vampires and shifters were first created—which is still boggling my mind, by the way, I'm not that old—who knows."

Coming forward with a rub of his hands, a blue glow began that formed into a rune when Reggie separated them. Jay glanced at Bari, who was staring at the bright display, and imagined Bari could see a golden aura hovering over the spell as a signature of Reggie's magic.

"Speaking of thralls, since you're Mr. Magic now, Bari my boy," Reggie said, taking one of Bari's hands and fusing the rune right into his palm until it vanished, "you should be the one to use this. No one else will be able to see the activation, and all you need to do is touch the people you suspect."

"Touch them?" Bari repeated.

"Well, if your new magical radar does the job for you, wonderful, but doubtful. A vampire's thrall isn't normal magic. Come on, now. You're the touchy type." Reggie threw an arm over Bari's shoulders and tugged him close, to which Bari playfully pressed a hand to Reggie's chest. "No one will notice anything amiss, eh? And if you can get this rune to reveal a thrall in action, we can use the magical trail to follow it back to its source."

"And maybe finally end this," Bari said like a sigh.

End it? Would it be that easy? They didn't know anything, not really. Jay felt like he hadn't known a goddamn thing in years.

He stepped away from the others, walking out into the lounge.

"Jay?" Bari called after him.

Jay closed his eyes, recalling the words of the prophecy and speaking them aloud.

> *"Plans set in motion spanning years in the making*
> *Her desire for the past still ripe for the taking*
> *One city saved won't prevent a revising*
> *Keep watch on the lonely for the blue moon rising."*

He turned back around when no one said anything. "There isn't a blue moon this year. That was last Halloween, over a year ago."

"So?" Bari broached, stepping toward Jay. "These prophecies are rarely exacting. It could mean any number of things besides an actual blue moon. The idea of a blue moon is an extra full moon in the same month, correct? Could mean an extra anything in this case. Extra cities involved, which we know, extra—"

"Vampires. Not necessarily on her side, but what if the lonely are vampires?" Jay turned to look at Reggie as he said it, who, for the first time since Jay had known him, looked truly melancholy. "Are you, Reggie?"

"Now that's a personal question," Reggie failed at attempting a joke.

"All these years, teasing you about people leaving the basement, all your conquests. Were they? Or just donors?"

A more obvious cringe crossed Reggie's expression. "Difficult to be with someone knowing you're lying to them, isn't it? Humans are too fragile anyway. And the shifters who know what I am…. They're very kind and understanding but still generally wary. It's been a while."

"Oh, darling." Bari returned to him and touched his arm. "Maybe we can change that."

"Volunteering, are you?" Reggie waggled an eyebrow.

"I meant change things systemically, but I do so love your humor."

Reggie chuckled. "Tell everyone I'm a vampire and hope for the best, eh?"

"Change has to start somewhere. And if our enemy is planning to use what defeated the vampires the first time around to win this time— powers and people like me—maybe our best chance at beating her is having a few vampires on our side to even the odds."

"You're being rather understanding when a vampire is to blame for all this."

"As if I'd suspect you're in league with her. Do you want to rule over all shifter- and humankind?"

"Goodness, no." Reggie winced. "Think of the responsibility! When would I ever have time to relax?"

Bari laughed, and it wasn't long before Reggie joined him.

How did Bari do it, Jay wondered. How did Reggie? How did anyone? It felt like all the walls were closing in on him, and his eyes were hot, like he hadn't experienced since he was a child, or first asked to be Councilor, or first asked to be Alpha. He was supposed to be stronger than this, better. He was supposed to be the one who kept everyone else safe.

And he'd failed.

"Excuse me, but I better eat something." Jay turned toward the stairs so neither of them would see the moisture in his eyes. "We need to be ready for whenever the others return home, and the last thing we need is for me to faint."

"I'll join you," Bari said.

"Can you… give me a minute, actually?" Jay asked, not trusting himself to turn.

"Oh, um… of course."

"Thank you," he said and continued for the stairs.

BARI WASN'T good at listening when others told him what to do. And though he wanted to respect Jay's wishes, he had an awful sinking feeling that right now he shouldn't.

"Reggie darling, can you get all this warded up again?" Bari gestured at the morgue. "Wouldn't want anyone suspecting anything if they came down here."

"I can do that. Feeling fit as a fiddle now." Reggie smacked his chest in a show of vitality, which nearly upset his sunglasses, still tucked into his shirt. He took that moment to put them back on. "Much better. If you need anything, love, I'm here."

Bari hurried up the stairs after Jay. The first place he checked was the kitchen, and though that was where Jay had gone, he stood gripping the door handle of the pantry, knuckles white, staring at nothing.

With a snarl, Jay swung his free hand, holding the pantry door in place, and punched into it so hard, he literally punched a hole through it.

The act was impressive, but now wasn't the time to get hot over Jay's strength.

"Whatever the door did to you, darling, I'm sure it deserved that."

Jay spun, his still closed fist looking scuffed but not bleeding. He hadn't even shifted to accomplish the feat.

"I know you said you wanted to be alone—" Bari approached him gingerly. "—but I don't think you should be."

Jay didn't say anything, like he didn't trust himself to speak and was barely holding himself together.

"Jay, please. I know things seem bleak right now—"

"Bleak? I've been an Alpha for five years, and I've already doomed my city. I had no idea any of this was going on. I believe Reggie means well, but he couldn't tell me the truth, even after years of friendship, and he's still keeping secrets. My circle and people don't trust me—"

"The people love you—"

"Loving me doesn't keep them safe!" Jay yelled and then sagged to a meeker height. "I'm sorry. But the wolves at the very least think I'm incompetent and weak, and I am. I don't know how to take control anymore." He closed his eyes like his burst of anger had deflated into grief and it was all he could do to keep from crumbling.

Bari was supposed to be the emotional one, the one who couldn't hack it as a leader or stick around when things got tough. It was strange, seeing that sort of meltdown from someone else. Sobering.

He didn't require Seer powers to know what Jay needed of him, though he was grateful for his Focus side, because he could feel the reach of it for the first time, the pulse around him as something he could extend and offer to others.

"You're not alone. You just have to decide if you're going to listen to what this power tells you and trust yourself or fight it."

Hearing Bash's words replay in his mind, Bari stalked forward, right up to Jay, and grabbed him by the shoulders, forcing Jay to look at him.

"You want to know how you take control? You do it. You want your circle to have autonomy, and they should, but you're still Alpha. Act like one. Stop trying to be nice so much of the time, and channel the dominant side that makes my knees weak, because that is how you take back your city.

"That doesn't mean being an asshole. I know what an asshole looks like, thank you, and he's currently rotting beneath my feet. It means if your people step out of line and act like assholes themselves, undermining the type of pack you want to cultivate, then you say something and stop that bullshit in its tracks. Period.

"You didn't doom this city, Jay. You wanted to save everyone in it, even when not everyone deserves the benefit of the doubt. Well, too bad. Someone here, in this house, is the bad guy, but we can still beat them. You can beat them."

Jay had almost looked affronted at the start of Bari's tirade, but he seemed doubtful now, in himself and his abilities. "Being an Alpha doesn't suddenly make you stronger or better at leading."

"It doesn't need to," Bari countered, "because an Alpha already is those things, especially if you were chosen. The people chose you, voted for you over everyone else. So show them they made the right decision. We're going to solve this, and it's not going to be because I can see visions or sense things in a new way, but because you have faith in me, and in your people, and that makes me have faith in you.

"Can you feel this?" Bari squeezed Jay's shoulders, letting the aura of power around him extend like he knew it could.

Jay gasped with a bulging of his eyes to experience so much focus actively given.

"I'm learning all sorts of new tricks," Bari continued, "but the thing is, I couldn't share any of this if the foundation wasn't in you. A Focus doesn't bring out the best in people, remember, just the most of what's already there.

"Now, do you feel like an Alpha, or am I mistaken?"

Bari knew the answer, because he could feel it, he could see it, the aura around Jay that was primal and powerful and proved he was born to lead. Bari's presence enhanced that. His intent to enhance it more bolstered Jay further, and as that washed over Jay, all indecision and dampness in his eyes faded.

He grasped the back of Bari's neck and jerked him into a hot and penetrating kiss.

Now this was Bari's Alpha.

"Behind every great Alpha," Jay whispered when he released Bari, "is a greater partner urging them toward that greatness."

"I believe the shifter version is a greater mate, but I can accept we're not there yet."

"Aren't we?" Jay kept his hold on Bari's neck, gently in the aftermath of his tight grip.

"Mr. Russell, is that a proposal?"

Jay laughed, still somehow managing to be his bashful, sweet self, wrapped in a commanding package. "Ask me again when this is over," he said and withdrew his hand, lingeringly slow, like a promise.

Bari was so going to hold him to that.

"Can you two keep the PDAs to private areas of the den, please?"

They turned to the kitchen doorway, where Maximus was entering.

"It wouldn't be PDAs then, now, would it?" Bari spouted back.

"There's still a P in private."

Smartass.

Theresa and William came in behind Maximus, and with their arrival swept a wave of dread into Bari's stomach. With one look at Jay, Bari knew he felt it too.

"Hi, Bari!" William bounded over. "I'm still sad Bash and Ethan had to leave so soon."

"I know, dear boy." Bari reached out to pat his head. "Hopefully, they can come back sometime soon. How was ice cream with your friend?"

The slightly darker hue that overtook William's cheeks said plenty. "Good."

"Listen." Jay took the initiative before the family could settle in. "I know you just got back, but... please go out front and wait for me."

"Out?" Theresa questioned with a frown. "Why—"

"I'll meet you outside and explain everything. Just go. Please," Jay added like the polite man he couldn't help being toward those he cared about, even if it had been an order.

Maximus took the hint that this was serious and ushered Theresa and William away.

Jay turned to Bari with hushed urgency. "I'm going to see them out, tell them to pick a direction and drive and stay away from the den until we inform them it's safe to return. We can't risk Theresa or William—"

"I understand. Go." Bari urged him. "I'll check back in with Reggie. Good luck convincing Max to leave you."

Jay huffed at the truth of that, but before he turned to go, he grasped Bari's face to kiss him one more time, hard enough that Bari teetered when Jay left.

Maybe he'd go the long way to Reggie's, through the courtyard. He could use a nice, calming view. And a cup of tea on the terrace.

Or a brandy.

"Ugh, you."

Fresh dread swept through Bari at Anjali calling to him when he was only halfway across the living room. "Um...."

"Where is everyone?" she asked, stepping briskly toward him. "I thought I heard Max. I've been looking all over this damn house."

"I-I... I'm not sure." Bari took a moment to calm himself, seeing that there was no previously hidden glamour about Anjali, so at least she wasn't a vampire. "Jay must still be out seeing Des. And I'm sure the happy little family is enjoying a free afternoon. I'm not sure about everyone else. I only just got back from the museum myself."

"Why are you so twitchy?" Anjali looked him up and down with the usual scorn.

"I'm not twitchy! A little woozy maybe. I was an unexpected blood donor earlier, if you hadn't heard."

"I did. Who do you think's been keeping everyone calm at the Shelter since you left?"

"Of course. And isn't everyone grateful for you. Goodness." Bari allowed himself to stagger slightly, reaching out to grasp Anjali's elbow to keep him steady. "Maybe I'm woozier than I thought."

She grimaced but didn't pry her arm away from him. When he glanced at the spot where they connected, there was nothing, not even a glimmer of magic.

No vampire thrall either.

"There are people home."

Bari nearly staggered for real, because behind him and Anjali from the dining room where he had initially been headed came Daisy and Clara.

"Anyone want to help us finish off a few more cupcakes?" Daisy asked. "I was hoping William might be back by now. I made tea!"

"This house gets so drafty in the fall," Clara added.

Jay was right outside, and Reggie just downstairs. There was no reason Bari should feel trapped. And he could not give away that he suspected them.

"I, for one, would love that," Bari said, releasing Anjali with a slow pivot. "I was just explaining that I'm a bit light-headed from earlier events. Do you need any help gathering things from the kitchen?"

"Just cream and honey," Daisy said as she moved past him. "Everything else is already in the dining room."

"Let me help anyway." Bari turned to follow her, reaching up to lightly touch her shoulder in a friendly pat. "Moving about helps keep me steady."

No thrall on Daisy.

"I'll get the honey," Bari offered hastily, giving him the chance to keep the hole in the pantry door hidden.

"Thanks, Bari," Daisy said, heading for the fridge to grab the cream.

He hurried to meet her again in the middle.

"You do seem out of sorts," Daisy said with a touch of concern, blessedly ushering him out of the kitchen with a loop of her arm through his. "Let's get a cupcake in you."

All Bari needed to do was stall until Jay returned. And sneak a touch on Clara too.

And Ursula—who was in the dining room with Clara and Anjali when Bari and Daisy entered.

Bari took a moment to breathe relief that their auras revealed no hidden vampires.

"Jay's with Des still?" Ursula asked, clearly having been informed by the others. She must have already been in the house or come in through the courtyard entrance if she hadn't run into Jay out front.

"I believe so." Bari swallowed down a stammer. He could do this, even if they were taking up one end of the large dining table and the only seat left open to him was the corner. He took it anyway, trying to smile affably. "Important work, you know, being a defense attorney."

There were plates, teacups, a steaming pot of tea with accompaniments, like the honey and cream they'd brought, and a tray filled with the remaining red and blue cupcakes.

When Clara reached for one, Bari used the opportunity to claim one himself—and bumped her hand.

"Excuse me."

Still no thrall.

"You think Des is innocent?" Anjali asked.

Bari sat at the head, with Clara and Daisy on either side of him and Ursula and Anjali beyond that. It wouldn't be easy to reach Ursula from here. "I, um… think the saying is innocent until proven guilty, isn't it?"

"According to the witnesses coming forward," Ursula said, "there's going to be plenty more proof soon."

"Witnesses?" Bari questioned.

"Placing Des at the apartment building at time of death."

"That's impossible. He wasn't there."

"And how do you know that?"

"He told Jay—"

"You said Jay was still with him."

Bari winced. It didn't help that he was speaking to a Warden, a trained interrogator, but he had to be better than this. "He called earlier to update me."

"Ah."

"You're a Seer like your brother, I heard," Anjali interjected, nearly causing Bari to whiplash toward her. "Everyone at the Shelter saw."

"Really?" Clara jumped in, already halfway through a cupcake. "Plus the Focus part? I can still feel you buzzing, even with the others gone."

Right, because the power Bari had projected around Jay was technically always with him, and he had to be careful who got its benefits.

"I hope this means you're finally starting to like me." Bari rallied a smile, pouring some of the tea for himself and adding a dab of honey.

"We never didn't like you," Ursula said, "just maybe not fans of your priorities."

Their eyes met across the table, and Bari focused on not letting his hand tremble as he lifted the teacup to his lips.

Poison rang out in his head. Joseph had been poisoned before he was killed.

Bari immediately set the teacup down again. Had any of the others drank from theirs yet? He couldn't remember.

"Not your flavor?" Daisy asked with her usual indomitable smile. "We have every kind of tea in the kitchen. I could make you something else—"

"Oh no, I… um…."

"Personally, I'm sure it's lovely as-is." Ursula stood to better reach across the table for cream.

Bari leaped to his feet and grasped her wrist midair. She was the only one left. She was the only one left. She had to be….

But no. Nothing. No flash or wisp of magic. No sign at all that the rune had activated, which meant no thrall—on any of them.

"Can I help you with something, Mr. Bain?" Ursula asked with a drop in her tone.

Bari let her go with a lurch backward, upsetting his chair. "Is it all of you?" he demanded with a suspecting glance at each of them. "One of you has to be involved, but is it all of you? And none of you are being controlled, you're just… doing it? Just murdering people?"

It was two by two on either side of him, with a wall behind Bari and no way out of the corner, as the contrasting friendly and hostile glances among the women coalesced into a singularly menacing stare.

The rest of them stood, and Bari would have scrambled back if he didn't nearly trip over his toppled chair.

"Pity," Ursula said, moving around Clara to reach Bari first. "I think you could have been useful. Jay could have been once too."

Bari pivoted around the chair to back up further, but Daisy and Anjali blocked his way to the door. As he retreated, Ursula came closer. "You don't understand what's going on," Bari tried to tell them. "You're not in control!"

"I think we are," Ursula said.

If Bari relied on his Seer intuition, he knew he could escape them, but he was too sickened by what they had done to consider fleeing. "I don't know how you can live with yourselves, killing innocent people, but you are being manipulated. You have to be! I know a vampire is behind all this!"

Clara and Daisy laughed.

"Are you a Seer or mad?" Daisy mocked. "We're following a wolf."

"You've seen her? Met with her?"

"I have," Ursula said. "Someone on the fringe wanting to help set things right and change what's become of too many cities. It's time wolves took things back. Jay might have been able to stay Alpha if he wasn't such a bleeding heart for the lesser races. Soon to be his loss, our gain." She started to shift, and Bari knew he was in imminent danger, but understanding the whole of this was too important. He couldn't run.

"Why kill one of each tribe? Why so specific?"

"For a spell," Clara answered giddily. "We needed the unrest to make Jay look weak so when we take over, no one will question us, but once we cast that spell, it'll ensure we regain power without anyone being able to stop us."

No, that wasn't everything. Bari could feel something was off. There was more to this, more hidden secrets.

When he looked into Ursula's glowing shifter eyes, he realized one thing for certain, even if the others had no idea.

They were following a vampire—and she was the only one who knew.

"All we need now are the tablets," Ursula said through a growl. "Those don't belong to you. Once you and Jay and that human are out of the way," she spat in regard to Theresa, "we won't have anything preventing us from getting to them and finishing this."

"Clever," a new voice said from behind them, causing everyone's heads to whip that direction, where Reggie stood grinning, one of his cardigan kimonos reacquired, as he leaned casually against the doorframe. "There are a few things you're not privy to, but at least now we know everything we need. It's enough."

Bari would have wondered how Reggie could remain so calm, outnumbered as they were—until Anjali turned on Ursula and pounced.

Chapter 17

BARI'S FIRST thought was he could have sworn Reggie said he couldn't enthrall a shifter, only for him to realize what was really going on.

Anjali was a double agent.

Anjali was a double agent?

Bari skittered along the wall to move around the table as Anjali tackled Ursula to the floor. There was so little room between table and wall that all Daisy and Clara could do at first was stare.

"Traitor!" Ursula roared. "And you wondered why I never let you know more!"

"Oh, please!" Anjali spat back. "You didn't suspect me for a second!"

Bari certainly hadn't. Anjali had been so believable as another bitter traditionalist, even his souped-up intuition hadn't been able to see through her guise.

He barely had enough time to finish getting around the other side of the table before Reggie launched what looked like a holding spell at Clara, but in that same moment, Clara returned to her senses and deflected it with an easy sweep of her arm to deploy a shield. The spell bounced and fizzled into nothing.

Not that it was any surprise, but Clara's magical aura was indeed blue.

Daisy howled, leaping around the grappling Anjali and Ursula toward Reggie, and grabbed the still-full teapot to smash over his head. He cried out from the heat, but that was hardly enough to incapacitate a shifter, let alone a secret vampire. Daisy obviously expected him to be more affected, because when Reggie glared at her and a glow started to form in his hands, she froze.

"Duck!" Clara called, and when her wife complied, she fired something at Reggie in retaliation. Bari couldn't tell what the spell was at first, because when Reggie was hit, nothing seemed to happen. Then, slowly, the drenching of tea all over Reggie began to seep into him like osmosis.

Reggie reeled, turned, and retched up a sickeningly dark red splatter onto the floor.

"Feeling a bit weak, Reg?" Daisy taunted.

The tea was poisoned!

But that wasn't a problem, Bari reminded himself, because a vampire wouldn't be affected. Once Reggie had purged himself of something not blood having entered his system, he wiped his mouth and grinned.

"You know, love, that would have been a brilliant move," he said to Daisy with a glance at Clara in admiration and then slowly removed his sunglasses to tuck them into his collar. "Except," he concluded and dropped his reapplied glamour to reveal glowing yellow eyes.

Clara shot out her arms and swept them wildly to the left, effectively moving Daisy out of Reggie's path with an extension of telekinesis. Reggie turned his sights on Clara instead.

And Daisy swiveled toward Bari!

The doors to the courtyard were behind Bari. He could run. He could get Jay! But no. That would leave the others outnumbered in the interim, and Bari didn't want to run. He was finally somewhere he felt like he could make a real home again, and he was not giving that up without a fight.

Daisy growled, her shifter eyes flashing and teeth and claws growing, and Bari shifted in echo. He steeled himself, prowling forward away from the doors.

"How can you do this?" he demanded. "Not only to innocent people, but to Jay? I honestly thought you cared for him."

They circled each other, only having enough room to do so because they were nearest the courtyard doors, while Clara and Reggie volleyed spells at each other from across the room, and between them grappled Anjali and Ursula, constantly impeded by the large dining table.

"We did care once," Daisy said, so strangely contrasting as a partially shifted wolf in a vintage mod dress. "We didn't want to overthrow Jay, but he's too soft, too misguided. Then, after all that mess with your brother, losing a mate to a fanger?" She sneered and cast a disgusted glance at Reggie when he was back in her view.

Bari glanced at him too, and good thing, because Reggie stomped the ground, narrowly missing Anjali and Ursula as a crack formed in the floor and shot across the room, snapping the table in half. Then Reggie used telekinesis to grasp the closer half and hurled it at Clara.

She countered with a fireball so hot and concentrated, the table burst into ashes that forced Anjali and Ursula to retreat from each other, clearing the soot from their eyes as it rained down on them.

"We need a strong Alpha." Daisy drew Bari's attention back to her. "One who will put wolves first. And that isn't Jay!" She howled and hurled herself at Bari just as he recentered himself and squared his stance in defense.

Daisy swiped at him, and when she missed with an expert weave of Bari's head, he remembered he could do this. He could use his abilities to prevent a single blow from landing. He did so, channeling the ease with which he had used his powers at the Shelter, and this time, he only had one opponent to focus on.

Daisy quickly grew frustrated as one strike missed, then another— then another!

"So much for being sick to your stomach when Angus was found!" Bari accused, trying to keep the fight to a constant pivot so they wouldn't stumble into the others' path. "You were willing to kill for this? A doomed cause?"

"We didn't do the killing! None of us needed to. Ursula's agents are loyal to her, not Jay. And I was sick to my stomach because I had to smell a rat in my house!"

Ursula's agents were accomplices. That's how the killer could be so many places at once, murdering five people at the same time, but all of it was orchestrated by Ursula.

No, orchestrated by the vampire, and Ursula knew her identity, knew what she was, and still followed her. Bari knew she knew.

"Daisy—" Bari tried one last time to appeal to her, but Daisy stopped her fruitless swiping of claws and smiled cruelly.

"I guess I did play my part in disposing of your ex. A lizard? Really? Uck. I can't believe you let him touch you. You're almost as bad as your fanger-whore brother."

Screw appealing to her better nature! "Joseph was a dick, but not because he was a lizard!" Bari channeled every ounce of power in him to feint right, feint left, crowding Daisy back near the courtyard doors, and when she least saw it coming, he curled his claws into a fist and decked her right across the jaw. "And it's not polite to call someone a whore."

Daisy slammed back so hard into the jamb between the doors, one of them popped open, swinging outward from her momentum, and cracked up the center as she toppled.

Win for Bari.

He whirled back around to take in the progress of the others.

Shit. Lose for everyone else!

It had been too much to think about—fighting Daisy, trying to understand her motives, avoiding getting caught in the other concurrent fights—that Bari hadn't projected his abilities as a Focus to aid his comrades. He simply was a Focus amid a crowd, empowering everyone around him, and Clara had succeeded in trapping Reggie in a holding spell like a glowing spider's web against the wall, while Ursula stood triumphant over Anjali's downed body.

At least neither of them went for killing blows, but only because they came together in the place where half the table had been torn away and focused their attentions on Bari.

He'd defeated five rats once—or at least four before the fifth clocked him—but this was a Warden and a Magister. Against magic as well as a trained fighter, Bari didn't know if he could win all by himself.

"Enough!" The blessed roar of Jay practically made the walls shake, and Bari could have kissed him right then as he stood seething in the dining room doorway where Reggie had made his grand entrance only minutes prior.

Ursula and Clara didn't look intimidated. They readied themselves to include Jay in however they attacked next.

Jay roared once more, already starting to shift, and tore open his button-down and vest so harshly it popped off several buttons just like he'd popped the ones off Bari's shirt once, easing the way for him to grow—and grow—to his largest Stage Three form with long werewolf snout and snapping jaws, beautiful brown fur, and an extra several feet in height.

Fuck yes, Bari thought and concentrated everything he had into Jay being the best damn Alpha there was, because he knew the groundwork was already there.

THE SURGE of power Jay knew was coming from Bari almost made him swoon, it was so invigorating, even more so than before their kiss in the kitchen. Having taken on his largest form, he felt larger still, his muscles pulsing and rippling beneath his fur as he snapped his elongated jaws and sprang forward after Clara.

Jay knew the exact spell she tried to throw at him, because he'd seen it recently—runes to drain his vitality—but he didn't even need to dodge, because as soon as it was cast, it vanished like neon lights fritzing out, unable to contend with the breadth of Bari's opposing influence keeping Jay empowered.

"She's mine!" Bari cried before Jay could do more than swipe at Clara, forcing her to leap away from him. "You take Ursula!"

There was no one's advice Jay would have taken to heart more right then, and he whirled toward Ursula instead.

She met him with an impressive grapple of claws, finishing her own shift to Stage Three as a beautiful white wolf. She was strong, but Jay knew he was stronger.

He thrust her backward, slamming her into the nearest wall. Half the table was gone, to where or how, Jay had no idea, but it gave them plenty of room to do this.

Reggie was awake to their left, trying to fight through Clara's hold on him. If Clara lost her concentration on that spell or Reggie broke through it, it'd be three against two, not that they needed the help. Jay was not going to let Ursula beat him, not when he felt an increase in power and confidence like never before that he knew was from Bari, but that could only exist because it was already in him.

"Why?" he roared as he swept after Ursula, trying to pin her to the wall, but she rolled out of reach just in time. "Tell me! Why?" His words came out barely human but clear enough to be understood.

Ursula circled him with an equally vicious snarl, an almost-smile on her snout as she tore away the remains of her ruined button-down and blazer. "Why? Because we are meant to be the race on top!" She leaped after him, forcing Jay on the defensive, but he used that to his advantage too.

Crouching and raising his hands to deflect her, he grabbed her claws as they descended and used her own momentum to fling her onward over his head. He spun but watched her land in a perfect roll, quickly back on her feet, facing him, before he could pounce in response.

"You're a fool being manipulated by a vampire, and you don't even know it!"

She hunkered low as if to leap again, but at the last second, she charged his legs instead. Foolishly, Jay swept down at her instead of pivoting out of the way, and she took his feet right out from under him. When he landed, she scrambled atop him to hold him still, and he thrashed against her.

"Isn't that the funny thing," she taunted, her voice a lower growl to keep quiet. "You think I don't know."

"What?" Jay gaped in surprise.

"Don't you understand?" Ursula snarled, pinning him firmer, with her blue eyes shimmering within her furred brow. "We should rule the shifters, but when vampires ruled above us, we owned the world."

"You know it's a vampire," Jay said aloud. He had to or he wouldn't have believed it.

Jay wasn't truly pinned, only dazed, and in the moment that Ursula took to beam down at him in her gloating, he had more than enough strength to roll them and pin her in turn.

"Who is she?" he roared.

She kept their trajectory going, rolling them once more, and rolled herself right off Jay and away from his grasp. Jay followed, not caring what the answer might be, because he knew she wouldn't reveal it, so he swept with his claws, again and again, forcing her to back up with no chance at getting in a swipe of her own.

But Ursula was good, one of their best. She knew how to use an opponent's skills against them, and she was faster than Jay, even if he was Alpha, knowing to dodge direct hits and stay out of reach like a skilled boxer.

In Jay's periphery, he could see Bari and Clara fighting like a mirror image of them, save barely being at Stage Two, with Bari dodging and weaving to avoid Clara's attacks just as Ursula was avoiding Jay's. Bari was more impressive, truly supernatural in how he seemed to know every incoming blow or spell, able to block or break through even some of the strongest magic Clara threw at him, leaving the walls around and behind Bari charred from misfired lightning strikes and fireballs.

Conversely, Ursula couldn't see Jay's attacks coming, relying on skill and intuition to guess. Jay had to think of something to spoil her expectations.

They were circling nearer to the busted table, and as soon as they reached it, once Jay had it at his back, he reached behind him, grabbed the table by the jagged side facing him, and flung it in a wide arch into Ursula, sending her flying toward the farthest wall, where she crumbled.

Bari and Clara were near where Ursula landed, and at last, Clara's constant spellcasting had her looking exhausted as Bari weaved, weaved, weaved again, and finally punched her. As soon as Clara hit the ground, the spell holding Reggie to the wall vanished, causing him to drop to the floor.

Bari looked across the room at Jay in triumph, seeming to very much enjoy seeing Jay hulked out to werewolf size. It would have been a nice moment, if Bari wasn't distracted just as Ursula got to her feet and turned her murderous glare on him.

Jay refused to sit back and risk Bari not being able to see her coming, so he did the one thing left within his power.

He roared.

This was like no roar Jay had ever bellowed before. It wasn't anger. It wasn't merely a warning. It was pure primal authority.

Ursula dropped to her knees rather than finish her attack, head bowed and werewolf form shivering in the wake of his command and the display of a true Alpha that for a while Jay had started to forget he needed to be.

"Stand down," Jay commanded, and it was only then that Bari spun to see the danger he'd been in, since for a moment, he'd looked like he was ready to drop to his knees too—for different reasons. "There is only one Alpha here, and it is not you."

Reggie had climbed to his feet, and everyone else was sitting up, back to consciousness. With a wave of his hand, Reggie put holding spells on Clara and Ursula before they could try anything else, this time like glowing manacles. As Ursula shifted human, the manacles shrunk with her to fit her smaller wrists, and Bari, chivalry incarnate as he was, removed his shirt to cover her. That was two he'd lost in one day. Jay would have to make it up to him, since it was three overall.

When Anjali rose to her feet with a groan, Jay growled and lurched forward, not understanding why Reggie hadn't shackled her as well, only for Bari to cry out.

"No! She's on our side! Slippery minx."

With a sag of his shoulders out of the tension that had reignited, Jay allowed himself to shift human. "I take it you're the final secret?" he asked, continuing toward Anjali.

"Forgive me, Alpha," she said with a small incline of her head. "If more people had known, these traitors might have figured out I wasn't really with them. We had to know where the orders were coming from, who was involved, and who was being targeted.

"A few weeks ago, after you left for Centrus, I started to suspect something was going on. I confided in Des, wary of telling anyone from the circle, and he told me about Reggie. Don't think a vampire in our midst didn't give me pause, but I trusted Des. We didn't dare tell anyone else, fearing even three might be too much. We still weren't able to stop the murders," she added with a cringe of anger and shame. "All I could do was slowly get the rest of Reggie's list into hiding."

"You did more than you know," Bari said as he moved up next to her. "This fight was too close. One person less and we might not have won."

"Agreed." Anjali granted Bari a rare smile. "One person less… and I don't think we'd have had a chance."

Brightly beaming in response, Bari nudged Anjali in the side. "What an actress! All that surly nonsense and not liking me was an act, hm?"

"I wouldn't go that far. I didn't know who from Centrus could be trusted, so blaming you after Angus's death may have been closer to my true feelings than I intended. You're also a bit…." Anjali waved a hand in an iffy gesture.

"Much?" Bari finished for her. "So I've heard. I'll wear you down."

"Ahem, not that I'd generally mind people having a little loyalty toward a vampire and all," Reggie said, slipping his sunglasses back into place, even if he didn't need to hide how his eyes changed anymore, "but did I overhear that right?" He turned toward Ursula, who hadn't moved from where she knelt. "You know a vampire is the one behind all this?"

"What?" Clara sputtered in disbelief.

Apparently, Ursula was the only one who'd known, and though she smiled, sinister and steadfast, she didn't respond.

"You've lost," Jay said, menacing toward her. "Give up the real person behind this. Who is she?"

"She is far more powerful than any of us," Ursula answered, avoiding the real question. "And she is going to keep coming, and eventually, she will win, and wolves will have our rightful place again."

"Your place," Jay growled, "is going to be the inside of a jail cell."

"Um?" Bari interjected with a wary raise of his hand, glancing around the room. "Are we forgetting someone?"

As if summoned, Daisy leaped to her feet from halfway out the terrace door, snarling with a flash of her eyes as if she had every intention of diving back into the fight.

Then a large, dark-skinned hand clasped her neck from behind, silencing her with a choke, and slammed her head into the floor, leaving her unconscious again.

Maximus stepped over Daisy to enter from the courtyard, while the rest of them stood stunned. "What? Like I was actually going to leave."

Chapter 18

MAGICAL RESTRAINTS had been replaced by human ones as the police took Ursula, Clara, and Daisy into custody. Between a little well-placed magic and real evidence, there would be enough for the three of them to take the fall planned for Des.

Bari was a little fuzzy on the details, but he trusted Jay knew how to game the system in just the right way to make it stick.

Once word spread throughout the pack about what had happened, it seemed those "witnesses" who'd been about to come forward against Des, and who, naturally, were Ursula's agents, had a change of heart. Furthermore, once Clara and Daisy realized Ursula really was working for a vampire, they gave up all the names they knew who had been involved and who committed the actual murders. Those people would receive shifter justice, and the families could rest easier.

"Do you think they're sorry, now that they know they were tricked?" Bari asked Jay as Daisy and Clara were put into squad cars.

"Not for the reasons we'd want," Jay said.

They had changed clothes and cleaned up the den as much as necessary, glamouring what was needed in preparation for police to search the house. Ursula still refused to give up the vampire's identity, but at least they had no worries about shifter culture being revealed to the masses. That much Ursula had sworn, that she'd play along as was expected and not admit anything that would expose their culture. She believed beyond a doubt that she was in the right and only doing what was best for her people.

As far as Bari was concerned, that only made it worse.

"You'll see," she'd said to Maximus before she was hauled away.

"How could you?" he'd demanded. "This isn't any vampire you're following, but one with no qualms about killing our kind, which apparently, you don't care about either. How could you... after the way Carolyn died?"

At that, Ursula had looked sorrowful, but only slightly. "Some sacrifices will need to be made, but you'll see. It'll be worth it."

All Maximus could do was stare in pained exasperation after someone who'd once been a friend.

Maximus had left with Theresa and William but came back alone, unable to leave his Alpha when it was a Second's job to be there.

"At least Jay had good backup." He'd smiled at Bari, Reggie, and Anjali. Whatever hatred he had for vampires—the ones who'd killed his wife or the one at large—he didn't put any of that on Reggie.

Things were finally starting to calm as the last of the police left, but Bari noticed some gawking neighbors he recognized. They were wolves—it was mostly wolves in this neighborhood—but they were among the ones who had attacked the Shelter.

They'd heard the truth by now and came over as a sheepish group.

"Can I help you folks?" Jay stepped forward to address them.

There were nearly a dozen, and as one, they all bowed their heads, while a man at the front said, "We wanted to apologize formally, Alpha, for taking measures into our own hands before. We had no idea what was really happening."

"We should have had more faith in you," a woman added.

"Yes," Bari said staunchly from the peanut gallery, "you should have."

Jay glanced at him with a small smirk before turning forward again. "What I expect from all my people is very simple, especially if you want to make this up to me."

The crowd of wolves raised their heads.

"Be better and you won't ever suffer the same consequences or worse than them." He nodded after the disappearing police cars.

The wolves all straightened their postures, understanding the warning.

A few of them looked cautiously at Reggie, who hadn't reapplied his glamour this time. Jay had asked him not to, and that truth had no doubt filtered into the community as well.

No one said anything.

"What now?" Bari asked once the wolves had left.

Jay glanced at each of them with an assured smile. "I'm going to make sure Des is home in time for dinner."

BARI WENT with Jay to expedite Des's release, mostly because he didn't want Jay out of his sight for the foreseeable future. They invited Des to return to the den with them to celebrate, and when they returned, other than a few missing members in the household, it could almost have seemed like things were entirely normal and no grand fight had occurred.

Because Anjali, Reggie, Maximus, and Theresa were playing hide-and-seek with William.

"Nice try!" William announced upon pulling the cover off the ottoman to find Anjali hiding inside.

"Can't blame a gal for trying." She shrugged as she arched up onto her feet and stepped out of it. "It was a good idea."

"When I did it," William uttered back.

Maximus and Theresa had already been found, and William turned, about to continue looking for Reggie.

From the entryway into the living room, Bari could just barely make out Reggie's flattened silhouette behind one of the curtains, floating to prevent his feet from being spotted the way Clara's once had been.

Cheater, Bari thought, and in response, he caught William's attention and pointed not so subtly in Reggie's direction.

William looked confused at first, since there were no visible feet, but then his eyes lit up and he dashed across the room and tore the curtain aside.

"No magic, Reggie! You lose!"

Reggie sighed in dramatic fashion and floated back to the floor. "Come now, love, I deserve a win, don't I? Got stomped in a magic fight and outed as a vampire in the same day." Even as he griped, he reached to playfully pat William's head, who didn't shy from him at all.

"It doesn't matter you're a vampire, Reggie," William declared. "Now I know two who are nice!"

"That you do, dear boy." Reggie patted him again.

"It's just kinda… weird, I guess, being less crowded here, ya know?" William said with a touch more melancholy. He was a very strong little boy that he wasn't saying what he truly meant, that it was painful knowing people he thought loved him, and maybe they did, were actually terrible, murderous villains.

"At least some good has come from this," Anjali said toward Des. "The right man has come home free."

He tossed her a smile in reply and recited grandly, "What immortal hand or eye could frame thy fearful symmetry?"

"Still not a tiger," she huffed and crossed to grasp him by the back of the neck, drawing him in for a deep kiss.

Bari wasn't the only one who gaped, though he was the first to find his voice. "Wait, wait, wait, you mean… you were a couple Reggie was helping get pregnant?"

"Don't be ridiculous!" Anjali refuted. "We're not even mated."

"Yet," Des said and brought her hand up to kiss the back of it.

Jay and Maximus seemed to be gawping the most.

"You were with Anji after seeing Reggie the day of the murders!" Jay realized.

"But… even with being undercover—" Maximus turned to her. "—you were always a traditionalist, wary of humans and the tribes intermating."

A touch of shame filled Anjali's face, but when Des took her hand again, she smiled. "What can I say? When you find love in the most unexpected of places, it tends to change your perspective. I get now how it happened to you, Max, and for what it's worth—" She turned to Theresa. "—if I ever made you feel unwelcome in this house, I'm sorry."

Theresa's eyes turned shimmery. "Thank you."

Rather than address any further that she had clearly been in a secret relationship for weeks if not longer, Anjali planted her hands on her hips and looked around the room. "Well? Is anyone else going to realize one of us has to cook if we want dinner?"

Right—no Daisy.

"Pizza?" Jay suggested.

William's eyes lit up, and no one argued.

Once the order was in, they spread out in the living room to enjoy a few moments' reprieve from the insanity of the past few days—the past few hours in particular.

"Well, JJ, time for a bit of circle restructuring, it seems," Reggie said from the chaise. He had his customary drink in hand, and while it looked like liquor, probably to avoid it seeming too nose-wrinkling to the others, Bari knew what it truly was. "Anyone who hasn't heard about all this by now certainly will have come morning, and they'll be expecting some sort of official statement. What's it going to be?"

"We're going to tell the truth," Jay said from where he and Bari shared the love seat, "including about you to anyone who doesn't know, if you're up for it."

Reggie caught Bari's eyes and said, "Change has to start somewhere."

Bari preened.

"Any ideas for Warden?" Anjali asked, seated in Des's lap in the wingback chair.

"Yes. You."

"I already have a title." She frowned.

"And I think you'd do better with a different one, and Des will take over for you."

"What?" Des sat up so straight, he nearly expelled Anjali from his lap. "But I… I never would have asked—"

"I'm asking," Jay said, "and I'd like you to be Councilor. I think you two will make a great team, taking those roles on together."

Whatever touch of offense Anjali might have been feeling faded as she looked at Des, and they exchanged a smile.

"That just leaves Magister," Maximus mentioned, on the sofa with Theresa and William.

"I'm sure you have plenty of magically inclined people who could handle the job," Bari said, patting Jay's arm.

"Only one who'd be perfect, though." Jay looked pointedly back at him.

"Me? I'm not even a member of your pack!"

"Then we should change that. Who better than you, Bari? You might not be a strong magic user, but the point of being Magister is to monitor it and keep people safe from those who wield it. You've proven you can see magic like no one else, dodge it, even dispel it in some cases. I want it to be you. A Magister needs to be knowledgeable with history, the people, and power. And you can still get as lost as you want in that museum and the occasional romance novel," Jay added with a smirk. "Please. It also unites our packs, like we intended."

"I suppose that's one way," Bari said with a pout.

Jay pulled Bari tighter against him. "I've been enjoying not rushing this, but… would you consider, at a future date, saying yes when I ask you to be my mate?"

Bari was very aware of all the eyes on them but kept his attention on Jay's sparkling blues. "Is that an engagement to be engaged?" When Jay merely kept grinning, Bari snuggled closer. "Do I still get something pretty to show off to my friends?"

Jay laughed. "We can figure something out. I owe you a shopping trip anyway." He tugged on the collar of the third shirt Bari had donned that day.

"Do we need to leave you two alone?" Maximus groused. He didn't actually sound annoyed, at least not anywhere near as much as he might have when Bari was first getting to know him.

"There is something else I want to discuss," Jay said seriously. "Housing. The Shelter is far too overcrowded."

"My apartment building is ready," Des offered. "I'd just been waiting for the right time to tell you about it."

"And I thank you for its donation." Jay nodded. "I am curious how you earned the money over the years to purchase it, but we can leave that be for now. What I really want to discuss… is adding the den as another donation."

JAY HAD expected more of a fight when he explained he wanted to donate the den as additional housing for people at the Shelter. It was another huge swath of tradition, mocking everyone with its frivolity. They could sell much of the furnishings to feed and house even more people and let several stay in a much better environment than warehouse bunks. Between that and the building provided by Des, maybe someday soon, they'd finally have the Shelter down to manageable levels, and even sometimes vacant if they could keep unrest down, though that was going to be up to the people.

Jay was starting to really like Bari's mixers idea….

For now, at least for a few hours, Alpha business would be put on hold. Jay was Alpha, and he wasn't going to forget it or let anyone else forget it anytime soon—except in one very special case when he wanted to place all the power in someone else's hands.

Once dinner was done and everyone dispersed, all Jay desired was time alone with Bari.

The second the bedroom door closed behind them, Bari had his hands all over Jay. Bari's fingers were cool as they slid up inside Jay's shirt along his warmer skin. The contrast made Jay gasp and fumble to grip Bari's arms as he was pinned, his lips ravaged with an eagerness that had been building since Jay's semi-proposal—or maybe since Jay gave that winning roar in the dining room.

Keeping his hold on Bari's arms and relishing in the frantic way Bari kissed him, deep and full-bodied, Jay managed to push Bari away just slightly to get the point across that he wanted to turn. Bari allowed the movement but didn't remove his lips or retract his hands from pressing to Jay's chest beneath his shirt.

Jay pivoted them as he returned every stroke of Bari's tongue, peeking an eye open to know the exact moment when Bari was the one with his back to the door. Then Jay pushed Bari up against it, and Bari grinned even as his eyes went wide from their sudden separation.

"Stay right where you are," Jay said—and dropped to his knees.

The flush that spread across Bari's cheeks was gorgeous, his eyes already hazy and darkened as he licked his lips. Jay undid Bari's slacks with deliberate slowness, sliding them down first and leaving them to trap Bari's ankles. The tent in Bari's underwear was all too appealing. Jay pressed his palms to either side of Bari's thighs, and Bari whimpered.

Obliging the plaintive request, Jay lifted the elastic and slid Bari's shorts just slightly down his thighs until he sprang free. He splayed his fingers across Bari's hips with Bari's erection framed between them. Holding Bari in place as he bent forward, Jay sucked him in, no tease, all the way to the base.

Bari's whimpers cut off in a low moan.

Jay hummed, satisfied with the reaction. He focused on Bari's smell, on that hint of jasmine he couldn't get enough of, bobbing back and in again. Bari's skin was so soft in the intimate places of his upper thighs and between his legs.

Jay ran his tongue along the underside of Bari's cock as he bobbed more slowly, then slower still, and then began to speed up, only using his mouth and tongue, with his hands steadying the more frequent jerky movements of Bari's hips.

"Jay," Bari moaned, hands falling to Jay's shoulders with the right running, reverent and adoring, over the crown of Jay's head.

Jay flicked his eyes up to see how hooded Bari's eyes had become—heavy-lidded, pupils blown, mouth slack. He couldn't help grinning at leaving Bari speechless.

After twirling his tongue around Bari's head, Jay pulled away just long enough to say, "I am going to make you come. Then we'll work on seeing how easily you bounce back."

A moan replied as Jay resumed his fervent work. Bari's hand tightened around the curve of Jay's head, his own falling against the door as if in relief that he'd been given permission to finish.

"Jay," Bari huffed again, this time with urgency, and Jay knew he was close. He hollowed his cheeks, continued with enthusiasm, and then pulled back to lick up Bari's length one last time, and finished him off with a swift hand.

Bari came fast and hot, relaxing into smiling relief. He blinked lazily down at Jay.

Most of the mess coated Jay's hand, so he swiped at Bari's still mostly hard cock to gather the rest and stood. "I'm going to clean up. You better be undressed the rest of the way when I get back."

Bari nodded vigorously, already a blur of movement by the time Jay turned for the bathroom. He washed his hands, removed his shoes and socks, started to undo his jeans, but left himself in a half-dressed state.

When he exited into the main room, he found Bari fully nude, stroking himself to hardness again, sprawled out over the sofa. That was a sight Jay would catalog for later and never, ever tire of.

"Don't get too comfy," Jay told him, crossing to the nightstand and taking out the bottle of lube. "I thought we had an arrangement on how this was going to go."

Bari's brow furrowed and then smoothed as his eyes went wide. He remembered.

Jay peeled off his shirt and tossed it to the floor. He slid his already undone jeans down, tugging each end from his ankles. Then he paused to take Bari in again, his lean naked form, as Bari eyed him with rapt attention.

Jay fluidly slid his shorts down to join the rest of the pile on the floor. He turned, putting his back to Bari—his full nude form presented—and peered over his shoulder to find Bari flipped onto his stomach, peeking up over the arm of the sofa like a curious cat.

Leaning forward, Jay rested his upper half on his elbows on the bed with nothing left to the imagination about what he wanted. "Are you going to leave me hanging… or give me what I asked for?"

Bari made a noise like a wounded grunt, like he might come again, right there into the sofa cushions, just from looking at Jay positioned like that.

He moved from the sofa at record speed, and soon, a warm hand was sliding down the curve of Jay's ass, slowly, as if merely wanting to touch him with gentle fingers. Bari molded his body to Jay's, his cool chest against Jay's warm back, his lips pressing to Jay's neck, his cock twitching between Jay's thighs.

"You look so good like this…," Bari said when he pulled away, running both palms up Jay's back, his heated length sliding against Jay's skin, eager to find a harbor. He moved his hands down to Jay's hips and smoothed over his cheeks, his thumbs teasing the line between them. "Are you sure you can handle me, Big Bad Alpha?"

"You be Alpha tonight, Bari. I have complete faith in you."

Bari grinned and reached toward the nightstand to snatch up the bottle of lube. "Since I can speak from experience, darling, I find that whoever is in this position," his right thumb flicked the cap open while his left gave Jay's ass a firmer squeeze, "tends to make more noise. I know I do. So I have to wonder… how noisy are you going to be?"

Jay shivered. "How noisy do you want me?"

"How thin are these walls?"

"Only Max and Theresa would be at risk of hearing us."

"Now, that just sounds like a challenge." Bari hummed, poured some of the lube into his hand, coating his fingers, and set the bottle aside. Jay was already so hard, just from the lead-up to this and imagining what Bari would feel like, that he was doubtlessly weeping precum onto the bedding.

The first touch of Bari's slickened fingers was a tease along the line of Jay's entrance down to his balls, where Bari palmed them, stroked down the length of him, gathering the leaking wetness and coating Jay fully to make the slide of his hand smooth. But he didn't linger, stroking only once more before he moved his fingers back up and passed his thumb over Jay's puckered skin, not yet pressing inside.

Instead, Bari moved his hand down again, repeated how he'd started, even stroked Jay twice like before, and again when he returned to Jay's entrance, he merely brushed his thumb and the tips of his fingers.

Jay whined before he could stop himself, unsure if he could take the sweet, torturous pace Bari was setting.

"I'm curious what other sounds you'll make," Bari said softly, his voice raspy with arousal, and as he spoke, he finally pressed the first digit inside.

Bari's fingers were long, and even a single press and curling gesture hit the spot Jay had been craving. He whimpered far more needily than Bari had against the door.

"Fuck," Bari said in response and stroked that same spot again.

Usually, in the past, with other partners, Jay always held back if he was in this position. There was no one he had ever been with who he'd wanted to be fully open with, fully revealed and bare. Fucking fulfilled a need, not a connection, but with Bari, Jay could have both, wanted both, and had amazed himself twice already how much making love to this man made him feel complete.

Jay moaned, loud as he naturally wanted to be, and felt Bari rock forward, twitching against his thigh. Bari knew to make the motion of his finger a stroke rather than a thrust, knew to twist and curl just so, far more experienced and talented with a single finger than should be fair.

"Remember when I told you... I touched myself thinking about you?" Bari asked.

Jay moaned again as the words were accompanied by the first press of a second finger, deliberately, teasingly slow. "Hard... to forget."

"Well, you had me draw things out with a repeat performance as wonderful torture, and if, tonight, I'm Alpha, then this time I get to torture you and hear you moan my name."

"Bari," Jay moaned, not intentional compliance, but because he was unable not to after the two fingers slowly stretching and scissoring within him started to slow, while simultaneously going deeper.

Jay growled through the second moan that followed, feeling himself begin to shift.

"That's it... I want to see those claws tear the bedsheets."

"Fuck... fuck, Bari...."

"Mm... just like that," Bari said with a grin in his voice.

Jay dug his face into the comforter, almost wishing he had a pillow to tear into with his teeth. He forgot how good Bari was at saying all the right things to drive him crazy.

And it felt so nice to not have to be in control.

While the fingers stretching him were human, Jay felt the tickle of claws at his hip as Bari traced nonsensical designs over his skin. A low growl was rumbling in Bari's throat like a constant purr, and when he lay across Jay's back again and bent lower to kiss his neck, and then lick, and then bite, Jay felt the tender prick of fangs.

"I pictured this…," Jay said, groaning between words, with the slow curving motion and press within him of Bari's fingers. "The first time I saw you… walking into my hotel room… so different from your brother. Better. I pictured this, wanted it, imagined how good it would feel… to be fucked by a man who doesn't know he has the heart of an Alpha."

Bari gave that straggled, wounded grunt again, and pulled his fingers free. The lube was snatched from the table once more, and Jay pressed himself deeper into the bedding, so ready, so eager for this, he moaned just thinking about it.

"I pictured it too… every which way and then some," Bari said, the slicking noise of him stroking lube over himself only making the anxiousness coiling in Jay's gut boil hotter. "But back on that train ride here… I never believed I could be this lucky."

He reached forward to press his fingers back inside Jay to make sure he was stretched and ready.

"Because you… you…." Bari's voice changed to such a deep rumble, with the added softness of fur edging his body, Jay imagined him halfway between Stages Two and Three, and he tumbled into a fresh moan as Bari finally pressed to his entrance. "You are so fucking sexy and all mine."

The first push burned just the right side of almost too much. It had been a while for Jay, and Bari was much larger than two fingers, but Bari knew to wait past the first breach, give Jay time to adjust, and before he pressed in any farther, he whispered for reassurance.

"Is it okay?"

All that alluring bravado paled in comparison to Bari's good nature. Jay nodded but had too little breath to say much more than, "Good… so good," and waited for the next push.

Jay's hands reached forward to twist into the comforter, his claws already starting to make tears, as he tightened his hold reflexively with each new inch of Bari, and a broken moan tore from his throat when Bari was fully seated inside him.

"I'm the noisy one, right?" Bari said in a husky whisper. "So… let's see if we can make you sound more like me."

Jay whined, nodded, and gripped the bedding tighter.

The first backstroke was subtle, just slightly out and in again, then again the same way. Each time, the thrusts got deeper, and Jay moaned into the fabric, louder—louder. Bari was going at such a gradual pace, enjoying each stroke with a huff and shudder of his rumbling breath.

They'd barely started, however, because Jay knew without asking that Bari being a Focus could translate to this too. He could feel it already, like Bari was holding back what would be a wave of empowerment to add to the sensations already coursing between them.

"I don't want you to come too soon," Bari said with a teasing lilt. "You were so nice to me against the door… I want to be nice to you."

He didn't sound so nice right now. He sounded positively villainous, and Jay couldn't help a swell of excitement.

Bari's hands slid around Jay's hips, down the front of his thighs and up again along the grooves. His clawed fingers grazed between Jay's thighs, just barely skimming his balls, and Jay could feel himself weeping, dripping onto the bed.

"Fuck, Bari… touch me…." Jay begged when Bari continued to run his hands around the prize but never on it, while his agonizingly slow thrusts, constant and deep—deeper each time—spilled the neediest noises from Jay's lips. "Please…."

"Mmm… I think you need to be louder," Bari said in a gruff giggle. "I want to be sure you've earned it."

He wanted to be sure he wrecked Jay apparently, which was exactly what Jay had been hoping for. He could play along, though he already had ideas of how wrecked he'd make Bari next time.

So Jay let the teasing pleasure build—Bari fucking him, with brushes of fur along his skin, the grazing of fangs on his neck and shoulder, the feathering of claws down and up and so close to taking hold of his cock but never quite on him—and moaned, cried out, whimpered with the best of them, even sputtered, "Bari!" and "Yes!" and "Fuck, harder!" just to prove he meant business.

Bari moaned in kind to hear it all. And finally, finally, his right hand slid around to cup Jay's balls, careful with his claws but not retracting them. He playfully passed them over his palm and stroked up through the silky mess of lube, gathering the much more liberal wetness at Jay's tip, and then used it to add to the hot slide of his hand. He started to pump Jay with a tight grip.

Jay could admit, he was close already, so close that he knew as soon as Bari started to bleed some of his Focus intensity into their connection, he wouldn't last long. And then he felt Bari letting that energy flow.

"Bari!" he cried out and released a long, resonating moan to follow it, because the increased sensations were all through and around him, all at once suddenly, like every nerve in his body had ignited.

And somehow, somehow, despite the flux of power like licks of raw magic, Bari's thrusts maintained the same slow, penetrating pace. Jay's knuckles had to be white from gripping the bedding so hard, and he could hear the fabric tearing.

"Yes... you love it, don't you, darling? The feel of me inside you, sharing myself like no one else can. No one. Just me... just you...." Bari was leaned over him as he stroked Jay's cock, nearly flush against his back, lips close enough to his neck and ear for Jay to feel the dusting of breath.

"Yes," Jay growled in reply. "Bari... please... please make me come...."

Bari took that as a worthy challenge, his pace picking up both behind Jay and in the palm of his hand, until Jay was overrun. He cried out affirmations and Bari's name more times than he could count, until at last he came in Bari's hand feeling buzzed and tingling.

Bari followed moments later, pulling free to spill against Jay's back. They huffed, breathing in ragged sync together, until Bari collapsed onto Jay, not caring about the mess. For a moment, it felt so nice to lie in contented exhaustion. They'd earned it.

"Who'd have thought... my newfound abilities... would be so useful outside a fight?"

Jay laughed helplessly into the comforter. He couldn't move, but he let the small bit of wolf he'd released fade away, feeling Bari do the same as the places that had been soft fur became the smooth caress of skin.

And a bit of stickiness between them.

"Shower?" Bari breathed against Jay's shoulder, and then kissed the spot the air had tickled.

"In a minute. I'm going to have to toss this comforter anyway." Jay didn't warn Bari before flipping him onto the bed over his shoulder and climbing up after him.

The comforter was already ruined. It didn't matter if it also wiped away their mess, as Jay gathered Bari against him, who was giggling and so marvelously beautiful with a sheen of sweat about him and a glow to his eyes and skin that didn't have anything to do with a blessed birth as Focus and Seer, but just Bari, simply as he was.

"You know… before I met your brother, this was what I'd hoped for," Jay said, tracing his fingers over Bari's chest.

"Being bent over a bed by a beautiful man?" Bari asked with a dramatic shake of his hair.

"That—" Jay chuckled. "—but also…. Bashir was never going to be the sort of mate who wanted all I am and only me. Maybe with Ethan he can be, but not with me. You're all I'd ever hoped for and dreamed of in every foolishly romantic way I could have imagined and more."

Bari's eyes shimmered with moisture, but it was a happy shimmer. "You say the nicest things."

Jay responded by kissing him, slow and sweet. The book was hardly closed on all his city needed to heal, and there was still an unknown vampire plotting against them, but for now, this was more than enough to feel accomplished and whole. "Engaged to be engaged? And only because I'd like to court you a bit longer. We have technically only had one real date outside this house."

"This house." Bari dropped his head back with a groan. "I am going to miss this place, you benevolent bastard."

"Do you wish I'd made a different decision?"

"Not even a little. But could we maybe keep one of the wingback chairs and a clawfoot tub?" Bari batted his eyes.

Oh, Jay was starting to truly love this man. "I think we can manage that."

Chapter 19

"I KNEW Reggie felt familiar!" Ethan exclaimed from Bari's—well, really, Jay's—bedroom mirror.

They were finishing another Brady Bunch update, as Bari had decided to call them, having only offered a text the night before to say all was well and that he'd brief them in the morning.

"I must have been able to tell he was a vampire somehow, like how you could eventually see through his glamour. Which is super cool, by the way!" Ethan gushed.

Bari had explained in detail everything that had gone on after Bash and Ethan left for Centrus City, even having to admit that his brother was right about him being able to handle things on his own—though thankfully not completely on his own.

"Okay, okay, now for the dishy details," Deanna said.

Their positions in the mirror were the same as last time, with Deanna, Bash, and Ethan across the top, Bari in the center bookended by Preston and Luke, and Nell, Siobhan, and Rio along the bottom.

"Engaged to be engaged?" Preston jumped in with a sneer. "What cop-out is that?"

"It's romantic!" Bari defended. "He wants to court me. Besides, you know I'll need at least a year to plan a proper wedding."

"And you're Magister too," Bash said with a subtle smile. "Good for you. You'll make a good one."

"I hope so. This city needs good leadership in its circle."

"Including a vampire!" Ethan gushed again. "That is so awesome!"

"Guess you're not the only good fanger around." A younger female voice preceded Jesse popping onto screen, this time with Luke instead of Preston.

"Language, young lady," Preston reprimanded across the mirror.

"Oh, whatever, I heard you called him that too."

"Not after I knew him!"

"While this is all good fun as always," Bari interrupted, "I don't have time to dish more, I'm afraid. You know the important bits. I have a museum to get to."

"You're really sending the tablets back?" Nell asked.

"My hope is it'll lead us to whoever tried tipping us off, and maybe to our villain too. Or rather, lead you three." He nodded to the people on either side of him. "You're heading to Glenwood?"

"Should arrive the same time the tablets do," Luke said proudly and then hooked an arm around Jesse's shoulders to hug her to his side. "But we're gonna have fun while we're there too, right, Jess?"

She had clearly already patented her "embarrassed by her parents" expression.

"The curator is still being a pain," Bari said, "but hopefully Glenwood's Alpha can help."

"That's it, though?" Siobhan asked. "No leads on our mystery baddie?"

"Not yet. If she wants the tablets herself, she'll show. So be careful, all right?" Bari added at Preston and Luke, especially since Jesse would be with them.

"I'm also a Magister, remember?" Preston raised one hand that erupted a fireball above its palm, and the other crackled with lightning. "And I pack the big guns. We'll be fine."

"Um, what if she tries killing more shifters again to do that spell or whatever they mentioned?" Rio asked, always sounding a little unsure, since he was newest to the group.

Bari sighed heavily before answering, "That's why I have to destroy one of the tablets, so there can never be a full set again. I might cry," he said half seriously. "And I will definitely need a drink later."

"What about recording the history?" Nell pressed.

"I have it all down," Bari allayed her concerns, "and plenty of people know between our two circles. Jay and I agreed we might want to ease the rest of the packs in with that knowledge, though. The truth needs to be told, but we don't need to throw everyone's worlds for a loop twice in the same week. Speaking of... same time next week, darlings? Assuming no other emergencies arise."

There was a flurry of goodbyes and well wishes, ending with Bash saying, "I'm happy for you, brother."

"Me too."

After the connection closed and the mirror was just a mirror again, Bari checked his reflection, declared he was fit to be seen in public, and headed out the door.

It was still early, and he knew Jay had already gone down for breakfast, planning to head to his office soon. Bari wasn't sure where anyone else was, but as he was about to pass Maximus's door, he remembered he was meant to borrow Max's car, since Jay needed his. He gave the door an obligatory knock before opening it.

"Max, are you—oh!"

He now knew where Maximus and Theresa were—which was on the bed, with Maximus stripped to his underwear, wrists tied to the headboard, while Theresa straddled him in a very skimpy black lace nighty. Her blond hair was down about her shoulders, as was Maximus's dark braids, and they both looked very startled at being interrupted.

"Oops. Was your anniversary today?"

"Bari…," Maximus growled in warning.

"Have fun!" Bari said with a parting wave and quickly closed the door again, adding with a soft utterance to himself, "Good for you, Max."

He was fairly certain he heard the sound of Theresa locking the door as he headed away. Smart call.

While it was early, it was the weekend, and William was up playing with a couple of houseguests—his friend Emily and the young cat shifter Jordan. Bari was surprised to see Jordan run past him with the others as he came down the stairs, since Jordan was too much younger than the other two to be a fellow classmate or friend, until he spotted Jordan's mother on the living room sofa, chatting with Des and Anjali. From what he could overhear, they were discussing her new job as a bank teller, how it was going, and how her experience had been at the Shelter. Already hard at work, those two, to find ways to better things for the pack.

Bari was quite proud to be part of it—even if he was seriously going to miss this house. They'd be staying in the top floor of Des's apartment building eventually, so the circle would all be together but not anywhere loftier than where their people stayed. It was the right gesture for squashing traditionalism, just a little bittersweet. It helped that Jay had promised Bari could do all the decorating once they moved.

Bari was also determined to get his mixers idea off the ground and desegregate the indoor parks. Keeping them separate was just silly when even more housing could be created.

"Excuse us, love." Reggie breezed past Bari, followed by a young couple—a rat and a cat, Bari noted by the smell of them. "Appointments all day. No rest for the wicked." He winked back at Bari as he reached the door to the basement and opened it for the couple.

By the excited smiles on their faces, Bari knew they were from the other half of that list, hoping for a child together and no longer trying to hide it. He wished them well.

Bari was going to miss this house, but the people in it were the important part.

He planned to seek out Jay before leaving, but as he was grabbing his jacket from the front closet, Jay found him first.

"Are you sure you're okay going alone?"

"To the museum? Darling, that's my happy place!"

Jay wrapped his arms around Bari's waist—his burly beautiful arms that were currently stretching the sleeves of a T-shirt almost inappropriately that Bari very much appreciated. "I'm just going to be a little protective of you for... probably ever."

Bari wrapped his arms around Jay's neck in turn, adoring that he got to touch this man whenever he wanted. "You go right ahead. But I know you've been itching to return to casework. See what's out there. There are many ways we can help this city and its people."

That was apparently the perfect thing to say, because Jay smiled and pulled Bari in for a long goodbye kiss. When they parted, Bari went right back in for another and let one of his hands drift up to trace the cartilage of Jay's crooked ear. They still needed a second date one of these days, but until then, he'd take what he could get whenever he could get it.

He almost headed out the door when he had to spin back.

"Oh! Do you have a spare key to Max's car? He's... indisposed."

IT TOOK Bari a good long while to prepare the packaging for the tablets. They couldn't just be slapped into boxes, after all, and would need to be carefully wrapped—other than the one he planned to smash. The thought nauseated him, and he decided to save that for the very end.

He was all set to begin wrapping the tablets, separating them from how they were still laid out in their correct order across the table, when he reached into his jacket pocket for....

For….

It felt like glass. It was glass. They were glass, and there were five of them, clinking around in Bari's pocket.

He pulled one of them out, shocked to find a small vial filled with something dark, thick, and red.

When had Bari grabbed these? He didn't even remember going into the basement to take them from where they should have been stored in Reggie's morgue.

He reached back into his pocket to pull out the others. All five— one from each of the five victims.

The tablets.

Bari's head reeled from the sudden press against his mind.

Spill them onto the tablets.

He gasped at how much it felt like a vise had his head in its clutches and was squeezing.

Spill a drop from each onto each tablet.

Bari set four of the vials on the table, keeping one that he started to uncork.

Wait! What was he doing? Why was he doing this? Then, as those thoughts broke through the cacophony of pressure in his mind, he saw the rune on his hand glowing.

Bari was being enthralled!

Do it!

He practically threw the vial onto the table with the others and backed away. "Get out of my head! Who are you? Where are you?"

He'd swear he heard a sigh, and then the low, controlled female voice came into his mind again. You are a conduit as much as you are a challenge, Mr. Bain.

"The spell…." Bari continued to talk aloud, though he doubted the vampire needed him to use words. "It wasn't to ensure Ursula and the others took over without trouble. It was for you. To empower you." The truth clanged in his head almost as noisily as her commands. "You'd be able to enthrall everyone, wouldn't you? Like Ethan's father tried to have him do in Centrus. Because you don't have that power on your own."

I will, one way or another. It's a pity you aren't more easily controlled. But even spoiling my plans here changes nothing. I have so many other wheels in motion.

The pressure returned with a vengeance, and it hurt so much trying to fight it, Bari nearly felt his knees give way beneath him.

He just needed to spill a little blood on the tablets....

No! With a growl, Bari snatched the vials from the table, turned toward a nearby trash can, and threw them so hard into it, he heard them shatter at the bottom.

"We are going to find you," he bit out with shaking fists as the pressure in his head abated, "and stop you."

Mr. Bain, I survived the first purge, and this time, I am going to orchestrate one. See you soon.

He felt her leave, however she had casually stepped into his mind from who knew how far away. She was ancient and very strong, but somehow, he'd resisted her. He looked down at his hand, reassured to see the glow gone.

After taking a few cleansing breaths, Bari returned to pack away the tablets, and when only one was left, the one he'd first realized was unique, depicting a vampire above shifters, he no longer had any qualms about smashing it to pieces at the bottom of that same trash can.

Later, when Bari returned to the den, he'd have Reggie follow the trail from the thrall she'd tried to use on him back to its owner, but his Seer intuition already told him he knew what direction it would point.

Glenwood.

Keep reading for an excerpt from
Their Dark Reflections
by Amanda Meuwissen!

Chapter 1

SAM KNOCKED on the paneling of the wrought-iron doors, trying to peer through the glass. It was frosted, offering no insight into what lay inside. Mr. Simons's instructions were for him to let himself in, but he still wanted to announce himself.

Hearing no response, Sam tried one of the handles, and it gave way with ease.

"Mr. Si—" He cut off with a gape as he entered. He'd known the house would be impressive from the outside, but this was Real Housewives kind of ostentatious, opening into a huge two-story entryway with a grand staircase leading to the second floor.

The décor was antique and modern mixed, with standing radios from the '20s or '30s on either side of the doors, resting atop trendy black-and-white tiles. Two matching art deco tables bookended the staircase in similar fashion, sporting their own vintage radios. This guy must be a collector.

Good. That meant there would be even more worthwhile prizes than what Sam planned to steal.

"Please close the doors behind you, Mr. Coleman," a voice called from the second floor.

Sam obeyed, noticing how the opaqueness of the glass kept out any natural light. The nearby curtains were closed as well, making it harder to blink upward through the dimness and see his host.

Sam had ridden there on his motorcycle to throw off his new "client." Any other professional with his resume would drive something more practical. The bike added a distinctive edge, so that when his skills proved worthy, Mr. Simons would be that much more intrigued by him—and easier to con.

Little good that did when the man couldn't see outside. Sam openly gawking around the foyer like an amateur didn't help either. He was twenty-three, not a child. He needed to act like it.

"Mr. Simons," he said, clearing his throat to start over, "a pleasure to finally meet you in person. I hope you don't mind me parking my motorcycle in the driveway."

"Not at all." He must have seen the bike after all or wasn't that easily surprised. At first, he made a somewhat hazy figure descending the stairs until he was close enough for Sam to see him clearly. "And call me Ed."

Sam nearly gaped again, because Ed was not the old rich guy he'd expected.

First, he couldn't have been older than thirty, with well-coifed strawberry-blond hair, green eyes, and a tall, slender frame dressed primly—and maybe a little ridiculously with a sweater vest and bow tie—which all amounted to a nerdy boy-next-door who didn't seem to realize he'd grown up hotter than his wardrobe.

"It's a pleasure to meet you too." Ed smiled warmly and extended his hand.

Hot and nice. This wasn't turning out like Sam had planned at all.

"IF I can call you Ed, then please, call me Sam."

Attractive and well-mannered. This wasn't turning out like Ed had planned at all.

Sam's skills and experience had been listed as housework, groundskeeping, scheduling, even personal finance—everything Ed needed in a temporary assistant. He hadn't expected someone so young, though, or with such a roguish smile.

Ed never realized how much he'd enjoy curls on a man, either, rich black with a few unruly ones falling into eyes that were almost black themselves and easy to get lost in.

Ed had to focus.

"It's cozy in here," Sam said.

"Yes, I keep the house fairly warm, since I tend to run cold. I'm sure you noticed." Ed waved his hand.

"Cold hands, warm heart, right?" Sam flashed a smile again. "Are you an antiquities collector? I couldn't help noticing the radios."

"A little," Ed admitted. "I love theater, but there's something special about purely spoken stories."

"A radio drama fan? That's rare. I enjoy the old oral traditions too." He cocked his head with a stretch to his grin that made Ed forget himself for a moment.

"I-I, um…. W-we should…." He paused to collect himself. "How about I give you a tour, and then we can discuss your schedule?"

"Sounds perfect."

Ed led Sam into the living room that spanned almost one whole side of the house and connected to the back patio that opened to the fenced-in backyard and pool. "I know it's a lot for one man, but I like my space, and I have numerous possessions I don't want to part with."

"I can imagine," Sam said, looking at Ed's framed photographs on the wall. Ed's three favorites were prominent: The Grand Canyon just after sunset, Times Square in 1957, and one of Big Ben first being built, two-thirds to completion. "This last one must be over a hundred years old."

"A hundred and sixty, give or take."

"Famous photographer?"

"Just a family heirloom."

"Must have been a cool family. I take it groundskeeping will include cleaning the pool?" Sam moved to the patio doors and pulled aside the fitted curtains.

"I like to swim at night under the stars," Ed said, holding back in the shadows, "so it can be your last duty of the day."

"You only swim at night?"

"I have photodermatitis and light sensitivity, so the sunlight can be dangerous. That's why I keep the curtains closed."

"I'm sorry." Sam let them fall back into place.

"The tools you'll need are in the pool house, but let me know if anything is missing."

"Stargazer too?" Sam indicated the telescope near the doors.

"Yes, I bring that outside on clear nights. I'm a Pisces myself."

Sam looked at him as if in surprise.

"Not that I take astrology seriously! I just think it's fun. Besides, the stars have their own stories to tell, and how people choose to interpret them can be fascinating, don't you think?"

With his grin creeping up again, Sam sauntered closer to Ed. "Pisces, huh? No wonder you like to swim. I'm a Gemini. What's that say about me?"

Ed felt his face flush as Sam drew closer. "Th-that you're adaptable, curious, witty. You can be the exact person someone needs you to be."

"Lucky you," Sam said. Then, when Ed stood staring like an idiot, he followed with, "For the job."

"Right! You're quite the Renaissance man, from your credentials."

"I hope I live up to what you expect of me, Eddie. Can I call you Eddie, or is that too informal?"

Ed could usually read people well, but he didn't often have them in his home for very long. He must be imagining that Sam was flirting. "I don't mind." Although no one ever called him Eddie. "Shall we?" Turning swiftly, he continued toward the dining room and kitchen around the other side of the house.

Sam followed. "This Renaissance man can also cook. Did you want—"

"No need," Ed broke in. "I order in all my food and don't eat much. It'd be a waste to have you cook for me. You're welcome to help yourself to anything in the pantry or fridge, though, and since you'll be staying over lunchtime, feel free to make requests."

"I'll take you up on that."

They came around to the staircase again and headed up to the parlor, which Ed considered to be the best place in the house to read, since it looked out over the high ceiling down to the foyer. He still had a book resting beside the armchair where he'd been awaiting Sam's arrival.

"The Tempest?" Sam read the title.

"We are such stuff as dreams are made on, and our little life is rounded with a sleep," Ed recited, and then chuckled bashfully when Sam grinned at him. "I, uhh… like to reread classics between new titles."

"Impressive library," Sam said, scanning the bookshelf behind the armchair.

"That's just for what I'm currently reading or about to start. The rest are in the real library." Ed motioned for Sam to continue down the hall, enjoying the shock that briefly filled his features.

They passed a bathroom, the office, a guest room, and entered the second guest room that Ed had turned into his library. He'd not only covered every spare inch of wall space with ceiling-high bookshelves, but had placed standing bookshelves in rows like a true library in order to hold everything he owned. He rarely got rid of books and kept adding to his collection.

"Harry Potter next to a first edition of The Canterbury Tales." Sam sputtered a giddy laugh as he looked around, but then the humor seemed to leave him, and he frowned as he continued scanning.

"What's wrong?"

"There's no order to any of this. Not by title, author, genre."

"I was more concerned with getting them on the shelves."

"Is that how all your organizational attempts pan out?" Sam looked at him with something akin to pity.

"I just don't like the tedium of it," Ed defended.

"I meant no offense." Sam held up a hand and gave a short laugh—hypnotic really, or magical, because it loosened Ed right up again. "Luckily for you, I live for tedious planning. Shall we move to the master bedroom?"

Ed was close to reprimanding Sam for such cheekiness when he realized he meant the tour. "Yes! Last stop." He moved swiftly once more to prevent Sam from seeing how red his face had become. He'd avoided real interaction with people for so long, he'd forgotten how to act normally.

Or Sam was just that charming.

The master bedroom was large, with its own bathroom, and housed a four-poster bed and matching dresser, along with a shelf for Ed's cameras—some modern, some antique—but he spent the least of his time in that room. It was mostly only for his safe, set into the wall by the closet.

"You know, people usually put paintings over those," Sam said.

"I will eventually. I just haven't decided which one yet. Besides, I wanted you to see it, since you'll be helping me with my finances. It mostly only holds cash and the logins to my offshore accounts on a flash drive. I can't let you have access to any of that or the safe, but you can see printouts of my holdings once we get to that part."

"No problem. That's all I'll need. Do you only collect cameras and photographs or take your own?"

"I take some. Whenever something beautiful catches my attention."

Eager to be out of the bedroom given Sam's effect on him, Ed started to lead them downstairs, but Sam pointed to the pull ladder at the end of the hall.

"That's to the widow's walk."

"May I?"

"Be my guest."

Sam pulled the string to bring the ladder down. The sun spilled into a little pool at the base, which Ed sidestepped with a simple pivot. Once Sam was almost to the top, he turned back.

"I suppose you can't join me, huh?"

"Still a little too bright for me. Go ahead."

Sam nodded and finished the climb. He disappeared for a spell, but then his voice filtered down. "You should bring your telescope up here!"

"I'm not a fan of heights either!" Ed called back. He could never quite get over that sudden feeling of vertigo when he was high up.

Sam returned and carefully replaced the ladder. "No basement?" he asked as they headed to the main level.

"No." At least, not that Sam needed to know about.

"Are you sure you only need me for two weeks?"

"We can play it by ear," Ed said, but he had no intention of extending the contract. Any longer would be too risky. "Shall we plan out your first few days?"

"Absolutely. I'm all yours, Eddie."

Definitely only two weeks.

DEFINITELY NO more than two weeks.

Ed wasn't like the others Sam had conned. Sam considered himself a Robin-Hood-for-hire, targeting rich assholes who had it coming. Granted, he kept all the money for himself, his crew, and his employers, but at least he only stole from bad people.

Until Ed, who didn't seem to have an ounce of badness in him and had no idea who he'd just let into his home.

Sam Goldman, not Coleman, who was currently scamming him for every cent in his offshore accounts.

"You got a full tour of the house, know exactly where the safe is and what's in it, and he's lax on security?"

"I even know the model number to the safe."

"Then all you have to do is play it cool for two weeks, and we can make a clean getaway."

"Yep."

"He probably won't even realize he's been robbed for months, with how much he has."

"Yep."

"It'll be the easiest job we've ever pulled off."

"Yeah...."

"You like him, don't you?"

Sam stared at Mim beside him at the table, his best friend and confidant, practically family, who knew him better than anyone—save maybe Gerry, the other member of their "family," who knew him even better from sheer force of will and prying.

Mim was tiny, blond, gorgeous, but packed a mean punch when she wanted to. She was playing with a knife, twirling it around her fingers while they talked, the complete opposite of Gerry.

"Do either of you know what this cord is for?" Gerry called from across the room.

He would have been an imposing man if he wasn't tall, dark, and bumbling more than any other adjectives, a cream puff in the body of a bouncer.

"I mean, it's HDMI to HDMI, which is always useful, but I already packed the other adapters except for what I need for my laptop. Although, since I have the others, I can probably get rid of this one."

"Gerry—"

"Only the moment I do, I just know I'm going to find whatever this goes to and wish I still had it. I better keep it."

"Gerr—"

"Of course, if I do realize I need it later, it's not like it's hard to replace—"

"Gerry, will you shut up?" Mim snapped, pulling him into their close-quartered conversation.

They shared the one-room loft. Logan, who owned Lucifer's Rest downstairs, had a soft spot for them, offering free room and board for doing odd jobs and occasionally bartending or waiting tables.

It was meant to only be temporary, but two years ago Sam had finished his twenty-first birthday passed out on that floor.

"There might not even be a payday," Mim said.

"What?" Gerry lumbered over to them, still carrying the cord. "What are you talking about?"

"Sammy's smitten with the target."

"I'm not—"

"Ew." Gerry stopped with a grimace.

"It's not like that. And he isn't some aging sleazeball. This one's different. He's young and handsome and… kind of stutters when he gets flustered."

"He's smitten with you too?" Mim groaned.

"Took to my flirting like he is."

"Sam."

"What? I've flirted to finish a job before."

"Not with someone you like."

Sam fell silent. That was their one rule.

Assholes only.

The three of them had no one else in the world, only each other, grifters since they could fit a hand in someone's pocket. Well, Sam did the pickpocketing, Mim handled muscle, and Gerry was in charge of the technical side. They were criminals, and they enjoyed being criminals, but that didn't mean they hurt good people.

"So that's it?" Gerry said, sinking into the chair at Sam's right. "No big score?"

"I don't know, but I'm not telling the Cramers we're backing out of a retirement-sized payday after only one meeting with this guy. Someone this rich has to have skeletons in his closet. Even if it's also filled with sweater vests and bow ties."

Brock and Celia Cramer, an up-and-coming power couple who'd just moved to Riverside, had come to them with this job. It had seemed like a dream come true when they told them of another transplant, a full-blown whale coming to town and bringing a fortune with him. Sam had never done a job in Riverside before—he wasn't an idiot—but this time, they'd be leaving afterward, so it didn't matter. Finally, all the scraping by he and his crew had done over the years would pay off, and they'd never need to con again, at least not to survive.

He couldn't call it quits after one day.

"Aw," Gerry said, bumping Sam's shoulder. "You do like him."

"That isn't a good thing, Gerry. The Cramers are expecting us to finish this job."

"We could always do it anyway, even if Simons is a nice guy," Mim said, picking at her nails with her knife.

Sam and Gerry glared at her.

"Can't blame a gal for trying." She shrugged.

"If Simons is on the level, we'll bow out, but the Cramers swore he was a worthwhile target, so keep packing," Sam told Gerry, "and start working on how to crack that safe. Simons has to be hiding something."

AMANDA MEUWISSEN is a bisexual author with a primary focus on M/M romance. She has a Bachelor of Arts in a personally designed Creative Writing major from St. Olaf College and is an avid consumer of fiction through film, prose, and video games. As the author of LGBT Fantasy #1 Best Seller, *Coming Up for Air*, paranormal romance trilogy, The Incubus Saga, and several other titles through various publishers, Amanda regularly attends local comic conventions for fun and to meet with fans, where she will often be seen in costume as one of her favorite fictional characters. She lives in Minneapolis, Minnesota, with her husband, John, and their cat, Helga, and can be found at www.amandameuwissen.com.

MOONLIGHT PROPHECIES

BY THE RED
Moonlight

AMANDA MEUWISSEN

Alpha werewolf, crime boss, and secret Seer Bashir Bain is neck-deep in negotiating a marriage of convenience with a neighboring alpha when a tense situation goes from bad to worse. A job applicant at one of Bash's businesses—a guy who was supposed to be a simple ex-cop, ex-con tattoo artist—suddenly turns up undead.

A rogue newborn vampire would have been a big wrench in Bash's plans even without his attraction to the man. After all, new vampires are under their sire's control, and Ethan Lambert doesn't even know who turned him. When Bash spares his life, he opens himself up for mutiny, a broken engagement, and an unexpected—and risky—relationship.

Ethan just wants a fresh start after being released from prison. Before he can get it, he'll need to turn private investigator to find out who sired him and what he wants. And he'd better do it quick, because the moon is full, and according to Bash's prophecy, life and death hang in the balance.

www.dreamspinnerpress.com

THEIR DARK
Reflections

AMANDA
MEUWISSEN

Personal assistant Sam Coleman can do it all: housekeeping, groundskeeping, bookkeeping. The catch? It's a con.

Ed Simon, his newest millionaire boss, doesn't know Sam Goldman is a Robin Hood for hire who targets rich jerks. Sure, Sam keeps the money for himself, his crew, and his real employers, but at least they only steal from bad people.

Until sweet, fumbling Ed, who doesn't seem to have a single vice. Too bad the people who hired Sam won't let him back out. They want Ed's money, and they'll hurt Sam and his friends to get it.

For years Ed has kept people at arm's length, but Sam's charms wear down his defenses—just as he learns their budding relationship was an act. Sam isn't who Ed thought he was, but Ed has a dark secret too: he's a vampire. And someone is framing him for a series of bloody murders.

When the real villains force their hand, Sam and Ed must choose: work together, trust each other, and give in to the feelings growing between them… or let what might have been bleed out like the victims piling at their feet.

www.dreamspinnerpress.com